The
Gate House
Secret

Debra Burroughs

This is a work of fiction. Names, characters, places and incidents either are the product of the author's imagination or are used fictitiously. Any resemblance to actual persons, living, dead (or in any other form), business establishments, events, or locales is entirely coincidental.

Lake House Books
Boise, Idaho

First eBook Edition: 2018
First Paperback Edition: 2018

THE GATE HOUSE SECRET by Debra Burroughs,
1st ed. p.cm.

Visit My Blog: www.DebraBurroughsBooks.com

Contact Me: Debra@DebraBurroughs.com

ISBN-10: 1722300914
ISBN-13: 978-1722300913

DEDICATION

This book is dedicated to my amazing husband, Tim, who loves me and encourages me to do what I love – writing. And to my children, Sean and Jenessa, who inspire me to be my best every day.

TABLE OF CONTENTS

ACKNOWLEDGMENTS

I would like to acknowledge my awesome Beta Readers,
Cathy Tomlinson, Janet Lewis, and Buffy Drewett,
who inspire me and help me with
their words of encouragement and critique.

I want to also acknowledge my brilliant Editor,
Lisa Dawn Martinez.

CHAPTER 1

JENESSA JONES RACED TO HER CAR, not daring to look back, and flung the door open. She jumped inside and slammed it shut, hitting the lock button. Her heart hammered against her ribcage until it reverberated in her ears. A light sheen of sweat broke out on her forehead as she wound her fingers around the steering wheel so tightly they were turning a ghostly white.

This had to be a bad dream…a nightmare.

The morning had started out pleasant enough, helping Logan get the children off to camp, then making a stop at the cemetery to talk to her mother. But everything had spun on a dime, leaving her shaken to the core, with her breath coming out in rasping heaves.

If this man wanted to destroy her, feed her to the wolves, he would have a war on his hands. She would not go quietly into the night. No. The only way she was going down would be kicking and screaming.

The terrifying scene replayed in her mind.

The dew on the grass had sparkled in the early morning sun, glistening like a carpet of gleaming crystals. But Jenessa hadn't been out for a stroll in the park. Instead, she had stood alone in the cemetery—a place she hadn't been in far too long...

In the coolness of the brisk August morning, she wrapped her arms around herself for warmth. Or maybe it was for comfort.

As she glanced down at the gravestone, her chest tightened. She ran a finger along its edges, feeling the slickness of the dew-dampened granite. Swallowing down a lump, she took a deep breath and blew it out. "Hey, Mom. It's me, Jenessa. I know I haven't been by in a while."

A "while" was an understatement. It had been more than a year since she'd stepped foot in this hallowed place. The last time was when she buried her father in the plot beside her mother's.

It wasn't as though she hadn't often thought about coming, but actually doing it, visiting her mother's grave, that was different. Jenessa didn't like being reminded that her mother was dead, cold and buried in the ground. Sure, it was selfish of her, but there it was. It helped to keep the grief at bay.

Jenessa knelt down and placed a small bouquet of pink peonies at the foot of the headstone. "Sorry I didn't come sooner." As she ran her fingers over the carved letters of her mother's name, tears welled up with ferocious speed, spilling down her cheeks before she could raise a tissue to stop them.

"I'm getting married." Jenessa spit the words out between sniffles.

As a little girl she had dreamed of saying those words to her mother...it just wasn't like this, it wasn't here. She had always thought the two of them would conspire like criminals as they giggled over the bridal books and planned her wedding.

But this was something entirely different.

She unraveled the crumpled tissues in her hand and dabbed at her damp cheeks, then took a long breath. "I've dreamed of this day, Mom, of sharing this news with you. And you'll never guess who it is...I'm going to marry Logan Alexander."

"Over my dead body," a deep voice growled from close behind her.

She startled, every muscle in Jenessa's body tensing at the sound of that ominously familiar voice. It could only belong to the one person on earth who hated her— Logan's father.

But surely it couldn't be him. She must be hallucinating. Grey Alexander was in prison—and she had been instrumental in putting him there.

Rising slowly to her feet, she pulled in a couple of deep breaths. Hopefully when she turned around there would be nothing there—his voice only a figment of her imagination.

Steady, Jenessa, you can handle this...you're just overwhelmed.

Maybe she'd be lucky, and it would be the ghost of Grey Alexander, coming here to haunt her. The graveyard seemed like a fitting place for his evil spirit to lurk about.

Turning with dread, eyes shut as she mustered strength, she straightened. Even if it was him—which it couldn't possibly be—she could face the man and not crumble. Couldn't she?

She opened her eyes, praying for empty space, or even the ghost in her imagination. A small gasp escaped her lips. It was the real Grey Alexander, in the flesh.

Jenessa refused to let her legs give out, refused to let him see even the slightest hint of weakness. She wouldn't give him the satisfaction. She didn't know how he managed to get out of prison, or how he'd tracked her down here—the one time in forever that she had come to the cemetery—but she did know she could not let him win.

"Lurking in the cemetery these days, Mr. Alexander?" she said, keeping her voice flat but firm. "You can't possibly be out on good behavior."

"Funny," he huffed, his eyes narrowing as he said it. "You always were a sassy-mouthed girl." His gaze was riveted on her, dark and brooding, like threatening storm clouds. His lips were drawn tight as he spoke. "As a matter of fact, I am out on good behavior. No thanks to you."

He brushed his hands down his sleeves as though wiping away the filth of his dirty deeds. "I've been out two days, actually. In case you were wondering."

She hadn't been, but she was wondering a bunch of other things now. Like where had he been since Thursday? And did Logan know he was out? Not to mention, what the heck was he doing here, at the cemetery, when she was?

Had he come looking for her?

She stifled another gasp. Had he been stalking her?

He paced around her like a satisfied lion, having cornered its kill. "You have questions. I can see it in your eyes, so I'll get to the point. Yes, I followed you here. I was going to talk to you today anyway, but the venue you chose," he swept his arm in a wide gesture, "well, I couldn't have chosen better myself."

What did he mean by that?

He closed in on her, taking a stance right in front of her, his face inches from her own. "I've come to give you fair warning, Miss Jones."

Fair warning? That couldn't be good. She straightened her shoulders, refusing to slump in his presence. "What do you mean?"

"I heard about your impending *marriage* to my son."

The man actually used air quotes when he said the word marriage. What was he? Fifteen? Granted, she wouldn't have expected congratulations, but this, this sounded more like a threat.

Grey's forehead wrinkled into a deep frown. "Now, Miss Jones, you of all people know I can't let that happen."

She pulled herself up a little straighter, if that were possible, as she fired back. "Thankfully, it's not up to you."

He inched closer and glanced around. Did he not want to be seen talking to her? Or was he making sure there would be no witnesses when he strangled her to death beside her parents' graves?

She shuddered and edged back.

"You may change your attitude about that, young lady."

It would be a cold day in hell before she would do that. Jenessa crossed her arms in defiance.

"Go ahead, Miss Jones, be smug." A devilish grin spread across his lips. "I had my attorney hire someone to do a little digging as soon as I found out about this so-called marriage."

A tingle of fear crept up the back of her neck. What on earth could he be referring to? She hadn't been a model citizen, but she surely had no monumental skeletons in any of her closets. "What kind of digging?"

"Into your past. Into those twelve missing years."

Missing years? Who was this guy kidding? She had not been missing. She'd gone to college and then worked on several newspapers in Sacramento. Perfectly normal stuff. No secrets there.

And she had been back in Hidden Valley for the past year, the thirteenth year since being whisked away to her grandmother's at seventeen, until she could give birth to her baby. His son Logan's baby, grandson to the mighty Grey Alexander and rightful heir to the Alexander fortune.

Sure, he had managed to orchestrate the baby's adoption, hiding her son away from her all these years. The boy had been hidden in plain sight, no less, being raised by Logan's cousin in another state. But she and Logan knew the truth about their son now, even though she was fairly certain Grey didn't know they knew. She was keeping that one under her hat for the time being.

She stuck out her chin in defiance. "You know exactly where I've been," she said, struggling to stay in control of her escalating emotions.

"I do know. *Exactly* where you've been and what you've done."

What I've done?

Grey's dark stare bore deep, as if searching Jenessa's eyes for a flash of fear. "My investigator has provided me with some very damning information about you. Something that, dare I say, will be sufficient to break whatever hold you have over my son."

Damning? Her heart hammered as his words flew through her brain, the pounding vibrating through her entire body. What could he have found? She was almost afraid to ask. "Like what? I haven't done any—"

He closed the distance between them again, grinning like a cat with canary feathers stuck between his teeth. "Apparently what happens in Vegas does not always stay in Vegas." He raised a brow, watching for her reaction.

Vegas? What was he…? And then it hit her. *Oh, no.*

Her throat squeezed shut as if the man had clamped his hand around it. She could hardly breathe. Vegas was a long time ago, and it was so out of character for her…just a stupid mistake. A big one, yes, but a mistake that had been rectified.

It had been rectified, hadn't it? She had no reason to think not. Sure, she'd never followed up to see, but, surely, after all these years…

Jenessa's stomach churned, and bile rose in her throat. She was certain her face was turning a thousand different shades of green.

Did Grey know something she didn't?

His eyes flared with satisfaction at her reaction. "That's right, Miss Jones. I know everything, and I will be forced—no, forced is not the right word—I will be happy to make public what I've learned, unless…"

Unless what?

He stroked his chin, appraising her with a wicked glint in his eye.

"So, would you like to call off your engagement to my son, or should I?"

And there it was.

She wanted to pinch herself, but Jenessa knew this was no bad dream. It was colossally bad timing though. She hadn't even thought of that night in years.

"Whatever you think you know, Mr. Alexander, I assure you, you're wrong."

"Are you really that certain, Miss Jones?"

Oh, God. Maybe he did know something Jenessa didn't. He was sure acting as if that were true. Why couldn't he have stayed locked up in prison? At least for a couple of weeks longer, long enough for her to marry Logan. Long enough for him to have no power over her anymore.

Jenessa's blood began to boil. She fisted her hands but kept them restrained to the sides of her body, afraid she might actually pop him one, right in the kisser. He was such an arrogant jerk. "Why are you doing this?"

"Because you're nothing but an unadulterated, gold-digging…well, you can fill in that blank." The man crossed his arms as though putting finality to that statement, as if his body language made it true.

But it wasn't true. His accusation was outrageous and unfair. Her head was swimming, her temples throbbing, and she couldn't find the words to reply.

"You were a gold digger when you tricked my son into getting you pregnant all those years ago, and now you're trying to have a second chance at getting your hands on our money."

She opened her mouth to defend herself, but the words still would not come. Where was her usual witty and biting comeback? What happened to her sassy banter? It was gone. Because if what he was suggesting were true…

It would mean the end of her and Logan. At least until she could find a way to fix things between them. *If* she could.

And if she couldn't, she might never become mother to his adopted children. Lily was such a sweet little girl, but Grayson, he was a different story entirely. He was her son—hers and Logan's—only he didn't know it yet.

They had agreed to wait until sometime after the wedding to explain things to the kids. Those children had been through too much to have to deal with that as well, and only a few months after their mother's death from cancer, adoptive or not. It was difficult enough to be a child and watch your mother die, but to have your entire world turned upside down—no, that was unthinkable.

"Look at me," he snapped, bringing her attention back. "I'm warning you, Miss Jones," he spat, each word dripping with contempt, "break things off with my son, or I swear I'll splash your dirty laundry on the front page of the newspaper."

"You wouldn't do that," was all she could manage to squeak out.

But he would, and worse. First, he would do everything in his power to drive a wedge between her and the young man she'd loved since they were teenagers. And if that wasn't enough, he could annihilate her...or at least her professional life. She was a reporter at the town's newspaper, but he was the owner. Not only could he force her boss to publish the story to expose and humiliate her personally, but he could also have her fired and destroy her reputation, blackballing her so she'd never work in journalism again.

But how could she stop him?

Grey leaned so close to her ear that she could feel the heat of his wretched breath on her cheek. Her stomach twisted, and chills skated across her stiffened shoulders.

"Do as I say," he whispered. "You have forty-eight hours to kill your wedding plans or the whole town will know your dirty little secret."

CHAPTER 2

STILL SHAKING FROM HER ENCOUNTER in the cemetery—and praying she could finally stop replaying the incident in her mind—Jenessa pulled her sportscar into a place in front of The Sweet Spot. Grey Alexander's threats put her on edge and she needed a mocha, or maybe a shot of tequila, and a vent session with her best friend, Ramey. The café was buzzing with morning customers, sitting at little tables, sipping their fancy coffees, and munching on an array of tasty baked goods.

She wouldn't find any Jose Cuervo here, but two out of three would suffice, and, fortunately, the line was short. After Ramey waited on a couple more customers, it was Jenessa's turn.

"Good morning," Ramey greeted with a smile and her usual bubbly warmth, her curly red hair piled atop her head. "You look like you could use a stiff drink. What's your poison?"

"After the morning I've had, I *was* just considering a shot of tequila, but, no. Give me a double espresso and a big fat cinnamon roll. That will have to do."

"I do have a bottle of pinot in the back from last Christmas, but something tells me that wouldn't cut it. Better just go with the double espresso." Ramey leaned over the counter, her smile disappearing, her expressive blue eyes narrowing. "What's going on, Jenessa? I mean, you only have seven days until the wedding…and you told me you wanted to cut back on the cinnamon rolls or you wouldn't fit into that gorgeous wedding gown."

It was gorgeous, but would she end up wearing it?

Jenessa didn't know what to say. What could she say? Especially here, in front of all the patrons in the small café.

"I know that look." Ramey studied Jenessa's expression. "This seems serious. What happened?"

This was not the time or place to explain. Nosy ears and wagging tongues surrounded them. "I'll have to tell you later. But I do need that cinnamon roll…the more frosting on it, the better."

"Okay, it's your funeral…I mean wedding," Ramey chuckled, moving to the display case, grabbing a hefty cinnamon roll and setting it on a plate. "We do have the final fitting at the bridal shop this morning at ten, so maybe then you'll tell me?"

"That's today?" *Shoot.* With the confrontation with her nemesis that morning, it had completely slipped her mind. "Yes, right, today," she recovered. "We can talk then, sure."

Telling her best friend about Grey Alexander's

threats was one thing, but how was she going to tell Logan about her secret indiscretion? Grey assumed Logan would break off the engagement if he knew the truth. Maybe he would...but hopefully he wouldn't.

Jenessa sighed. It was all she could do for the time being. "Now, about that espresso..."

"And the fat cinnamon roll?" Ramey held up the plate. "The operative word being *fat*."

"Okay, on second thought, skip it. I have a fabulous wedding dress to fit into."

I hope.

~*~

The little brass bells on The Sweet Spot's door jingled as Logan strolled in, talking on his cell phone. At the sound, Jenessa and Ramey turned to look.

Logan caught Jenessa's gaze and smiled. "Let me know, Sam." He hung up and stuffed the phone in the pocket of his jacket.

A smile spread on his face and he went straight to Jenessa, slid his arms around her waist, and pulled her in for a proper kiss. "Good morning, sweetheart. Fancy meeting you here."

She laced her arms around his back. "You say that like this is the first time you've seen me today," she said.

He released her from the hug and leaned back to give Jenessa a quizzical, blank stare, playing along.

"Don't tell me you forgot I helped you get Grayson and Lily off to camp this morning?" Jenessa raised an eyebrow.

"Of course not. How could I forget getting up at

five am?" He grinned and planted a soft kiss on her lips.

Jenessa wrapped her arms around his waist and laid her head on his chest. "I miss them already."

There was something in her voice that sounded forlorn. He lightly kissed the top of her head.

"Are you all right, babe?"

"I'm fine." She dropped her hold and took a small step back, giving him a halfhearted smile.

"You'd tell me if—"

"Yes, yes," Jenessa interrupted, "I'm fine."

"Well, I think it was a simply brilliant idea, Jenessa," Ramey said, "sending the kids off to camp the week before the wedding. Now you can concentrate on all the last-minute details."

"Yes, I need to concentrate," Jenessa muttered, tucking her long dark hair behind one ear.

His fiancée seemed stressed, her jade-green eyes having lost their usual spunk. Was it just pre-wedding jitters, or had something else spooked his bride-to-be? Hopefully she wasn't getting cold feet. His phone rang in his pocket, but he chose to ignore it.

"Aren't you going to get that?" Ramey asked.

"Nope. Not when I have the most beautiful woman in Hidden Valley standing next to me."

"Just in Hidden Valley?"

Jenessa was teasing him again. That was a good sign. Maybe he'd misread her expression a moment ago.

"Okay, you got me," he said. "The most beautiful woman in the world. Better?"

She nodded with a little grin. "Better."

"And before I forget," Logan circled back, "make

sure you have it in your calendar that the kids will be home on Friday around five—"

"Friday, around five," Jenessa repeated.

"So we'll need to pick them up before the rehearsal dinner."

"Of course, the rehearsal dinner."

Jenessa appeared distracted again. Perhaps the good-natured ribbing was just a ruse.

"Are you sure you're okay?" he asked.

"Yes, of course. Ramey and I are off to the bridal shop for final fittings," she said with a bit of a smile. "My sister and the others are meeting us there."

"Sara has already left," Ramey said to Jenessa before turning to the groom. "And, Logan, do you have the tuxes taken care of?"

"Yep. Got the guys fitted weeks ago."

"Rings?" Ramey pressed.

"We have platinum wedding bands," Jenessa added.

Logan took Jenessa's hand. "Only because we haven't been able to nail down more than that."

"What?" Ramey gasped. "Still?"

"Jenessa wants something special," his attention shifted to his fiancée, "and we haven't found the perfect ring yet."

"We will," Jenessa said with a bob of her head and a little smile. "But for now, I'm fine with us getting married with simple wedding bands. Aren't you?"

"Absolutely." Rings or no rings, Logan wasn't going to let the love of his life slip away again. "Speaking of tuxedos, I'm not sure what to do about my father."

Jenessa's eyes popped wide. "Your father? What

does he—"

"With him being in prison and all…well, I'm not really sure what the etiquette is in this situation. I was just on the phone leaving another message for Dad's attorney. He hasn't returned any of my calls. I need to know whether or not they are going to grant my father furlough to come to the wedding."

Jenessa looked as though she were going to faint. He slipped a reassuring arm around her waist. "Are you okay?"

Jenessa straightened. "You don't need to keep asking me that."

"Aren't furloughs only for funerals of close family members?" Ramey asked.

"Maybe, but I at least had to try. He is my father."

"You were seriously thinking of inviting him? To our wedding?" Jenessa muttered.

Logan nodded. "I'm sorry, sweetheart. I should have talked to you about it before calling his lawyer."

She sighed. "No, that's okay. He's your father."

From the look on her face, though, it was far from okay.

"Anyway, like I said, it's probably a moot point," Logan went on. "I doubt he'll be able to make it."

"Why would Daddy Dearest even try to make it to a wedding that included Jenessa?" Ramey crossed her arms and glared. "There's no love lost there."

Ramey had her own issues with Grey Alexander. It hadn't been very long since they all found out that Ramey was Logan's half-sister—with Grey having had a brief affair with her mother and paying the woman to keep it quiet. Ramey's mother died before ever telling her. It was Jenessa who had uncovered the truth.

"He is part of the family." Logan frowned at Ramey. "If he weren't in prison, he'd come with or without an invitation from me. And who knows, he always seems to get what he wants, so—"

"Yeah, he does," Ramey interrupted.

"So...let's not worry about him." Logan gave Jenessa a light squeeze. "No matter what, I won't let him ruin our wedding."

~*~

It was truly a beautiful day. At least physically. The sun was already warming the air considerably, burning off the last traces of the morning dew that had chilled Jenessa at the cemetery. Too bad that big ball of fire couldn't burn off the chill that Grey had left her with.

She and Ramey walked down Main Street for a few blocks, chatting about the plans for the wedding cake Ramey was making, but Jenessa's mind was not in the game. All she could think of was her conversation that morning with Logan's father...and the one with Logan himself at The Sweet Spot a short while ago. He obviously had no idea Grey had been released from prison.

Should she have told him?

But, since he had no idea, Logan also had no way of knowing that Grey had accosted her while she visited her mother's grave.

Had Jenessa just lied to her future husband?

Well, it wasn't technically a lie, was it? She'd

omitted some important truths, yes, but to say it was a lie? Besides, what choice did she have?

Yes, what choice indeed…Grey hadn't given her a choice at all. No, he'd lurked about in the cemetery, waiting to pounce on her with these outlandish threats and allegations. Things she hadn't thought about in years. Why would she have? As far as she had been concerned there was nothing to think about. A stupid mistake that was made in haste and was rectified just as quickly.

Hopefully.

Jenessa let her gaze wander to the other side of the street, catching a glimpse of a ruggedly handsome dark-haired man—one not from around here, but one whom she thought she recognized.

No. It couldn't be.

"Jenessa, you haven't heard a word I've said," Ramey admonished. "What is it? What are you looking at?"

Jenessa brought her focus back to her friend, then did a quick double-take to the other side of the street, but the man was gone. "It's nothing. I thought I saw someone I once knew, but I was wrong. Now, what were you saying? Something about pink roses?"

"I don't believe you. Something is wrong, but you don't want to tell me." Ramey wrinkled her brows at Jenessa. "But yes, I was saying the florist needs you to make a final decision on the flowers you want. Pink roses for the wedding? What do you think?"

Jenessa pasted a smile on her face and linked her arm through Ramey's as they walked. "Yes, pink. Pink is nice. Maybe some peonies too, with white stephanotis."

Grey had her rattled. No matter how absurd his threats were, on some level, she feared them. She feared him. After all these years she had come full circle with Logan. They were in a good place. About to be married, and they had found their son. They were finally going to be a family, if Grey didn't bring everything crashing down.

As they strolled past the flower shop, a tall man with a large bouquet charged out the door, right in front of them.

"Michael," Jenessa exclaimed, almost plowing into him. "Hello...uh...uh..."

CHAPTER 3

MICHAEL LOOKED SURPRISED BY JENESSA, taking a small step back. "Jenessa. Ramey." He seemed nervous, uncomfortable, like he didn't know where to look or what to say.

"Nice flowers," Ramey remarked with a grin.

"They're for my mom. Uh…it's her birthday."

"Yes, they're beautiful," Jenessa said, feeling awkward herself. "Tell her—"

"Sorry, but I've got to go." Michael dashed away, down the sidewalk.

"See ya." Ramey breathed a laugh. "How funny to run into your ex-boyfriend on the way to your wedding gown fitting."

"Not funny." Jenessa clutched Ramey's arm tighter and pulled her toward the bridal shop down the street. She had broken his heart and there was nothing funny about that.

"Here we are," Ramey said, when they stopped in front of Evelyn's Bridal Boutique.

Jenessa studied the display window. It was the picture-perfect wedding scene. A female mannequin dressed in a flowing white gown of lace and pearls, and the male wearing a finely cut black tuxedo. There were satin banners and flowers adorning the backdrop. The whole scene gave Jenessa a sense of calmness, serenity. She was going to marry her high school sweetheart—and no one, not even Grey Alexander, was going to stop her.

"This is so exciting," Ramey beamed, admiring the stunning gown in the window. "You've been waiting for this for such a long time."

Yes, Jenessa had been waiting a long time. Thirteen years, to be exact.

"I can't wait until it's my turn." Ramey sounded wistful. "Someday, Charles and I…"

"Soon, I hope." Jenessa tugged at her friend's hand. "Come on. Let's go inside."

"No hurry, we're early." Ramey tore her gaze away from the window and followed Jenessa. They stepped through the door of the stylish boutique, which was filled with racks of gorgeous gowns, veils, and headpieces. A sparkling crystal chandelier hung in the center of the entry, with polished dark hardwood floors from front to back.

Jenessa paused, studying the intricate chandelier as thoughts and questions swirled in her head. That is, until she turned to see Ramey staring at her with a quizzical expression. "What?"

"If I didn't know better, Jenessa Jones, I'd say that you don't seem very excited about trying on your wedding dress. You're more interested in that light fixture than the bridal gowns."

"No, I am, Ramey, of course I am. I just have a lot on my mind today."

"Ah, yes, what you were alluding to at the café." Ramey stepped closer, her hand flipping through a row of dazzling gowns. "Since we have a few minutes, why don't you tell me what's going on with you."

"Oh, Ramey," she groaned, "I don't even know where to start." If she couldn't even broach the subject with her best friend, how could she ever hope to find the words to tell Logan?

"The beginning is always a good place." Ramey lifted her brows for emphasis.

"Funny." Only Jenessa wasn't laughing. Her gaze drifted out the window and across the street again, but no sign of the man she thought she'd seen. Perhaps he was never there, a figment of her active imagination.

She looked at her friend, who was wearing a serious but caring look on her face. "Come on, Jen. You're my closest friend. You can tell me anything."

"I know."

"You're not getting cold feet, are you?"

Jenessa shook her head. Cold feet? No, it was just the opposite. She was practically desperate to marry Logan. They'd talked about having a long engagement, to get to know each other again after all the years she'd been gone, but once they discovered Grayson was their long-lost son, well, Jenessa was eager to become Logan's wife. And Grayson and Lily's mother.

It was gnawing at her not to be able to say anything to Grayson. Every time she was around the boy and his little sister, it took all she had in her not to yank him into her arms and never let go.

She thought of all that the kids had been through in such a short amount a time. She could wait. After all, she'd waited this long, hadn't she? But she had to nail down the legalities of this marriage in order to feel like she could finally exhale. Then, at least, Grayson and Lily would be hers, even if it had to be as an adoptive stepparent…technically. For now.

"Fine, Ramey. The beginning, then. I went to the cemetery this morning to put flowers on my mom's grave."

Ramey draped an arm around Jenessa's shoulder. "I know she would have loved to be helping you plan your wedding and to be here for this fitting today. Is that what has you down?"

"No." Her throat tightened, and tears threatened to come, but she blinked them back. Her mother would have loved this whole wedding planning adventure, probably would have even wanted to bake her wedding cake. Lydia Jones had started The Sweet Spot bakery and café with Ramey not long before her tragic accident, and that did have Jenessa down, but it wasn't the thing that was forefront in her mind right now.

"What then?" Ramey asked.

"Grey Alexander ambushed me at the cemetery."

"What! He's out of prison?" Ramey's eyes rounded, her brows knitting together, incredulous at the thought. "How? When?" she sputtered.

"Apparently since Thursday." The idea of it twisted in Jenessa's gut.

"But when Logan told you—"

"I know, Ramey, but I couldn't talk about it."

"Why not?" she pressed.

"Because Grey threatened me." Jenessa glanced around and lowered her voice. "He said he had dug up some dirt on me and would make it public if I didn't call off the wedding."

Ramey lowered her voice too. "He's just trying to stop you from marrying Logan—what a son of a…" A scowl bloomed on Ramey's face.

Though it had been determined that Grey was her biological father, Jenessa had never known Ramey to ever consider him to be her dad.

"Wait. What kind of dirt?" Ramey's eyes widened as she whispered her questions. "What could he possibly have on you, of all people?"

Jenessa pursed her lips. "Does it matter?" A shrug. What difference did it make? Dirt was dirt.

Ramey lightly touched Jenessa's arm. "Is it true? What he's threatening you with?"

Jenessa looked down at her feet, then plopped onto a tufted settee near the front door, grateful no one was nearby. "Yes, it's true. It was a stupid mistake, a long time ago. It was nothing really, but I know Grey Alexander, and he'll find a way to make it seem worse than it really was."

Ramey's expression softened, and she took a seat beside Jenessa. "What else? Tell me. I want to help."

Help? No one could help.

"Please, tell me," Ramey pressed.

Jenessa lifted her eyes to meet Ramey's and took a deep breath, nodding. "Eight years ago, I went to a friend's wedding and met a man—"

"A man? What kind of man? You never told me—what happened?" Ramey's deep blue eyes lit up as though she had a thousand questions.

"His name was Rafe Santiago and he was a reporter."

"Like you?"

"No, he was a foreign correspondent. More serious stuff. Global."

Just then, the door to the bridal shop opened, and Jenessa's younger sister, Sara, burst in. "Global what? Warming?"

CHAPTER 4

AN IMPECCABLY DRESSED older woman came from behind a spotless glass counter, approaching as Jenessa and Ramey met Sara at the door. "I have your aunt and cousin in the back, sipping tea."

Aunt Renee was there? Thank goodness she hadn't come out while Jenessa was confessing to Ramey. That would have been a tough one to explain, although she hadn't gotten far with the story.

"Is everyone else here now?" the woman asked.

"We're just waiting for one more," Sara replied, almost apologetically.

Ramey looked around. "Who's not here?"

"That other bridesmaid," Sara said. "The one Jenessa used to work with."

"Evangeline?" Jenessa asked.

"Yes. She called Aunt Renee's this morning looking for you, Jen."

"Did you speak with her?"

"No. She left a pretty vague message. Something about a story, maybe?"

"Why didn't you tell me?" Jenessa snapped.

"Don't bite my head off," Sara said. "I'm telling you now."

"Sorry." Jenessa glanced out the large storefront window, Grey's threat and the memory of what she had done in Vegas were working her last nerve. She hoped her friend, Evangeline, wouldn't make things even worse by not being able to come for the wedding.

"It's just wedding jitters," Ramey said to Sara.

Jenessa turned away from the window. "I am sorry, Sara. I'm just afraid if Ev drops out of the wedding party, that will throw things off. That's all."

But was it?

It was after Evangeline's wedding in Las Vegas that Jenessa had made what was now turning out to be a critical mistake. Thinking of Evangeline brought to mind Rafe again, and the day they had met at Evangeline's nuptials.

Would Ev have invited Rafe to come to Jenessa's wedding as her plus one? That might explain why she may have seen Rafe earlier, if it was him. But that was unlikely. For all Jenessa knew, Evangeline hadn't seen Rafe in all these years either. At least, she'd never mentioned it when they had spoken on the phone every so often.

Jenessa gave her head a shake. "Let me give her a quick call, see what's holding her up."

She pulled out her phone and realized there was a missed call from Evangeline. She immediately dialed the number, and Evangeline answered on the second ring.

Jenessa explained she was at the bridal shop for the final fitting and asked if she was on her way.

"I'm so sorry, Jenessa. I left a message with your aunt. I'm stuck in Sacramento on a breaking story. There's no way I can get away until at least Monday. I hope that's okay."

It would have to be, now wouldn't it? "If it can't be helped, sure."

As she spoke with Evangeline, the image of Rafe refused to leave her mind. He and Evangeline's husband had been good friends, and Jenessa and Rafe had both been in their wedding. Evangeline might at least know where he was, and hopefully she wouldn't say it was Hidden Valley.

"This is going to sound a little weird, Ev," Jenessa took a couple of steps toward the display window for a bit more privacy, and lowered her voice, "but I wonder if you know where Rafe Santiago is."

"Rafe? No. We haven't heard from him in years. Why do you ask?"

"I'm sure I'm wrong, and this is going to sound kind of silly, but," Jenessa peered out the front windows toward the street, "I thought I saw him this morning."

"In Hidden Valley?"

"Yes, of all places." Jenessa laughed a little to cover her nervousness. If he were in Hidden Valley, it would have to be Grey's doing. "I was probably seeing things, right?"

Please say I was seeing things.

"Last I heard he was covering a story in Afghanistan," Evangeline said, "or some other God-forsaken place. Rudy and I tried reaching him for a while, but it seemed like he'd dropped off the face of the earth or something. Finally, we stopped trying, figuring wherever he was, he didn't want to be found."

The other side of the world, that was a much better place for him to be. "Yeah, you're probably right. He's likely been busy covering important global stories."

Hidden Valley had its share of news, some might even be considered rather big, but it didn't come anywhere close to the constant stream of news out of the Middle East.

"That makes more sense, Ev. I mean, with him being a bigtime foreign correspondent and all. It must have been my imagination. I was remembering your wedding this morning—" thanks to Grey Alexander, "—and I probably just had Rafe on my mind." Her friend must have thought she was nuts, seeing things. "Anyway, I'd better let you go and get back to your hot story. I'll see you on Monday. Call me when you're on your way."

Jenessa put her phone away and pasted a smile on her face as she joined the others. "Evangeline can't make it until Monday."

Aunt Renee stepped out from the back room. "There you all are. We've been waiting, wondering when you girls would get here."

"Sorry, Aunt Renee," Jenessa offered.

"No worries. I've enjoyed getting to know your cousin. But it's time to get on with this fitting, and I want to see you in your dress."

Jenessa linked an arm through her sister's and one through Ramey's as they headed toward the back of the shop where the modeling platform and changing rooms were located. "Let's get this party started, shall we?"

"I'll second that," Sara said.

Seated, facing the platform, was a young woman who turned at the sound of their entrance. Selena Vergara was a cousin of Jenessa and Sara's, on their mother's side—Aunt Renee had met her once and had very kindly offered to let her stay with her for the wedding. Selena's features were classic Latina—warm brown eyes, long dark hair like Jenessa's, and golden-brown skin covering a stunning face and an hour-glass body. She stood as the women approached.

Close in age, she and Jenessa had been the best of friends while growing up in San Francisco, before Jenessa's family moved to Hidden Valley. Through their college years, they had kept in contact off and on. After graduation, Selena, being fluent in Spanish, had taken an internship at a television station in Spain, which turned into a great job opportunity. They had drifted apart over time and had lost touch until recently.

Now back in the states, Selena was working for a Spanish television station in San Diego, which thrilled Jenessa because it meant she was able to be her third bridesmaid, not to mention she could reconnect with her cherished cousin.

"Jenessa!" Selena went to her and gave her a warm embrace. "Oh, how I have missed you."

"Me too! I'm glad you could make it."

Selena moved to Sara next and gave her a big hug too. "So good to see you, Sara."

Jenessa proceeded to introduce Selena to Ramey, as Sara explained to her friend that their cousin was a news reporter for a television station in Southern California. Ramey giggled and bounced like she was meeting a movie star. Sara rolled her eyes.

Jenessa gave her aunt a light hug. "How are you doing, Aunt Renee?"

It had only been a few months since their aunt had been hospitalized with heart problems, which had scared them all to death. The girls were doting on her less and less, but the concern still had a way of slipping out from time to time.

"I'm fine, of course." She waved a dismissive hand toward Jenessa.

"Have you heard from Cousin Isabel?" Selena asked. "Will she and Alex be coming for the wedding?"

Ramey's brows lowered. "Who is Cousin Isabel?"

"Her mother and my mother were cousins, so she's actually second, or is it third, cousin—I never get that right." Jenessa turned to Selena. "She RSVP'd, so yes, they should be coming."

"And she's an FBI agent, Ramey," Sara pointed out. "So Jenessa had better be on her best behavior."

Jenessa shot her sister a smirk. "Very funny."

"Is she coming from Washington DC?" Ramey asked.

"No, from Paradise Valley, Idaho," Jenessa replied. "She works in the Boise office."

Just then a diminutive, middle-aged redheaded woman with glasses and sensible shoes stepped through the draped doorway from the changing rooms. With a tape measure hanging from around her neck, it was obvious she had to be the seamstress.

"Pay attention, girls," Aunt Renee said.

Jenessa looked again to her aunt. She was beaming as if she were the mother of the bride. Since Lydia Jones' passing, Renee had been the closest thing to a mother that Jenessa and Sara had had. The sister of Jenessa's late father, and a sophisticated social pillar in Hidden Valley society, Aunt Renee watched over the girls, including the motherless Ramey.

Renee clapped her hands together lightly a few times. "Time is wasting."

"Your dresses are hanging in the fitting rooms," the sales lady said. "Come out as soon as you have them on, and Mrs. Meyers here will mark any alterations that still need to be made."

The young women filed into the back rooms, as requested. Ramey offered to help Jenessa into her gown, which Jenessa gladly accepted.

"There's no way I can get all those little buttons fastened up the back."

Once in the fitting room, with the door shut, Ramey quietly spoke. "Your cousin is so beautiful. Wow. And a celebrity too." She began to carefully pull Jenessa's gown from the hanger. "But this mysterious man you started telling me about...who is he and what's his connection to you?"

"Not so loud," Jenessa said softly, but Ramey didn't seem to hear her.

"Is there a reason he'd be in town for your wedding? I don't recall you ever mentioning him before."

"Shhh." Jenessa put a finger in front of Ramey's lips. "Keep your voice down," she whispered as she stepped out of her sundress.

Ramey bobbed up and down restlessly. "Come on, I'm dying to know."

"Fine," she said, stepping into the dress that Ramey was holding out for her. "He was the best man at my friend Evangeline's wedding, and I was her maid of honor."

"How come I never heard of this before?"

"It was a long time ago, after college. Evangeline and I worked at a Sacramento newspaper together. She needed a maid of honor, so I said I'd do it. It was nothing."

"Doesn't sound like nothing."

"She and Rudy had a quick Vegas wedding, some older family members came, a few friends. No big deal."

"Hmmm." Ramey crossed her arms and shifted her weight. "So, where's the big mystery? There has to be more to it than that."

She fixed her eyes on Jenessa and refused to back down.

"There's no big mystery, Ramey." At least, not one that Jenessa wanted to share. She ignored Ramey's inquisitive gaze and slipped the gown up over her shoulders, snaked her arms through the lacy cap sleeves, and adjusted the fit.

Ramey began working the delicate tiny buttons into their loops all the way down Jenessa's back. "So then, why were you so upset this morning at the café, if it was no big thing?"

"I already told you, Grey ambushed me at the cemetery."

Ramey stopped with the buttons and spun Jenessa around to look at her. "Yes, you told me he ambushed you—the thought of it makes my skin crawl—but you never finished telling me the rest. What did the old man want?"

Jenessa went to the door and peeked out, making sure no one was standing close enough to overhear them. "Listen, Ramey," she closed the door and locked it, "you can't repeat any of this, to anyone. Understand?"

CHAPTER 5

HOLED UP IN THE BRIDAL BOUTIQUE dressing room, Ramey nodded at Jenessa's directive to keep her confidence, her face lighting up like a child who was about to find out the secret to their favorite magic trick.

"Okay, then," Jenessa went on. "Like I told you, Grey said he had uncovered some incriminating information about me, and he threatened to expose it if I didn't break up with Logan—in the next forty-eight hours."

Ramey sucked in a quick breath. "Forty-eight hours?" she blurted then brought her volume back down to a whisper. "You? What incriminating information could he possibly have on you?" Her eyes grew round and her expression changed as though a lightbulb was flicking on inside her head. "It's something about your mysterious Rafe isn't it?"

But before Jenessa could acknowledge—or deny— the allegations, there were two quick raps on the dressing room door. "Are you almost ready, girls?" Aunt Renee jiggled the doorknob. "Mrs. Meyers is waiting."

Mrs. Dobson, the Alexanders' housekeeper since Logan was around eleven—for about twenty years—had phoned him and asked him to come by his father's manor estate. Although he had no idea what she could be calling him about, Logan didn't hesitate to tell her he would come right over. In her mid-sixties now, she was more like a grandmother to Logan than a housekeeper. She had known of Grey's abusive behavior and had tried to shield Logan whenever she could.

Logan pulled his BMW onto the long circular driveway. The expansive white-brick mansion he had grown up in loomed grandiosely ahead of him. Though his legacy came with a great deal of money and prestige, he preferred living in his own condo, even though this place remained empty, aside from the staff, while his father was incarcerated. Logan couldn't bring himself to live there, no matter if the house was spectacular or if one day it would be rightfully his.

Who knew how long it would sit idle, waiting for Grey Alexander to make his grand return...and, truly, who really cared?

The kids had been happily living with Logan since his cousin Summer, their adoptive mother, had died. It was particularly hard on Jenessa, Logan knew, not being able to have her own son living with her after all the years of searching for him.

Soon that would change. As soon as they returned from their honeymoon the two would take the children and make a new life with them, raising them in Jenessa's comfortable family home.

Something caught Logan's eye as he came to a stop, off to the side of the main house. His gaze was drawn toward a figure stalking across the side lawn toward the house.

No. It couldn't be.

But it was.

Grey Alexander strode hurriedly from the gatehouse with a stern look on his face, his father not appearing to have seen him.

A fire rose up in Logan's chest at the sight of that gatehouse. He despised that place. From the outside, it appeared charming, but it was anything but that to Logan. No, to him it represented so much pain that he shuddered at the mere memory of it.

That gatehouse was full of hidden secrets. Awful things. None of which had any justification, but all of which his father had attempted to either ignore or validate in some way. It was where his father went to get away from the family when Logan still lived at home. No one, not even Logan's mother, was allowed to set foot in that place unbidden.

Grey had told them it was where he conducted business, or unwound after a hectic day, but Logan knew much more went on behind those closed doors. It was where his father went to entertain someone privately...often someone of the female persuasion. If that was all, he could stomach that.

But it was also a place of discipline when Logan was younger—severe discipline. Things he had never spoken about—to anyone. He'd alluded to it before with Jenessa, but even she did not know to what extent the wrath of Grey Alexander could rain down. Logan shivered at the memories of what had happened to him there, then brought his attention back to the shocking visage in front of him.

How on earth had his father gotten out of prison, and how long had he been here? Why had he not told his own son he was being released?

And why was his father coming from the gatehouse? Was he checking on his belongings, to make sure they were as he had left them?

Logan had more questions than answers as he parked the car up near the front door—the fastest place to make a quick getaway, if necessary. He had no idea what would transpire when his father saw him there.

Was this why Mrs. Dobson had called him? Was it at his father's request or was it intended to warn him before his father could wreak havoc on Logan and Jenessa's wedding?

He considered the family business. What did this mean where that was concerned? Logan had been running his father's companies since the man was sent to prison, and the board members had been happy with his work. "Extremely pleased" was how one of them had put it.

There were rumblings that they would prefer to keep Logan on and oust his father as president, regardless of any potential release from prison, whether early or not.

Had Grey caught wind of the rumors? Of the board's possible intentions? Is that why he had found a way to get released? Had his team of attorneys kept their ears to the ground and reported back to him? If his father knew what the board was up to, he would consider it mutiny, and they would surely go to war.

~*~

Something painful twisted in Logan's gut as he rang the doorbell.

Within moments, Mrs. Dobson answered the door and the pain began to subside. A smile spread on the older woman's face.

"Hello, Mrs. Dobson." Logan stepped into her open arms for a tight hug. "It has been too long."

"Oh, Logan, it is good to see you." She released him from her embrace. "And I have to say, I am just thrilled that you and that young lady have finally found your bearings." She shook her head. "It was a crying shame what happened to you, how you two were torn apart."

Logan let his hand linger on the woman's shoulder and he gave it a gentle squeeze. Mrs. Dobson was part of the family. He was drawn to her warm personality and the way she had watched over him as a child, especially after his parents divorced when he was twelve and Logan was too often alone in the house with his father.

He glanced around nervously. Where had dear old dad disappeared to so quickly?

"Sorry I haven't come to visit," he said, truly meaning it. Since his father's arrest, more than a year prior, he'd decided he no longer had a reason to darken the doors of this house. At least his father had done the honorable thing and kept Mrs. Dobson and some of the other staff on to maintain the place until his release, even if it was for selfish reasons.

"No need to be sorry. I can't blame you, Logan. Running your father's businesses must have taken a lot of your time. And, besides, why on earth would you *choose* to come back here when you didn't have to?"

"Yes, business has been keeping me jumping. And I'm getting married in a few days."

"I know." Her expression took on a look of pride. "I received an invitation and already returned my RSVP."

Jenessa must have sent it. He had meant to put Mrs. Dobson on the list, but there was so much going on that he had forgotten. "My fiancée is handling all that, as you might have guessed, but I'm thrilled you can make it."

"Do you know why I called you?" She closed the large front door.

"I have a feeling," he said.

"So, you saw your father then?"

Logan nodded.

"Well, then, I shouldn't be keeping you, Logan. He is expecting you, and you know full well he doesn't like being kept waiting."

So, she had phoned him at his father's request. Too bad she hadn't given him some warning.

"I saw him coming from the gatehouse, but I suppose he's back in his office by now?"

Her hand went to her chest and her brows knit together in a frown. "The gatehouse," she muttered.

"Something wrong?" Logan asked.

She looked past him as if to see if his father was approaching. In low tones she said, "He had me change the linens and put out fresh towels first thing this morning. I can only assume someone is planning to stay there."

"Any idea who it might be?" Logan whispered, leaning closer to her.

A colleague? One of his attorneys? Had he made a new female *friend* already since getting out?

"I don't know," she replied with a slight shake of her head. "Your father was rather tight-lipped about it, and I know better than to press him."

Yes, Grey Alexander did not like to be questioned…or opposed. A light film of sweat bloomed on Logan's forehead at what might be ahead. There was no benefit in putting this off. "I'd better go find him."

"Logan!" his father called from down the hall. "You're late!"

"Be strong," Mrs. Dobson whispered as she squeezed his arm and looked him in the eyes. "You are a grown man now."

Logan straightened as he turned. Yes, he was a grown man now—strong and smart, a leader. Everyone saw him that way. Everyone except his father. He'd have to make his dad see him like that, as well.

He squared his shoulders and sucked in a deep breath. "I'm coming," he called out, "and I'm right on time."

~*~

Jenessa and her bridal party poured out of the wedding boutique. They clustered around her on the sidewalk, chatting about the wedding and the dresses.

"So, Jenessa, you said the kids got off to camp all right?" Aunt Renee asked.

"The kids?" Selena asked. "What kids?"

"They were Logan's cousin's kids," Aunt Renee replied. "She died and left them to Logan."

"That means soon you will be a mother," Selena commented, looking to Jenessa. "Interesting turn of events."

"Yes," Jenessa replied to her aunt's question, ignoring what Selena said, "Logan and I managed to get them to the buses on time, in spite of the early hour."

"Do you think they'll be okay?" Aunt Renee's face morphed from glowing aunt of the bride to worried matriarch. "I mean, going away so soon after losing their mother and…well, you know."

"It's okay." Ramey placed a hand on the woman's shoulder. "Charles took Charlie this morning too. Grayson and Charlie have become pretty close buds in the last several weeks. Two peas in a pod."

"I suppose with both losing their mothers." Aunt Renee seemed pleased to know that.

"Charlie has been a big help to Grayson," Ramey continued. "And I think it has helped Charlie too."

"How's that?" Sara asked.

"Well, Charles says Charlie might be coming around, where I am concerned." A smile swept across Ramey's face at that. "I think he's getting ready to propose."

"That's wonderful, Ramey." Jenessa was tickled pink that her best friend was so happy and in love with a good man.

And Charles was a very good man, loving and kind, hardworking and stable. Sometimes he was a strict boss, but he was only trying to keep the newspaper afloat amidst what might be a dying industry.

The Hidden Valley Herald was a small paper with a small staff, and the locals seemed deeply steeped in tradition, which helped the business. The more resistant the townspeople were to be switching to Internet news, the longer she would have a job in this town.

That is, unless Grey Alexander had his way.

"I'm taking Selena home with me," Aunt Renee announced, bringing Jenessa's attention back to the group.

"No, no, I have my own rental car, Renee," Selena said, giving Jenessa's aunt a hug. "I want to pick up a few things first, so I can just meet you at your house. Text me the address."

Renee's eyes grew round. "Text you the address?" She sounded like someone had asked her to program the space shuttle launch.

"I'll do it." Jenessa smiled and pulled out her cell, texting the information. "There."

"Can you and Logan come over for dinner tonight?" Aunt Renee asked.

Texting she could do, but Jenessa couldn't possibly make plans for this evening. She needed to figure out a way to come clean with Logan about what happened with Rafe all those years ago—before his father did.

"I'll have to check with Logan," Jenessa said.

Jenessa and Logan shared an incredibly complicated history and yet their relationship had only been blossoming for a few short months. Everything, both good and bad, was still so fresh and delicate. She should probably just beg off for tonight, as much as she would love to see her aunt and catch up with her cousin, Selena.

"Actually, we have a lot going on right before the wedding, Aunt Renee," Jenessa said, "so tonight is probably not a good time."

"I'm sure you do, but your cousin is only in town until the wedding, so..."

"Yes, I know. I'll try," Jenessa said to appease her aunt, "but don't count on us." She gave the woman a warm hug. "I've got to get to work. Thanks for the help today."

"You're welcome, my dear. Hope to see you tonight."

Everyone scattered to go their separate ways, but Ramey followed Jenessa.

"So, you have a cousin that's in the FBI? How cool is that?"

CHAPTER 6

"I'VE NEVER MET A REAL FBI AGENT BEFORE,"
Ramey said, clearly impressed. "That is way cool."

"I never thought of it that way," Jenessa replied, as
she kept walking, "but yeah, I guess it is pretty cool. I
really can't stay and talk about it."

Ramey tugged on Jenessa's arm. "Hey, we need to
finish our conversation about what happened—"

"With Grey?" Jenessa stopped and turned to reply,
catching a glimpse of a dark-haired man ducking into the
hamburger place across the street. Could it have been
Rafe? She gave her head a shake and brought her focus
back to Ramey. "I know, and we will, I just can't right
now."

"I didn't mean now." Ramey looked at her watch.
"It's almost eleven thirty and I promised Maria I'd be
back to help her with the lunch crowd. Just tell me
when."

"You go and help Maria, and we'll talk later. I promise I'll tell you everything."

Ramey's deep blue eyes twinkled as she grinned with anticipation and then turned to walk away. "I'm holding you to that, my friend," she said over her shoulder as she hurried down the street.

Jenessa had to know if her mind was playing tricks on her or not. She dashed across the street and hurried into Dad's Hamburgers. A small crowd of people were lined up at the counter to place their orders.

The third person in line looked like Rafe from the back, at least from what she remembered—straight black hair, over six feet tall, muscular build—but was it? She stood just inside the door and watched him move to his chance at the counter. He placed his order and turned, assumingly to find a seat. As he surveyed the place for an empty table, he locked eyes with Jenessa, briefly.

It was not Rafe. *Whew!*

Was she losing her mind? Fear was doing that. Grey Alexander was doing that. She was angry at herself for letting him get to her.

She stood by the door like a statue, staring, relief washing over her. What would she have said to him if it had been Rafe? That the night she had been with him was now about to blow her happy world apart, as had the pivotal evening she had spent with Logan all those years ago?

When she was seventeen, the trajectory of her life had veered off course in an unexpected direction when she had gotten pregnant. She had spent the next twelve years trying to rebuild her life and find the baby boy she had given up for adoption.

Finally, a little more than a year ago, she had found her way back to Hidden Valley, back to Logan. She was happy now—indescribably happy. But now Grey Alexander was giving ultimatums that could destroy that. If Rafe was in Hidden Valley, Grey had to be the reason. Why else would he show up here after all these years?

But no, this man wasn't Rafe, she reminded herself. Thank God for that. If she was lucky, Rafe would never show up here.

Jenessa sighed, spun around, and stepped outside. She didn't have time for little side adventures like thinking she had seen a man from her past, a man whom their mutual friends had not even heard from in years either.

She sucked in a deep breath and blew it out to release the pent-up stress. She headed off, down Main Street, to grab a coffee and a sandwich at The Sweet Spot before going in to the newspaper.

"Jenessa," a man whispered.

The late summer sun was warm on her bare arms, but a chill rippled down her spine. Surely, she was hearing things. Her mind had to be playing tricks on her again. She turned toward the voice to find a head peeking out from around the corner of the building.

Rafe.

He motioned for her to come to him.

She flinched, and then darted her eyes in all directions, fully expecting to see her fiancé's father standing nearby too. There was no way she was going to let either of them destroy her dream of a family.

"Come this way," he urged.

There was no running from this. The man in front of her was real this time. She quickly scanned up and down Main Street. No one could see them together. It was the last thing she could allow.

Nobody seemed to notice her—and Grey did not appear to be anywhere in sight—so, she rushed around the corner of the building and into the alley.

"Hello, Jenessa. It's been a while." He reached a hand out, but she stepped back. His smile faded and his eyebrows dropped at her evasive response.

She didn't care. It wasn't like they were friends. Too much time had passed between them, and him showing up now, like this, it brought up too many suspicions—and it reeked of Grey Alexander.

"Sit down, Logan." His father gestured toward a leather chair across from his desk.

No pleasantries of any sort. No "Hey, Son, Dad's back from prison," or even "Logan, I'm so glad to see you." It was simply business as usual, at least from his father's handbook of corporate practices. Just sit down and shut up, let the boss do the talking.

The man had only been in prison a little more than a year. He had been sentenced to three, but somehow, clearly, with his money and connections, he had finagled a way out early.

Logan took a seat, however grudgingly. "I'm surprised to see you. You didn't give me any warning they were letting you out early, Dad. I would have come and picked you up." Although it wasn't true.

His father's gaze lingered on him. He probably knew it wasn't true, as well. "There's a lesson to be learned here, Son." He tapped his finger on the desk for emphasis. "Always use the element of surprise to your advantage."

Even with his own son?

"To your advantage how?" Logan knew what his father meant, but he hoped to draw out information by playing coy.

"Against your enemies."

"Am I one of your enemies?"

"Of course not, Logan. Don't get smart. I meant that bunch of clowns who sit on our company's board of directors."

"You think they're your enemies? They've helped me keep your companies running while you've been gone."

Anger darkened his father's eyes. "Are you in cahoots with those traitors?"

He would never tolerate his son turning on him.

"Of course not." Logan leaned forward in his chair. "Why do you think they're traitors?"

"My attorneys informed me that they've heard rumblings, talk of a coup."

"I don't know where they would have—"

"They are trying to gather support to unseat me as president, Logan!" His eyes were bulging as he screamed it, and his cheeks flamed red.

"Now calm down, Dad. You don't want to have a heart attack over rumors."

Grey's eyes narrowed. "Are you saying it's not true?"

Logan didn't want to lie, but there was no way he was going to give away the fact that the board wanted to make him the new president. "I'm saying it's probably just rumors. Calm down until you know something definitive."

He would find out the truth soon enough. The board had not been aware of Grey's early release. Or, if they had, they hadn't seen fit to inform Logan of it. Likely they would be scrambling as soon as they learned he was back.

The timing could not have been worse. The wedding was only five days away, and Logan did not need any more drama. At least not until after he and Jenessa returned from their honeymoon.

Logan rose to leave. If he stayed a moment longer, his father might be able to get something out of him that Logan would certainly regret having spilled. Even now, as a grown man, it was nearly impossible for Logan to resist his father's intimidation.

"Where are you going?" He leaned his hands on the desk as though about to get up. "We're not done here. We need to figure out what to do to stop the board members from overthrowing me."

"You need to wait until you have the facts before you go off all halfcocked, Dad."

His father leapt from his chair and dashed around his desk to face Logan toe to toe. "How dare you talk to me like that? You don't know half of what it takes to run a large corporation like Alexander Enterprises."

Logan stood his ground, feeling the spit flying from his father's mouth as he spoke, his eyes squinting with anger. Logan held his breath, working up the courage not to back down. He could do this. Logan exhaled.

"I know you don't think so, Dad, but I have been running the companies while you've been in jail and running them quite successfully, no thanks to—"

His father took a step back, his lips pinched together, anger still etched on his face. "Why you little—"

As Logan stood basking in his small victory, he failed to notice the back of his father's hand as it flew toward his face, smacking hard against the side of Logan's mouth. He shouldn't have been surprised. He raised his finger to his lips and drew it back, seeing the blood there, the evidence of his father's continued quick temper.

The anger drained immediately from his father's face. "I'm sorry, Son, I didn't mean—"

Logan stepped back as he clicked his jaw from side to side. "Right, *Dad.* I know just how sorry you are."

His father stood there, staring blankly back at Logan. No words came. But then again, no words could suffice, under the circumstances. They never could, but it was the same every time. Grey Alexander's incendiary temper went from flaring to detonation, and back to a sputter in mere seconds.

There was always an excuse followed by a quick, rote apology. The boy Logan used to be always accepted his father's apologies, actually believed he'd meant it. Until the next time, which could be days or weeks away, but sometimes only moments.

But the man Logan was becoming...well, that was a different story. He used to keep his mouth shut. "What would people say?" That was how his father managed to maintain a rein on Logan's so-called loyalty. But, increasingly, Logan was caring less and less about what *people* might think.

Still vibrating with anger, he glared at his father. "I have to meet Jenessa," he announced, willing himself to look his father straight in the eye before turning to leave.

Logan moved toward the door, then paused, turning back. "I'm guessing you own a tux."

There was no pretense of subtlety. There was no need for it. It was as likely as hell freezing over as it was trying to stop his father from inviting himself to the wedding, now that he was out.

"I do." Anger pooled in his eyes once more. "Lucky me. I got out of prison just in time to see my only son marry a conniving gold digger."

And there it was. The apology phase was over in that instant.

Logan took one large, quick step toward him and stopped. "Never, ever talk about her like that again," he ground out in a low, controlled voice, fury rising inside him. He carefully measured his words and the volume, refusing to cower in front of the man as he had when he was a child. "Jenessa *is* going to be my wife, and you'll just have to deal with it."

A devilish smirk spread across his father's mouth. "And that's precisely what I intend to do."

CHAPTER 7

JENESSA CROSSED HER ARMS AND stood facing Rafe in the alley. A part of her wanted to pinch herself to make sure she wasn't dreaming this up, and another part wanted to pretend she was.

"What are you doing here, Rafe, in Hidden Valley?"

"After all these years, this is how you greet me?" Rafe said, feigning that she had hurt his feelings. "No hug or kiss for your—"

"Look, I'm sorry I don't have a better greeting for you, Rafe, but that was a long time ago," Jenessa huffed.

He rubbed his stubbled jaw. "I was kidding."

She was not in a joking mood. "Why are you here? Why now?" It seemed a little too coincidental. "We have no contact for years, then all of a sudden—"

"I was in prison in Afghanistan."

"Oh, my gosh, no." She calmed a bit and uncrossed her arms. "Why?"

"As a foreign correspondent, we get sent to dangerous places. You know that."

She did know. "What happened?"

"I was working on a story and got scooped up with some Taliban insurgents I was trying to get intel from. When the Afghan troops discovered I wasn't a rebel, they threw me in a hole for a few years, hoping to get some ransom money."

He went on to explain his imprisonment and torture, and how he was finally released by US-led NATO troops.

She began to cross her arms again, then dropped them to her sides, not wanting to appear hostile or uncaring.

"You don't believe me? I can show you the scars."

Rafe started to pull up his shirt when she put a hand on his arm and blurted, "No, don't."

He dropped his shirt at her request.

"I have no reason to doubt what you're saying," she said. He had obviously been through a lot since they had parted ways. Her problems seemed trivial in comparison. "So, is that when you returned to the US?"

"No, there were other assignments, other countries."

"I get it, the exciting life of a foreign correspondent."

He cocked his head and pumped his brows. "Hey, that's what attracted you to me, doll."

"That and a lot of alcohol. Evangeline and Rudy's wedding was crazy, wasn't it? I never drank so much before, or since."

"Don't you Americans have a saying like 'What happens in Vegas stays in Vegas' or something like that?"

"That's pretty much how it goes, yeah." She laughed at the memory of their brief time together. Then the reality of it set in, of him being here, in Hidden Valley, of talking with Rafe after all these years, and her muscles tensed.

"With all that traveling, when did you find time to file those papers?" she asked.

"Papers?" His face went blank.

The pressure in her chest tightened, her eyes grew wide, and fear settled down, deep in her stomach. "You're joking, right?"

His face remained blank, his mouth seeming like he wanted to say something, but couldn't.

Jenessa waited, her breath held. "Rafe?"

Finally he said, "Oh, those papers."

"Rafe, no. You swore you would take care of it."

His gaze dropped to the ground, avoiding her eyes. "I know I promised, Jenessa, and I meant to, it's just that, well, like I said, I had a lot going on."

The muscles in her shoulders tensed. "But you did take care of it eventually, didn't you?"

He lifted his dark eyes to her, wincing as he gave a shrug. "Not exactly."

Not exactly? That meant not at all. She had been young and stupid. At this time in her life, she would never have relied on a man she barely knew—but she had back then, naively, and she'd gone on with her life, trusting he did the right thing. *So stupid!*

Her heart pounded so hard it hurt. *This can't be happening.* Her throat tightened, and her stomach churned. Grey Alexander was going to destroy her.

"What do you mean *not exactly?*" she squeaked out.

~*~

The tires of Logan's red BMW squealed as he tore down the driveway of his father's estate. He'd stormed out of there, not even stopping to say good-bye to Mrs. Dobson. Heat began creeping up the back of Logan's neck.

He'd done a good job taking over the businesses, in spite of being thrust into the position with little warning. There was the newspaper, the bank, the real estate agency, to name a few…would it take his own father's death before Logan would be allowed to fully come into his own?

He felt a little like Prince Charles waiting a lifetime for his mother to pass to sit on the throne and become the King of England. Logan shook his head. Perhaps that was overdoing it. Maybe he felt more like Tom Brady's backup quarterback…

Either way, it wasn't fair. Not fair at all. He'd more than proven himself. If he hadn't, there was no way the board would even be considering him to replace his father as head of Alexander Enterprises.

He had been able to squirrel money away, not living as lavishly as his father. Maybe this would be the perfect time to start his own business and get out from under his father's thumb once and for all.

Logan turned into the parking lot of his downtown office. Time was against him, and he had better warn the board members of his father's intentions—and that the man was out of prison. From his parking space he phoned Max Lindsay, who was the head of the board.

Once Mr. Lindsay picked up, Logan relayed the conversation he'd had with his father.

"I'm not one bit surprised," the older gentleman said. "I had heard rumors about his early release, but I thought it was simply speculation. I've already spoken to several of the board members about holding a meeting this afternoon—strategic deliberations, about transferring the reins to you, Logan—but now we'll just have to add Grey's early release to the agenda. We need to figure out how we should deal with him."

"You know as well as I do that he'll do whatever it takes to hold on to his position as president. My father can play pretty dirty when he wants to." Logan stroked the side of his jaw, which still ached.

"Yes...I'm well aware of that."

"What time do you want me there?"

"Perhaps your time would be better spent keeping your father away from the meeting. Take him golfing or something."

"We exchanged some pretty heated words this morning...I'm sure he'd know something was up if I called and said I suddenly wanted to take him out for a round of golf."

"Apologize. Lie if you have to. Tell him you are very sorry about the way things went this morning and, to make up for it, you want to treat him to a game of golf. He would buy that, wouldn't he?"

Could Logan get those words out of his mouth without gagging on them? "Maybe."

"Golf, fishing, a late lunch—do whatever you can to keep him busy from three to four this afternoon. It's your best chance of keeping your position as acting president."

Logan agreed and said his good-byes.

After the things his father had said about Jenessa, how could Logan manage to stay in the same room with the man? And after the way Logan had stood up to him, walked out on him, would his father agree to be in the same room as Logan?

He wanted to hear Jenessa's voice. Perhaps that would calm him down. She was the one true thing that had always gotten him through the tough times. Even before she returned to Hidden Valley. He always held her in his mind as the gold standard. It was a pity, but all the women he had dated over the years couldn't even come close to Jenessa. None had stood a chance of truly capturing his heart.

He had once tried dating Sara, Jenessa's sister, but even she couldn't hold a candle to the flame that Jenessa had ignited within his heart. And now, to have her back, to have their son back…Logan would do anything to protect that. Anything. Including kissing up to his old man.

He dialed Jenessa's number, anticipation building as he imagined her voice saying hello, but after several rings it went to her voicemail. Leaving a message would have to do.

"Hey, babe. Call me back when you get this message. Can you believe we're getting married in only five days? I love you." And he hung up.

As he sat in the car, the words *my father can play pretty dirty when he wants to* echoed in Logan's mind. That was, in truth, an understatement. If he fought his father for the presidency of the company—oh the things Grey might choose to do. He would likely even go so far as to try to orchestrate something to blow up his and Jenessa's wedding plans.

He climbed out of the car and beeped the key fob to lock it. It was all on him now, and he would have to find a way to stop his father.

~*~

Rafe looked at his watch. "I've got to go."

"Wait."

"I've already told you about Alexander." He peeked around the corner of the building, up and down the street. "We'll talk more later," he said, his expression serious, "but there's something I've got to do right now."

"No, wait," she urged, but her phone began to ring. It was her editor. "Give me just a minute."

She turned away to take the call, but when she turned back he was gone.

Still not knowing for certain what had happened to the annulment papers, she could safely assume from what Rafe *had* said, that they were missing in action, much like he had been.

She headed to work, shaken by her encounter with Rafe. She hoped a juicy story would help take her mind off this mess, even if only for a few hours. But Charles had assigned her some local stories of society events and wedding news—no juicy stories to be had, except her own, which she was not going to write about.

Sitting before the computer, she found her mind wandering. Of course she did. What Rafe had told her had shaken her to her soul. It had been bad enough when she'd thought she was faced with having to admit to Logan what had happened in Vegas, but now, having to tell him that the mistake hadn't been rectified.

Rafe had seemed cagey, and he wouldn't tell her much, except that Grey Alexander's investigator had found him and had paid him a great deal of money to come to Hidden Valley to destroy her upcoming marriage to Logan.

Why would Rafe agree to that, to hurt her? Truth was he hardly knew her, so was it just for the money?

She believed the part about Grey tracking him down, paying him an exorbitant amount of cash. That man would apparently stop at nothing to ruin her life and keep her away from his son. But something about the rest of it didn't sit right with her.

Rafe had said he needed the money to finish something he had started. What did that mean?

Ultimately, where Rafe had been all these years was of little consequence. The fact that he was here now, less than a week before her wedding—his timing could not have been worse.

How was she going to explain to Logan her connection to Rafe? And how would he react? Grey was obviously betting on his son calling off the wedding—would he?

Logan wouldn't have to. She was quite certain she was still married to someone else. She had better call her lawyer.

~*~

Logan sat at his desk and gazed about the office that was once his father's. Everything in it reflected Grey Alexander and his tastes—almost everything, Logan had placed a few photos on the desk, Jenessa of course.

If Logan wanted to keep this job, he knew what had to be done...he had to bite the proverbial bullet. He picked up the phone.

"Hi, Dad. Listen, about before..."

His father quite bluntly declined Logan's invitation to a round of golf. Said he had "business" to attend to, but Logan could decipher what that meant...something to do with the mysterious person staying at the gatehouse.

He couldn't quite put his finger on the why, but he had a sneaking suspicion that the person—whoever it was staying in his father's gatehouse—could only mean trouble.

CHAPTER 8

UNABLE TO FOCUS ON WORK, Jenessa left the newspaper and headed out for a walk down Main Street. Maybe she would be lucky enough to find Rafe again. It hadn't been that long since they'd stood in the alley, talking about desperately important matters—at least to her. But Rafe had darted off when she'd turned away to take a call from Charles, leaving her with more to say. Perhaps he might still be nearby.

Though the chances of her finding him were small, she had to at least try. Jenessa walked the streets for thirty minutes or so, then, on the verge of giving up, she spotted Grey Alexander's dark gray Tesla, parked in front of the drug store. No one else in town was wealthy enough to drive such an expensive vehicle—it wasn't as though Grey cared a whit about the environment, he just always wanted to have what others could not. So, it had to be him.

The windows were darkly tinted, but when Jenessa adjusted her position so the sun was behind the car, she was able to see movement inside the vehicle, two people sitting in the front seats.

She pressed her back against the wall and watched, hoping to not be seen. For all she knew, it was Logan in the car with his father, but she decided she would wait until someone got out or the car drove off without anyone showing their face. She hoped for the former.

As she stood squinting, almost afraid to blink for fear of missing something, Jenessa's phone began to chirp Ramey's ringtone. She reached into her pocket and silenced it with a press of the home button. Her friend would just have to wait.

Why were they taking so long? Jenessa was getting antsy. Time was ticking to come clean with Logan, at least according to his father's deadline. What were they doing in that Tesla? All she could see were shadows gesticulating inside the vehicle. Clearly at least one person was wound up about something. The driver. Grey Alexander.

Her phone jingled again in her pocket. It wasn't Ramey this time, it was Logan's ringtone. She had programmed his with chapel bells. It made her smile, but still she ignored the call, pushing the button to send it to voicemail. She'd have to call him back too. But the call had affirmed one thing—it couldn't be Logan in the car with Grey. There was no way he would stop to call her while in the throes of a heated debate with his father.

Or would he?

What if Grey was right then spilling everything to Logan, and Logan had pulled out his phone to call her to hear her side of the story? No, she didn't think that was possible. Grey had given her a deadline. In his sick, twisted mind he probably thought it would hurt more coming from her, assuring him that Logan would end their relationship, and their wedding planning. And any chance at a future together.

It *could* be anyone in that car with Grey, but Jenessa's gut told her it was Rafe. So, she continued to wait it out.

~*~

Eventually, the passenger-side door opened, painfully slowly. Finally, a denim-clad leg reached out, placing a booted foot onto the street, followed by the large torso of a well-built man. Namely, one Rafe Santiago.

She was eager to find out what Grey Alexander had been ranting about for the thirty or forty minutes—at least—she had been standing there waiting.

She watched as the luxury sedan sped off, leaving Rafe standing on the side of the street looking as though he'd bet all his money on the horse that lost.

Maybe after seeing Jenessa, talking with her, Rafe had changed his mind. Perhaps he could not go through with whatever nefarious scheme Grey had cooked up. Maybe Rafe had been trying to get out of it.

Something told Jenessa that Grey would never—willingly—take no for an answer. And the look on Rafe's face as he climbed out of the Tesla was not one of victory, but of defeat.

Jenessa scurried across the street, trying to catch up to Rafe, who had begun walking along the sidewalk, his head bowed down against the slight wind that was coming in from the east. Or maybe it was to hide his face, to keep from being seen in this town. Rafe was the epitome of rugged tall, dark, and handsome, with an exotic Spanish air about him, and he couldn't help but attract attention.

She had to admit, although it was the excess liquor she had consumed that night in Vegas, it was Rafe's looks and Latin swagger that had initially attracted her to him. She glanced around to make sure there was no one watching her as she quickened her step.

He was just ahead of her, but he seemed edgy, peeking around the building and onto the street before he crossed. Rafe was heading straight for The Sweet Spot, and Jenessa had to stop him, preferably before he got there. Ramey would be all over them like white on rice if she were to see Jenessa and Rafe together. No, she simply could not have that.

"Rafe," she said in a whisper-shout. He did not turn around. She tried one more time, this time from closer behind him. Her heart flew into her throat when he spun around. He looked haggard and worried. What on earth could Grey have said to him?

He pressed his back against the side of the building they were in front of, pulling Jenessa in by the arms. Then he ducked around her and looked both ways up and down the street. Satisfied at whatever he'd seen, or not seen, Rafe dropped his shoulders slightly, then fixed his dark eyes back on her.

"What are you doing here, Jenessa?"

But he didn't give her time to answer. "We shouldn't be seen together. Not now."

Something was off, Jenessa could feel it. "Why? What's wrong?"

"I can't talk about it."

"Does it have anything to do with your conversation with Grey Alexander in his car a few minutes ago?"

His eyes narrowed. "How do you know about that? Never mind. Yes, of course it does, but I can't say anything more. I'm sorry."

He did look truly sorry, but it was too late to expect her not to pry further. "Listen, Rafe, I can help you. You just have to tell me what Grey Alexander has planned."

"I don't know. The man is crazy, if you ask me." He shook his head.

"Does he know the marriage was never annulled?"

"I don't think so."

Of course, he couldn't know. If he did, all he'd have to do is inform Logan his fiancée was already married, and the wedding would be off for sure. "So, what is his game?" Jenessa pressed.

"I have no idea. I did my part, did what I was hired to do. Now I just want to get my money and get out of town."

He did his part? "What do you mean?"

He said his part was to make sure she saw him, but really? That was all that Grey Alexander had wanted from Rafe Santiago? Seemed a little oversimplified. Unless of course Grey was trying to torture her, prove to her that he could back up his threats, scaring her into compliance. But it didn't. It only served to strengthen her resolve.

Grey always did have a way of underestimating her.

When she and Logan were teenagers, he had believed his son, the heir to the Alexander fortune, would never fall for a girl like Jenessa, the daughter of one of his underlings. When she had come back to town and had helped solve a crime that had put him behind bars, he had been wrong about her then too. And he was doing it now, believing that she would cower and give up, like a frightened little puppy.

"Where are you staying?" she asked Rafe.

His eyes were darting around again, searching the streets. "I'm staying with Grey Alexander. I need to get back."

Shut the front door. He was what now? Staying with Grey? Logan didn't know that, did he?

Jenessa glanced up and down the street as well. "Who are you hiding from?"

"The less you know the better." He looked her in the eyes. "I don't want to put you in danger too. I've already said too much."

"You know, Evangeline is coming on Monday," she said in an effort to keep him talking.

"She's what? Why?"

"She's one of my bridesmaids. We have pre-wedding stuff to—"

"Bridesmaid?" he interrupted. "How can you still be going through with the wedding, knowing we're still married?"

"I'm working on it," she replied. "I have a call in to my attorney and I'm hoping—"

"What did you tell Evangeline?"

"Just that I thought I had seen you."

Rafe's dark eyes grew wide, his jaw muscles tightened. "Evangeline knows I'm here?" He grabbed her by the shoulders. "Who else did you tell?"

She pulled loose. "No one. I only mentioned it to her, that I thought I saw you."

"What did she say?"

"That she hadn't heard from you in years, that it was probably my imagination."

His jaw relaxed a little, and he checked the street again.

"Is there something wrong, Rafe? Should I not have said anything?"

"I wish you hadn't."

"Why not?" Her phone rang. It was Ramey again. She sent it to voicemail. Again.

"I can't say." He dragged his hand across his face, then up through his tousled black hair. "Did she say anything about Rudy?"

Jenessa shook her head. "She said he couldn't make it to the wedding...though, she didn't say why." Something was definitely going on with Rafe. More than what she knew, maybe more than she could even guess at. "Rafe, you're scaring me. What's this about?"

He took Jenessa by the shoulders again, his eyes fiery and intense. "Listen, I didn't work for a news agency like I told you."

"What?" What was going on here? "Then who did you work for?"

"I can't tell you."

"Why not?"

"I wish I hadn't dragged you into my mess."

This was getting worse by the second. What had started as a threat by Grey to prevent her marriage to Logan had turned into—what? What was this anyway?

"What mess, Rafe? I don't understand what's going on." Here she stood before a man she was technically married to yet barely knew, and somehow their lives had become entangled again, and it more than panicked her. It scared her to death.

"Listen, Jenessa, it's better you don't know. I only took Alexander up on his offer because I desperately need the money. It's critical I finish what I started."

"You're scaring me."

"In a few days I'll be out of here, and you'll never hear from me again."

"What about the annulment papers?"

"We'll work it out, but right now I have more important matters to attend to."

"But I need—"

"Listen," he snapped, his tone intense, his dark eyes boring into hers. "When you see Evangeline, tell her you were mistaken about thinking you saw me. It's better that no one from my past knows I'm here."

"But why?" Jenessa pushed. "Are we in some sort of danger?" Her phone rang again. Ramey's ringtone. To voicemail it went. She couldn't stop to answer questions about which type of icing she wanted on her wedding cake right now.

"I've said too much already, but this may be the last time we meet, so I will tell you this much." He tugged a leather necklace out from inside his shirt collar. Hanging from it was a large topaz with a metal backing. "I have something hidden in the back of this thing, something worth killing over."

"What is it, Rafe? Tell me. Maybe I can help."

"No. You're better off not—"

Jenessa's phone rang a fourth time in quick succession. It was Ramey of course. Four times in fifteen minutes or so, something must be up. "I'm sorry, Rafe. I'd better take this. I'll just be a minute." She turned away, facing down the alley.

"Ramey, what is so urgent?"

CHAPTER 9

"THERE YOU ARE," Ramey said. "I just heard from a customer that the pastor that was going to marry you this weekend got in a bad car accident."

"*Was* going to marry us?"

"Well, Mrs. Crownover said he's in the hospital with two broken legs."

One problem after another! Were the powers that be trying to tell her something?

"Listen, Ramey, we'll talk about this later. I've got to go."

She hung up the call and turned back to Rafe, but he was gone.

Again.

~*~

What was the takeaway from all this?

Jenessa had been through such an emotional roller coaster since she'd moved back to Hidden Valley. First, getting involved with Michael, and his son Jake, then breaking his heart—both their hearts—when she had decided to choose Logan.

Had she made the wrong choice?

She hadn't thought so…everything had seemed so perfect, maybe too perfect, with finding their long-lost child, then Logan getting custody of Grayson and Lily when Summer had passed away. Was it all too good to be true? Maybe it was…

She sighed and checked her watch. She had less than forty hours left to tell Logan everything. That sounded like a long time, but it wasn't—and it was getting shorter by the minute. She had to tell him tonight. Yes, get it out and deal with whatever fallout came. Delaying would only increase the torment, which Grey was most likely relishing.

She steadied herself and made the call, dialing Logan's number without checking her voicemails. They were probably all from Ramey anyway.

"Hey, Logan, it's me."

Logan had answered Jenessa's call on the first ring and had agreed to come over for dinner. As her doorbell chimed, she looked at the clock. He was right on time.

She had mentally rehearsed what she was going to say to him, but now that he was there, all she wanted to do was crawl under her duvet and pretend the entire day had been a bad dream.

But it hadn't been one.

It was time for Jenessa to face the music. She could delay, but to what end? *Better to just rip the band-aid off.*

She hurried to the front door and flung it wide. "Logan, I'm so glad to—" She stopped and sucked in a quick breath. "What happened to you, sweetheart?"

He gingerly touched a finger to his mouth and winced. "What? This?" He played it down. "This is nothing." He shrugged off his jacket as he stepped through the doorway. "No kiss?"

She gave him a gentle peck beside his swollen lip. "Well, it doesn't look like nothing." She took the jacket from him and hung it in the closet.

"Go, sit down," she motioned toward the living room. "We'll talk more about this in a minute. I have to check on dinner." Jenessa dashed to the kitchen to check on the frozen lasagna she'd put in about an hour earlier.

"Let me help. At least pour some wine."

"I have things under control," she assured him. "Put your feet up and relax. I'll be back in a minute." She needed a moment to herself to gather her thoughts before spilling everything to him.

Jenessa had phoned her attorney earlier that afternoon about the annulment, but it being Saturday, he was out. She'd left a short message with his answering service, saying it was urgent, but not mentioning any details, not wanting her secret to become public knowledge. The receptionist assured her he would get the message as soon as he checked in. But Jenessa hadn't heard from him yet and that bothered her.

She opened the oven and the cheese had begun to brown nicely, so she shut off the heat but left the dish inside to keep warm while she made the salad and garlic toast.

"Something smells good," Logan hollered from the living room.

"It's almost ready," she called back.

Jenessa was already jittery about having to tell Logan about Rafe. What on earth had happened for him to show up looking like someone had punched him in the face? Her hands were trembling, and she dropped the salad tongs on the floor.

"Let me get that," Logan said, scooping up the utensil and tossing it in the sink.

His sudden presence unnerved her. "You should be relaxing," she chided. "Go put your feet up while I finish here."

"Really, I'm fine, babe." He set her laptop on the counter. "Hey, I saw you were looking at wedding rings online."

"Vintage rings," she clarified. The truth was, she had been searching for the perfect ring, one that spoke to her.

"What about this one?" he asked, pointing to a spectacular emerald-cut solitaire with ornate carving and tiny diamonds around the stone.

Jenessa's breath caught at the sight of it. How had she missed that one? It was absolutely perfect.

"This looks just like my grandmother's ring." He clicked on the image to enlarge it. "It's a little bigger, but the cut, the design, it reminds me of…"

Logan's voice trailed off and a melancholy expression floated through his eyes. His shoulders slumped a little as if in defeat.

"Are you okay?" Something had to be wrong.

"Leave the food." He took her by the hand and led her to the couch.

"Jenessa," he peered deeply into her eyes with a seriousness that scared her, "we need to talk."

~*~

We need to talk? That's never a good sign. The words made Jenessa's heart drop all the way to her feet.

She tried to read Logan's face. Did he already know about her and Rafe? Know that she was still married to another man? His expression was unreadable.

Swallowing down the huge lump that had grown in her throat, she followed him to the living room. She sat on the edge of the sofa, turned only part of the way to face him.

We need to talk. Was Logan going to break up with her? Was her life as she knew it, or as she hoped it was going to become, over?

She met his gaze, searched his vivid blue eyes, but she had to turn away just as quickly. Pain was evident in them, she couldn't endure it.

He tucked a couple of fingers under her chin and raised her face to his. "I love you, Jenessa. I always have, since we were kids. I always will. But…"

Oh, God, here it comes…

"…seeing those rings, remembering my grandmother's ring and how she had wanted me to have it someday, well, it…

He dropped his hand from her face and looked away for a moment.

"What is it?" She twisted inside, seeing the man she loved in so much pain. "Logan, I—"

"No," he shook his head sadly, then lifted his eyes to her. "It's me. I can't do this anymore. I can't go on like this, with this secret between us."

That was it. He knew. It was all over.

She had waited too long, had spent the afternoon searching for Rafe rather than talking to the man she was about to marry—no, scratch that, *had been* about to marry. It was written all over his face. Sorrow. Loss.

And he had used the word *secret*.

Jenessa pulled in a deep breath to steel herself, waited. When Logan finally raised his head, he spoke the words she hated to hear. "I saw my father today."

"You did?" She struggled to keep her voice casual, not knowing how she should react. Should she tell him she had seen Grey also? If she admitted to having seen his father too, she would have to tell Logan about everything else.

As if he didn't already know.

But what if he didn't know? What if he was talking about some other secret? Goodness knows this town had its share of those, as did his family.

Maybe she should just shut up and let the man speak.

Logan opened his mouth, about to say something, when his phone rang in his shirt pocket. "Sorry." He yanked it out, peered at the screen with a frown, then answered it. "Logan Alexander."

He listened to the person on the other end for a few seconds, nodded his head and muttered a few affirmative responses. "I understand." His face softened as he hung up.

"Logan? Who was it?"

He stood without an answer. Jenessa rose too, a tingle of curiosity prickling her neck. He pulled her into his arms and kissed her softly, wincing from the obvious pain. "I'm so sorry. I need to go."

CHAPTER 10

JENESSA WATCHED FROM THE DOORWAY as Logan sped off, puzzled and shaken by what had just happened. What now?

The aroma of Italian spices wafted past her. *The lasagna!*

She turned and ran to the kitchen to retrieve the lasagna from the oven before it burned. Although she had turned the oven off, the residual heat had continued to brown the top.

She set it on the stove.

Now what?

A bottle of red wine sat on the counter. It had been one of the samples she and Logan had tried in anticipation of the wedding reception. They had both agreed on this one. It had a full, fruity aroma, an oaky flavor, and a smooth finish. Jenessa contemplated pouring herself a glass—something she rarely did, hence the atrocious mistake she'd made after Evangeline's wedding reception.

What was Logan about to say to her? And why had he dashed out of there in such a hurry?

Well, there was no sense sitting around all evening stressing over it. Jenessa wrapped the lasagna in an insulated bag, stuck the salad in another, and she headed over to Aunt Renee's. If she was lucky, they hadn't begun to cook dinner yet, and she could share hers with them, since she couldn't share it with her husband to be…at least she hoped Logan still qualified as that.

Logan left Jenessa so fast, he felt like a jerk for doing so. Here he was, about to confess things to the woman he loved that he had never shared with another soul. Things about his painful childhood and his abusive father. And he just took off.

But what else was he supposed to do? He couldn't very well drop a bomb like that in under two minutes, which was all the time he had before dashing off to an emergency board meeting.

It had been Max Lindsay on the phone. He'd said he had urgent news and needed to see Logan immediately, that his presence was required at the meeting. The board had reached a decision, he'd said, and time was of the essence.

Logan raced to the meeting, keeping an eye out for police lights and sirens. Had his dad gotten to the board? Or had they managed to get through the meeting this afternoon without it being crashed by his angry father?

There was only one way to find out. Logan pulled into his reserved parking stall and sat in his car for a moment, gathering his thoughts—and his strength. He was going to need it. Before long, Logan got out, beeped to lock it, and marched to the building's glass front doors.

"Here goes nothing," he muttered under his breath as he waved his pass by the scanner.

~*~

The board had just announced to Logan that they decided to oust his father and instate Logan as company president. He wasn't entirely surprised, but he wasn't quite sure how he felt about the offer.

It was one thing when his father was still in prison, but now he was out, and he was already furious with Logan for planning to marry Jenessa. Did he dare to risk alienating the man further? Should he?

He rubbed at his jaw, remembering just how mad his father could get—and how far he was willing to go to demonstrate that hostility.

One of the board members cleared his throat loudly, and Logan looked up. They were all staring at him, waiting for a response.

Everything in him knew he could do this job, he wanted to prove himself. Ever since he'd joined Alexander Enterprises he had focused on climbing to the top, to be the man in charge. He'd never really thought it would actually be possible—until now, that is. But what would this promotion cost him? And was he willing to pay that high a price?

An image of Jenessa flashed through Logan's mind, the expression on her face just before the board had called him tonight. He'd been on the verge of telling her about how his father had abused him when he was a child. She had looked so worried. Could she have sensed he was going to tell her something like that? Maybe she had guessed it, judging by the split lip he'd shown up with after telling her he'd seen his dad.

He had hated leaving her like he did. He was so close to having everything he'd ever wanted—Jenessa, the kids—life couldn't be any better.

It was in that moment that Logan made his decision. He would turn the board down, start his own business like he'd always dreamed about. But when he opened his mouth to speak, the double doors of the meeting room burst open and a red-faced Grey Alexander was on the pushing side. Right behind him was his entourage of stone-faced attorneys.

"I don't know what is going on here, but this company is mine!"

"Hello, everyone," Jenessa sang as she sauntered into her aunt's kitchen, carrying the food. "I brought dinner."

"We were just about to make spaghetti, but I suppose we can eat whatever you brought. Assuming it's edible," Sara teased.

Jenessa made a funny face at her sister. "Thanks for the vote of confidence," she chided. "Besides, it's a ready-made lasagna that I just heated up. Logan and I were going to have dinner and discuss...uh, a few last-minute details before the wedding."

She quickly surveyed the women's faces to gauge whether everyone within earshot bought her hasty cover up.

"Let me help." Ramey stepped up to Jenessa at the breakfast counter, where she was removing the dishes from the insulated bags. "Last-minute details, huh?" She gave Jenessa a look that said she didn't buy anything her friend was selling.

Ramey knew a bit about Rafe already, but she hadn't gotten quite as much of the story as she had been hoping for earlier in the day. It was obvious by Ramey's curious expression that she still had questions.

But that conversation would have to wait. The lasagna was still piping hot and the salad was ready to eat. Jenessa mouthed the word *Later* and began to cut and dish out the main course, while Ramey scooped the salad onto side plates, setting a slice of garlic toast beside each mound of lettuce.

As they all took their seats around Aunt Renee's dining table, Ramey leaned over to Jenessa's ear. "I'm going to hold you to that," she whispered.

Jenessa wouldn't expect any less. Nothing shy of a meteor hitting the side of the house could stop Ramey from cornering Jenessa the minute dinner was over, begging to be told the rest of the sordid story.

She sighed and cut off a corner of lasagna with her fork. "I'm starving," she said, sticking the pasta into her mouth. "Dig in, everybody, it's delicious."

~*~

Dinner was over and had proven to be rather tasty, in spite of Jenessa having picked it up in the freezer section of the local grocery store. Maybe it didn't quite measure up to Aunt Renee's lasagna or Ramey's, or even Sara's for that matter, but it wasn't half bad.

Her stomach was full, and Jenessa wanted nothing more than to relax on the sofa when Selena and Sara had offered to do the clean-up, but no. That would mean she would literally be a sitting target for Ramey's prying mind, so Jenessa waved them off. At least if she were busy at the sink she could avoid eye contact with Ramey.

But her friend would not be ignored.

"So, dish, Jenessa," Ramey said as she snatched the tea towel hanging off the oven door and began drying the salad bowl that Jenessa had finished washing.

"That's what it is," Jenessa replied, attempting to defer the conversation with a little humor. "A salad dish, to be exact." She picked up the tongs and began wiping them with the sponge.

"That's real funny, ha-ha. You know exactly what I mean, lady. Tell me the rest of the story about this Rafe fella."

"Keep your voice down," Jenessa warned.

"All I know so far," Ramey dropped her voice, "is that you met him at your friend's wedding and that it could get you in some sort of trouble with Logan." Ramey pointed the dripping tongs at Jenessa as she spoke. "There's got to be more."

"All right, I'll tell you, Ramey, but you have to promise to keep it just between us."

Ramey nodded with excited anticipation lighting up her face.

Jenessa lowered her voice and leaned closer to her friend. "It was all just a crazy mistake. We met at Evangeline's wedding, like I told you, and we hit it off right away. He was handsome and charming...and a reporter too...how could I resist?"

"Apparently you didn't."

Jenessa frowned. "Anyway, we were at the reception, celebrating the wedding, and we both had a few too many drinks at the open bar. We found that we were both unhappily single and ended up commiserating over our lost loves."

"You had a one-night stand?" Ramey looked shocked. "Jenessa Jones, I never would have believed—"

"Shhh..." Jenessa turned and rested her hip against the counter. "No, Ramey, I did not have a one-night stand. It was..."

CHAPTER 11

"NOT A ONE NIGHT STAND?" Ramey cocked her head to one side. "Then what? I don't understand."

"Worse," Jenessa sighed. "Way worse." She turned back to the sink and pulled the plug, letting the soapy water sputter down the drain. "We got married."

"You got married?" Sara strode into the kitchen. "You and Logan eloped? When? With all the work and expense that has gone into planning your wedding? You really went and eloped?"

Jenessa shook her head and raised her eyes to the heavens, hoping for some random act of God that would get her out of having to explain what her sister had just overheard. But nothing happened. No earthquake. No monsoon. No swarming locusts. Not so much as a thunderstorm to save her.

"Eloped?" Now Aunt Renee had joined the fray.

Cousin Selena wasn't far behind. "Somebody eloped?"

Jenessa turned to face her accusers—their eyes almost boring holes in her like lasers—and crossed her arms over her chest. She was caught. "Fine, I'll tell you all, but I need some dessert first."

~*~

"So that's it." Jenessa set her fork on her plate after finishing the last bite of triple chocolate cake. She had told them the whole sordid story about her debacle with Rafe, being careful to leave out the fact that she had seen him in town that day.

Sara was shocked. Aunt Renee was sympathetic, as was Ramey. But Selena had been oddly quiet through the entire story, taking it all in.

Curious, Jenessa asked her cousin if she knew Rafe, but Selena denied ever meeting him. It seemed plausible they might have met, after all, Selena had worked at a television station in Spain, and Rafe had been a reporter there at one point. Or so she had thought.

Before.

Before he mentioned something about not working for a news agency at all, that is. What did that even mean? Was he not a reporter, or was he simply a freelancer, not employed by any one agency?

Jenessa looked to Selena and wondered.

"Well, Logan loves you, Jenessa. I know that much." Ramey stood and began gathering all the dessert plates from everyone.

"I know."

But was love going to be enough?

"He won't care that you made one drunken mistake," Ramey said. "That was a long time ago. It's not like you had an actual marriage that you never told him about—another life, or another family. Right?"

"But that's just it." Jenessa grimaced as she handed Ramey her plate. "We're still married."

"You're what?" Sara's eyes widened, and she looked like she was going to fall off her chair.

"Not in the real sense of the word," Jenessa said, "but, technically, legally, I think we are still married."

"Have you called our lawyer to see what can be done about it?" Aunt Renee asked.

"Yes, but I could only leave a message." She probably wouldn't hear back from him until Monday. "Rafe swore he would sign the annulment forms and file them."

"And you trusted him to do that?" Sara questioned.

"I had no reason to doubt him. He didn't want to be married any more than I did. But then he left on an assignment overseas."

"So he never filed the papers?" Sara questioned.

Aunt Renee's hand flew to her chest. "The timing of this couldn't be worse, dear girl."

"I know." Jenessa noticed her aunt's gesture. "Are you okay, Aunt Renee?" The last thing Jenessa wanted was to send her aunt into another heart attack over this drama.

"I'm fine, just surprised."

"So, what was his excuse?" Sara asked pointedly.

"He told me he got deep in a story and was scooped up with some Taliban insurgents. When the Afghan troops discovered he wasn't a rebel, they held him hostage, hoping for some ransom money." She went on with the story and finished with, "When the war ended, officially, at the end of twenty-fourteen, he was freed."

"He was captured in the war?" Selena's interest seemed to pique. Though, in fairness, she was a reporter, and Jenessa herself knew how much hearing a good story could get her own investigative juices flowing.

In an attempt to think positively, Jenessa chose to move on, segue the conversation to less volatile topics, like where they were at on the RSVPs, the caterer, the venue, and the church. And, more importantly, did they have a pastor to marry them?

And, after all the details were thoroughly discussed, Aunt Renee announced that she had invited Detective Provenza to the wedding as her plus one.

Jenessa was delighted to hear that. Of course, hearing about Provenza reminded Jenessa about his partner, Michael, and that brought up a whole new set of emotions.

How had her life become so freaking complicated?

It had been too late to phone Jenessa when Logan had finally gotten home from last night's meeting, so he simply sent her a short text apologizing for leaving so abruptly. He didn't want to go into more than that.

What a crazy evening it had been after his father had stormed the boardroom, claiming mutiny and threatening the entire board with dismissal if they did not vote in his favor.

"You can oust me," he'd said, "but as the majority shareholder of this company, I'll fire you all and then hire a board who sees things my way. You serve at my pleasure, not the other way around!"

Reverting to threats in a pinch, no surprise there. The board knew Grey had meant every word, though, for his threats were never empty ones.

And to think that Logan had been ready to throw in the towel completely, give up his position with Alexander Enterprises, and take the money he had saved to venture out on his own.

But now...now he almost wanted to stay, just to spite his father. Just to see if somehow, some way, he could fight for control over the business. Sure, his father was the majority shareholder, with Logan and his mother combined having less stock in the company, but maybe there was a way...

"What's wrong with you, Alexander?" He stared at his reflection in the bathroom mirror and admonished himself. How could he be feeling like he had something to prove to his father anymore?

He was no longer a scared little boy, afraid of the swift hand of his father's misunderstood justice. He was a grown man now. He could stand on his own two feet, take care of his family, give them the life they deserved...without flying into a rage or ever laying an angry hand on his children.

His children.

Logan could hardly believe he was actually a dad, not just the hypothetical father of a long-lost son that he used to be. No, he was a real father now and he loved those kids. He could hardly believe how much he missed them already. They had barely left for camp, but he simply couldn't deny the hole their absence had left in his life.

~*~

"Evangeline, I'm not sure I'll be as graceful as you were." Jenessa swept through the front door of The Sweet Spot, talking on the phone with her old friend. "In fact, I'll probably fall flat on my face walking down the aisle. That's why I *need* you here with the other bridesmaids. How soon can you be here?"

Jenessa paused to take in the delicious aromas wafting around the quaint café. Walking through those doors always managed to lift her spirits. From the gentle tinkle of the bells on the door, to the smell of freshly ground coffee, and vanilla mixed with cinnamon, they were the things that gave her comfort, reminded her of her mother. Coming here felt like a warm embrace.

She spied Ramey, whose face lit up on seeing Jenessa. She raised a finger and flashed her phone to let Ramey know she'd be up to order as soon as she got off the call. In the meantime, Jenessa grabbed one of the few open tables left in the entire café and went back to her conversation.

"I'm sorry, could you repeat that last part?" Jenessa asked.

"I said, I can't get to Hidden Valley until Wednesday, around noon, I hope."

This is Sunday.

"Better late than never." Jenessa was just glad her friend was coming. Otherwise Logan would have one more groomsman than she would bridesmaids, which would make everything awkward, from the photos to the first dance—assuming there was still going to be a wedding.

"Where should we meet?" Evangeline asked.

"Hmm, not sure where I'll be on Wednesday at noon…better to call me when you get into town and I'll let you know where to find me."

With that, she disconnected the call and headed to the counter.

She smiled and greeted Ramey, remembering her confession to everyone the night before—everyone but Logan, that is—and how Ramey was always her number-one supporter.

"That was Evangeline. She says she'll be in town around noon on Wednesday."

Ramey frowned. "That's cutting it rather close."

"I know. But," Jenessa shrugged, "nothing I can do about it. I'm just glad she didn't have to cancel."

Ramey nodded her agreement. "That's the last thing we need. You've already been pitched more than your share of curveballs." She flashed the big cheerful smile that Ramey was known for. "Now go. Sit," she instructed. "I'll bring you your coffee and a snack. The usual?"

"Thanks, Ramey, but just the coffee."

"Because of that gorgeous wedding dress?"

"I've got to fit into it." Jenessa slipped out of her light jacket and placed it on the back of the chair, returning to her seat in the corner. As she put her phone on the table, Ramey was already setting her coffee down in front of her.

Her friend pulled out the other chair and took a seat. "Sorry, the cinnamon rolls need a few more minutes in the oven."

"I said just coffee." Jenessa eyed her friend suspiciously. "Are you trying to make me fat?"

"Of course not." Ramey laughed. "I just know you and thought you might change your mind."

"I do love your cinnamon rolls, but I'm only having coffee today," Jenessa confirmed.

"Okay, I get it." Ramey chuckled. "You know, Aunt Renee is simply over the moon about acting as your wedding planner. I haven't seen her this happy in a long time."

"I'm lucky to have her. And you, Ramey." Jenessa reached over and patted her friend's hand. "I couldn't have planned this wedding without you either."

A mischievous look flashed across Ramey's face. "Well, it seems you *did* plan a wedding without me once."

"Yeah and look how that turned out." Jenessa grimaced at the idea of it.

"Speaking of which," Ramey glanced around to make sure no prying ears could hear them, "now that it's just the two of us, tell me more about this Rafe fellow."

The door opened, causing the bells to chime. Jenessa didn't know if she was being saved by the bell or about to be sacrificed to the woman walking in.

Selena had a very curious look on her face as she strode over to the table. "Hi, Jenessa. Ramey." She leaned down and gave Jenessa a light kiss on the cheek. "I'm glad I found you here."

Selena turned to Ramey. "Would you be a doll and make me a café Americano, *por favor?*"

"No problem." Ramey smiled and stood, flashing Jenessa a look as she offered her seat to Selena. It was clearly a look of disappointment at not being alone with Jen to talk more about Rafe. Ramey's life, overall, was generally rather quiet. Though, Jenessa would gladly trade the eventful last twenty-four hours for a little boring same-old any day.

~*~

Reeling from what happened the night before, Logan's mind was swirling with questions. His empty condo was doing nothing but remind him that the kids were away at camp. And knowing that Jenessa was having Sunday morning coffee with Ramey at The Sweet Spot, Logan was free to do some sleuthing of his own. Jenessa didn't have to be the only investigator in the family.

His father had something up his sleeve—Grey Alexander always did—and Logan was determined to find out what it was.

CHAPTER 12

BEFORE LOGAN DID ANYTHING ELSE, he would drive to the estate to find out who was in the guesthouse. That had to be the key to whatever was going on with his father. He'd suspected something was up when he was there the day before, seeing his father slinking out of the gatehouse like a villain in the night...or a philanderer. But this felt like more than him just having a secret affair.

Logan took the last swig of his coffee, slung a light jacket on, and snatched up the keys to his car. He was going to get to the bottom of this, even if it killed him.

~*~

Jenessa and Selena chatted briefly about what had happened in their lives since they had last seen each other, both filling the other in on the highlights, while Ramey was kept busy by the steady stream of patrons coming through the door.

Observing Ramey for a moment, she let Selena prattle on. Ramey appeared to thrive on running the café, the baking, the chatting with customers—she seemed to love it all.

"Cousin," Selena leaned in closer, "tell me more about this fabulous man you are about to marry. I've heard he's quite handsome—thick wavy blond hair, engaging blue eyes." Selena's full lips tugged into a satisfied grin. "I'll bet he's quite a lover."

Jenessa eyed her for a moment, hiding the momentary hesitation that was bubbling up. "Is that what Sara told you?"

"No, Renee." The grin widened. "So, tell me more."

"Aunt Renee?" Jenessa was a little stunned. *Why, that old vixen.*

"Come on," Selena coaxed. "Spill."

Reluctantly acquiescing, Jenessa told her about Sara's brief fling with Logan, her relationship with Michael Baxter, and how her sister had been trying to fill the spot she'd vacated in Michael's and his son Jake's lives when Jenessa had chosen Logan.

Selena had just made a flip comment about romantic dramas in a small town when Jenessa was saved by the sound of an old-fashioned typewriter. It was the ringtone she had set for her editor, Charles.

"Sorry, Selena, I have to take this." Jenessa swiped the screen to answer the call. "Hello, Charles. What's up?"

~*~

Even now, as she raced to the scene, Jenessa couldn't believe the words Charles McAllister had said to her only moments before. A body had been found at the Alexander estate, and she was to hurry there to get the four-one-one and report back immediately.

Charles was fully hoping for a juicy headline. Jenessa was half-hoping the body would turn out to be Grey Alexander. Not that she wished the man dead, but he had caused her more than her share of grief over the years, and even more now that she had finally found her happy place in Logan's life. Assuming that wasn't just a temporary place.

As she pulled up to the estate, she noticed Logan's car parked along the side of the house, nearly hidden by some trees. A terrifying thought hit her deep in her gut. What if the body was Logan's?

Jenessa wanted to vomit.

She pulled her car up behind Detective Provenza's and clung to the steering wheel so tight her knuckles went white. Oh, God, no. She shook her head and forced her fingers to release their death grip on the wheel. *Please, God, don't let it be Logan.*

She didn't know what she would do without him now that she had finally found her way back to him. And what about the kids? What would happen to them if Logan was dead? Technically she had no parental rights to the children yet.

Even if Grey had killed Logan in a fit of rage and went to prison for it, there was no way he would ever allow her to get custody of Grayson. He would go to any lengths to ensure he could help himself to everything he wanted, including getting her out of Logan's life…one way or another.

He'd tried one way…what if this was the other one?

No. She shook her head violently, refusing to believe even Grey Alexander could kill his own son. He might be a cold-hearted S.O.B., but on some level, he had to love his son, right? Why else would he put so much effort into trying to get her out of Logan's life?

She bolted from her vehicle and rushed to the gatehouse, where most of the action seemed to be taking place, intending to slip under the crime scene tape. She waited patiently for the uniformed officer to be distracted, and she did just that, hurrying through the open door before anyone could stop her.

She knew Detective Provenza was not a fan of her sneaking into crime scenes, and Michael was even less so, but once she had crossed the threshold she felt confident she could sway him to her way of thinking. Provenza, that is. Detective Michael Baxter would be another thing entirely. She had mostly avoided him since they'd broken up a few months ago, except for that awkward run-in yesterday.

Hopefully he wasn't still carrying a grudge. She'd truly broken his heart. What's worse, she'd broken little Jake's heart too, and for that she was deeply remorseful.

Quite honestly, she tried not to think about Michael or Jake. She had been so immersed in getting back together with Logan, with getting to know the children, and with all the wedding plans, that she had easily avoided the subject of Michael.

Until now, that is.

~*~

Jenessa rushed in, finding Detective Provenza standing with Michael and the medical examiner. A man's body lay on the sofa in front of them, face up, the stillness of death clouding his handsome features. Jenessa gasped loudly, drawing the attention of all three men.

She stood frozen, gaping at the dead body. Had she known she would never speak to him again, she might have done things differently. But now, there he lay, his features gaunt, his charm no longer evident, just the shell of the man he had been. Jenessa was suddenly filled with regrets.

Provenza approached her, and just in time, for her legs gave way. He had to catch her and help her to the armchair nearby.

"Miss Jones. You shouldn't be here."

"I...yes, I see that now..."

Michael came over and handed her a bottle of water and a handkerchief to place over her mouth and nose to mask the smell that was beginning to permeate the room. Then he walked away again without so much as a word. But she could read the emotions in his eyes, or maybe it was her own that she was projecting there.

Was this death her fault? If she had chosen Michael instead of Logan, maybe this wouldn't have happened. She shook her head. Of course, it wouldn't have happened. This had to be her fault. If it wasn't for her being selfish and wanting to marry Logan, there would be no dead body lying on the sofa across from her. A man's life could have been saved.

"Is there something you want to say, Miss Jones?" Detective Provenza asked.

What could she say? That she'd had a relationship with this man and now he was dead? That it was all her fault? What would they think of her when she told them?

Her tongue felt numb in her mouth. Her lips immovable. Her eyes were riveted to the lifeless body as her heart beat hard against her chest.

"Something you want to tell us?" Provenza repeated, his eyes sliding to the dead body.

There was no more holding back. She found her voice.

"He's my husband."

CHAPTER 13

"HE'S YOUR WHAT?" Logan yelled as he burst through the open gatehouse doorway and rushed toward Jenessa, a look of utter disbelief frozen on his face. His hands fisted at his sides as though he was doing everything in his power to hold himself in check.

Michael and Provenza looked just as shocked.

"What did you just say?" Michael exploded.

Provenza huffed in disbelief. "Your husband?"

All eyes were on Jenessa and she sunk inside herself. This was not the way she had wanted Logan to find out about Rafe. If she had been stronger, if she had found a way to say something to him yesterday, maybe Rafe wouldn't be dead.

Or maybe he would.

A horrifying thought came to Jenessa just then. She hadn't spoken to Logan since he left her so suddenly the night before, and she still had no idea what he had been about to say to her before his phone rang. What if Logan had found out about Rafe, and what if he had rushed off to kill him?

No. No. Jenessa refused to believe Logan, *her* Logan, would stoop to murder. She could believe it of Grey, yes, but not Logan. Of course, people did have a way of convincing themselves of just about anything in times of stress.

"Logan," Provenza stepped toward him, his arm restraining Logan from getting any closer to Jenessa, "I'm sorry, but you'll have to leave."

Logan protested. "But I—"

"This is a crime scene."

Logan nodded, his gaze on Jenessa, his eyes pleading with her for some sort of silent assurance. But she was in such a state of shock, all she could give him was a shrug and a shake of her head. He turned to leave.

"But, Logan?" Michael said.

He glanced back at Michael.

"Don't go far. We'll need to talk to you."

Logan bobbed his head. "I'll be up at the house."

"And one more thing. Do you know where your father is?"

Logan answered that he hadn't seen him, that he'd just arrived and noticed the cop cars and crime scene tape. He had sat in his car for a few moments, deciding what to do, then came to the gatehouse.

Michael and Provenza dismissed him to go to the main house and wait to be questioned. Logan headed out. He cast a painful glance back at Jenessa, seated, still reeling from the sight of Rafe's body, laying lifeless and cold.

Provenza and Michael moved off to the side of the room. They kept their voices down, but it was clear they were engaged in a heated debate. Finally, Michael strode over to her.

"We need to ask you a few questions," he said.

She looked up at him from the chair. "And you drew the short straw?"

Several emotions seemed to flash across his face—surprise, irritation, uneasiness—before he finally answered her. "No. Yes. Well, not exactly the short straw." He stared at his feet momentarily before bringing his eyes back up to meet hers. "More like George volunteered me."

"I get it."

"Do you? According to him, I need some closure and now is as good a time as any, was how he put it."

Thanks, George.

"Your husband? Honestly?" Michael looked incredulous.

Before she could make a comment, Michael took a seat on the chair beside her. His familiar scent wafted around him—a mix of fabric softener and aftershave—and she felt a little shudder run down her spine at the smell of it. She may have chosen Logan, but that didn't mean her feelings for Michael had simply vanished. Maybe it was more like they had morphed somehow into something more in the friend zone.

He had been a good friend of hers, years ago, before she'd been run out of town by Grey Alexander, when she had become pregnant. And, he'd been good to her after she came back for her father's funeral. They had become more than friends this time. He'd been ready to propose to her, to welcome her into his and Jake's lives on a more permanent basis.

But then she'd panicked, had gotten so caught up in the mystery surrounding Logan's cousin Summer and a scandalous cold case from twenty years ago…well, next thing she knew, Logan was in the hospital because he had saved Jenessa's life, and they'd discovered, together, that Grayson was their son. In that moment, there had only been one choice for Jenessa. Maybe that was all there had ever been.

"Tell me the truth. You were married to this man?" Pain shimmered in his eyes.

"Yes." Should she elaborate?

He pulled out a notepad. "When was that?"

"Eight years ago."

"Do you know anyone who would have wanted him dead?" His eyes were on her.

"No. I hardly knew him myself."

"But you were married to him."

She explained the circumstances of their marriage, and he made a few notes, then paused and looked up. "How come you never mentioned that to me? Did Logan know?"

"I would have, eventually." Or would she have? She had assumed the marriage was annulled and had filed it away in the far recesses of her mind.

"And Logan?" he repeated.

"Logan? No. But what does that matter?" she asked.

He poised his pen. "Motive."

"Then no, he didn't know."

"He did seem shocked when he walked in on all this." Michael motioned toward the crime scene. "Could have been just an act though."

"I promise you, Michael, it was no act."

"Then I feel sorry for the guy, finding out like this, right before his wedding."

Michael's compassion was appreciated, although their wedding was seeming more and more unlikely.

He stood, signaling the interrogation was over, for now. "I should be glad it wasn't me finding out my fiancée already had a husband."

She rose too. "Michael, do you think we can move past this hurt between us and be friends again?"

It was something that they both clearly needed.

A small smile lifted his expression, he appeared amenable to that.

"You know," she ventured carefully, "I mentioned to my sister the other day that she should ask you out for coffee sometime."

Michael shook his head.

"Too soon?" she asked.

"I don't know, Jen. I'm not sure I'm ready to put myself out there again."

She resisted touching his shoulder to comfort him.

"I just thought," Jenessa started to say, hoping to give him the closure Provenza had suggested he needed. "I've heard she's really good with little Jake."

"Yeah," he looked at his notepad for a moment and paused, now allowing his eyes to meet hers. "She has helped him get over the loss of...well, the loss of you, Jenessa," his gaze shifted to her, "but I don't know. I wouldn't want Sara to be a rebound. That wouldn't be fair to her."

Michael might be right.

"Besides," he continued, "I don't have much faith in my choices these days where women are concerned."

Jenessa had to let it go. He deserved to make his own decisions and to get over her in whatever way felt best for him.

As Michael walked away, she thought of Logan. What must be going through his mind after hearing what he just had heard? To make matters worse, he wasn't even allowed to stay and listen to her explanation.

Oh, Logan, what have I done?

~*~

Logan's head was spinning as he dropped into a leather club chair in the main house. He was having a difficult time wrapping his mind around what he'd just heard. Not only was there a dead guy in his father's gatehouse, but apparently it was a dead guy that was married to his fiancée. The notion made him jump to his feet. How could that even be?

Was everything he knew—or *thought* he knew—a lie? He began to pace. Firstly, it wasn't a woman his father had been hiding out in the gatehouse. It was another man. A man who, apparently, was married to his Jenessa. None of this made any sense.

He sat again. His father must've known about the marriage. So, wouldn't he have wanted to put the information on the front page of his newspaper? Scream it from the rooftops? The Grey Alexander that Logan knew would have been overjoyed at the discovery and would have relished sticking it to Jenessa and letting Logan know all about it.

He couldn't sit still. He was restless, waiting to be questioned. He went to the window and watched for any movement from the gatehouse.

What did this all mean? Why now? Their wedding was only a few days away, how could Jenessa have been planning a life with him when she already had one with someone else?

The clicking of shoes on the entry tile drew his attention from the window. It was the grandmotherly housekeeper, Mrs. Dobson, crossing the hall into the kitchen, which spurred a memory. Logan thought back to the day he lost his grandmother's diamond ring, the one he so desperately wanted to give to Jenessa.

He had taken it from his mother's dresser when he was a kid, with the intention of pawning it for money to run away. But then he'd chickened out, and he lost it.

Logan remembered the beating his father gave him in the gatehouse the night he'd found out what Logan had done. Mrs. Dobson had been in the gatehouse cleaning up, likely after one of his father's many trysts. How much had she heard that night and did she recall it now?

Whatever happened to that ring, he did not know. When he'd decided he couldn't go through with pawning it, Logan had stuck the ring inside his pillowcase for safekeeping. But it hadn't been safe there, for somehow, someway, it had disappeared.

He'd always believed his father had been the one to find it and had taken it to make Logan regret having stolen it, which he did. The ring had been in their family for three generations, and his grandmother had told him that someday when he found the woman of his dreams, she would give him the ring to give to her.

Right before his grandmother had passed, she'd given it to Logan's mother to hold until the day Logan was ready to propose. If he hadn't been such a brat and taken it, he would have it now to give to Jenessa. And his father would not have beaten him black and blue that day. Of course, he would have found other reasons, other days.

Anyway, it seemed a rather moot point right then. As far as Logan knew, he didn't have a woman to marry, and there was a dead body in the family's gatehouse.

CHAPTER 14

THE POLICE QUESTIONED LOGAN at his father's house. It was short and not too stressful—aside from the fact that Michael Baxter was doing it. Still, Logan was relieved when it was done. Being in a room with Jenessa's ex was not on Logan's list of favorite things to do.

When Michael and Jenessa were still dating, Logan never even attempted to make his feelings for Jenessa a secret. If anything, he endeavored to make them quite well known, especially to Detective Michael Baxter. He wanted to leave no room in Jenessa's mind to doubt he was still in love with her after all these years. And now that she had left Michael to be with him, suffice it to say things were awkward.

Add to that being interrogated about a murder that had just happened in his father's gatehouse, not to mention the fact that the victim was, somehow, married to Jenessa. Well, it was complicated, at best.

Now that Baxter and his partner had left, all Logan wanted to do was hustle over to Jenessa's place and find out what, exactly, she had meant when she'd told the detectives that the dead man was her husband.

He tried to say good-bye to Mrs. Dobson, but she was nowhere to be found, though he had seen her earlier, just before he'd been sat down for questioning. And where was his father? Still very much MIA too. Stood to reason though, assuming he'd just killed a man. And Logan did assume that. Who else could have done it? Jenessa? Improbable. But his father? There was no doubt the man was capable of murder.

Logan rubbed at his jaw, remembering the recent smack his father had given him.

Yeah. He really needed to talk to Jenessa. And soon.

~*~

Jenessa paced the living room floor, waiting for Logan to arrive. There was no way she was going to relax. Her mind was reeling from the discovery of Rafe Santiago's body in Grey Alexander's gatehouse, and her heart was doing the same. Why did Logan have to walk in at the very moment she proclaimed the dead man was her husband?

The sound of a car door slamming brought her running to the door. She swung it open to find Ramey walking toward her with a cardboard carrier filled with two coffee cups and a small white bag. A mixture of disappointment and relief filled Jenessa.

"I thought you could use some moral support," Ramey raised the carrier as she stepped inside.

Jenessa hugged her friend, hard. "How did you know?"

"Charles called me, said you reported Rafe's murder to him. Let's drink the coffees while they're still hot."

The two went back to the kitchen and Ramey laid the goodies out on the small table.

"Now, sit down," Ramey said, "and tell me all about it."

"It was horrible," Jenessa slid into a chair and shook her head a bit as the vision of Rafe in the gatehouse flooded her mind.

"I can imagine."

Jenessa took a sip of coffee. "Provenza was there, and Michael of course. Then Logan came in just as I said to George and Michael that the dead man was my husband. As you can imagine—"

Ramey gasped. "Poor Logan."

"Provenza sent Logan to the main house to wait to be questioned."

"What about you?"

"Michael questioned me first. He seemed to accept my answers, but I wonder if he secretly suspects I may have killed Rafe? I did have more to lose than anyone else in town—and what alibi did I have?"

Ramey took Jenessa's hand. "You were seen at The Sweet Spot this morning. I'll tell them so. That has to count for something."

"Maybe, but I have no idea what time he was even murdered. So maybe it won't." Jenessa shrugged and took a sip of her coffee. "At least the dead body didn't turn out to be Logan's."

Ramey's eyes widened. "You thought it might be Logan?"

Jenessa nodded sadly. "Charles told me a body was discovered at the Alexanders' and when I got there I saw Logan's car."

"You poor thing. I see why you might—"

"Do you think Logan could be a suspect? And would Michael treat him fairly?" She shook her head with worry.

"I would hope so," Ramey said. "Michael is a good man, and an even better detective. You know that."

Where Jenessa could often convince George Provenza to bend the rules for her, Michael was usually steadfast in his beliefs, almost always wanting to go by the book.

Detective Provenza, only a couple months from retirement, was more inclined to let Jenessa in on a case, as long as she promised not to print anything without his permission. In fact, she had even helped them break a case or two.

"Logan texted me, before you got here, that he was on his way," Jenessa said.

"I should probably go then." Ramey picked up her coffee cup. "I'll leave the scones."

Jenessa walked her to the front of the house. She pulled back the sheer curtains and peered out into the street again. "Where is Logan?"

"He'll be here," Ramey said in a comforting way.

"What if he's had a change of heart and isn't

coming over after all? He *has* to. This whole mess is just a misunderstanding."

"A misunderstanding?" Ramey questioned with an arch of her brow.

Jenessa had not even considered Rafe Santiago in years. She certainly hadn't even remotely entertained the idea they were still married.

"I'll straighten it out," Jenessa replied as she peered out the window again.

Just then Logan's red BMW came down the street. *Thank God.*

She opened the door for Ramey. "I appreciate your stopping by." She gave her friend a hug. "It's better if I talk to Logan alone."

"I agree." Ramey stepped out, then turned back. "Good luck. Let me know how it goes."

Jenessa waited for Logan to get out of his car, but he stayed in it until Ramey drove off. At least if he was willing to speak with her it meant she still had a chance with him.

It was all she could do not to rush out to him. She didn't want to scare him off now that he was finally here, and the truth was out...sort of. At least what little he knew of the truth.

~*~

As Logan got out of his car and headed toward her house, Jenessa failed to get a read on his mood. She wanted to rush into his arms, kiss him, and tell him it was all a mistake, but she held back, instead waiting for him to approach her. His expression was so neutral, so deadpan, she didn't know what to do. She couldn't remember ever seeing him like this. It wasn't that he was cold to her, exactly, but he wasn't warm either.

"Logan," she greeted softly.

"Jenessa." His reply was flat.

"Come in." She held the door open and stepped back. "Thanks for agreeing to see me."

Thanks for agreeing to see her? That was not the way one was supposed to greet their fiancé, just days before the wedding. A chill flashed across Jenessa's shoulders and she shuddered as she closed the door behind Logan.

He walked straight into the living room and dropped down on the sofa, without removing his jacket or shoes. Was he planning on leaving in a hurry or something?

She hesitated, then joined him, uncertain of where to sit. She decided that sitting beside him would be too presumptuous, and so she chose the armchair nearby instead.

"We need to talk."

They said the words in almost perfect unison.

Jenessa nodded. "Okay. I'll go first."

He sat back and crossed his arms, then, appearing uncomfortable, he released them and leaned forward again, resting his arms across his legs.

"That must have been a big shock for you," she started.

"You mean arriving to find the cops all over my dad's place, with a dead guy on the couch, or finding out the woman I'm about to marry is already married to the dead guy?"

Fine. She deserved that.

"I didn't know," she said finally.

His eyes narrowed a bit. "You didn't know you were married? How does that work, exactly?"

Was it anger or hurt she read on his face? Either way, she had to keep going, no matter how he might want to lash out at her.

"No, I...I knew I had married him. I just didn't know we were still married."

Jenessa fidgeted with her hands. She really needed a drink of water. She felt like she had balls of cotton in her cheeks. "It's complicated," she continued, "I made an honest mistake."

"How's that?"

"You know my bridesmaid Evangeline? The girl I told you about?"

Logan nodded, but everything about him remained stiff and closed off.

"Well, it was after her wedding, after the reception. I had met Rafe at the ceremony, and we hit it off. We danced and talked, had a good time...too good, actually. It seemed we drank too much at the party and woke up the next morning in my hotel room to find ourselves married."

"You don't remember getting married?"

"Well..." she shrugged. "The details are still a bit fuzzy. But in the morning, we were both wearing cheap wedding bands and our heads were pounding from drinking so much. That's when we realized what we had done."

"So, you slept with the guy?"

"I can't be sure. I still had my bridesmaid dress on—wrinkled as it was—and my underwear, with no sense I'd been intimate with him."

Logan's lips thinned, his blue eyes dark with pain. He studied her as if he was trying to decide whether to believe her or not.

She continued, hoping to convince him. "I changed clothes and raced out to pick up the annulment forms right away. I signed them, and Rafe was supposed to sign them too, but he had to rush off to an important assignment. It wasn't until yesterday that I found out his assignment was overseas, and he'd never filed the papers."

Logan sat there staring at her, silent, looking stunned.

Emotion was thick in her throat. "Please, sweetheart, say something."

He shook his head. "I don't know what to say." He leaned back against the sofa, his eyes meeting hers. "Did you love him?"

"No. No, of course not." She got up from her chair and took the place beside him on the sofa, resisting the urge to place her hand over his. "You have to believe me."

"Then what was he doing here? And why was he at my father's gatehouse?"

And why is he dead, she wondered.

"Well, you kind of just answered your own question. Your father found him—"

"My father?"

"Apparently he had a private investigator digging around in my past, looking for something that would break us up, stop our wedding, and what he found was Rafe Santiago."

"So, my father knew you were married to this guy and brought him here to destroy our wedding?"

"Pretty much. At least from what I can tell."

"You know this how?"

"Grey ambushed me at the cemetery when I went to visit my mom's grave. He threatened me with exposure if I didn't tell you about Rafe. Of course, at that time I believed the annulment had been filed. All I thought I needed to do was tell you about it…which was hard enough."

"Then how did you find out you were still married?"

"Rafe told me."

"Wait. You knew my dad was out and didn't tell me. And you met with this guy? Behind my back?" Anger sizzled in his voice.

"Not on purpose. At least not the first time."

"The first time? You mean you've been with him more than once?"

"Don't say it like that, Logan. It wasn't like that. The first time I ran into him was on the street. It turned out that was part of your father's plan, for Rafe to let me see him, to know your dad was serious about his threats, I guess."

"You said you saw him a second time too?"

"Yes. That time I went looking for him. I found him in your father's car on Main Street, arguing with him, so I waited for him to get out. I had to talk to him, straighten this whole thing out. You have to know, Logan, I was terrified of losing you." She bit her lip. "I still am."

She sat silent, hoping for him to say she would never lose him, but that is not what he did. In fact, he said nothing. He simply crossed his arms again and leaned away from her. This felt every bit as horrible as she'd expected it would be. Worse even.

CHAPTER 15

BY THE TIME ALL WAS SAID AND DONE, Jenessa had blown up Logan's world. He could hardly wrap his head around it. It was so out of character for the Jenessa he knew to be so impetuous that she would run out and marry a stranger in Las Vegas.

Or was it?

He shot a quick look at her, seated beside him, her jade eyes begging for understanding. He looked away, questions eating at him.

They'd been through so much together, but had they really taken enough time to get reacquainted with each other before deciding to get married?

It had made sense at the time to hurry up and tie the knot. Jenessa was anxious to be with her son—and who could blame her?

Plus, she wanted to officially be Grayson's mother, stepmother at least, when they finally told him he was actually their biological son.

Grayson and Lily were legally his children now. It had all come to fruition after the reading of his cousin's will and the spousal abuse conviction of their adopted dad, who didn't have any problem relinquishing parental rights over the two.

All that was left—or so he'd thought—was to get married and make them all a family. Except that now, it appeared that was not how it was going to play out.

The police were looking for his father for questioning, for he was the most likely suspect...aside from Logan and Jenessa, that is. And Logan knew he didn't kill the guy. And Jenessa, well, had he known before what he knew now...

Was she capable of murder? He glanced at her again, finding her staring down at her hands roiling in her lap. Could she, if it meant saving her upcoming marriage to him and her chance to finally live with her son?

"Logan, talk to me," Jenessa implored.

He searched her eyes but remained silent.

Maybe he really didn't know his fiancée as well as he'd thought. For her to drink so much alcohol that she'd run to—what?—an Elvis chapel on the Vegas strip. To marry a man she'd just met? Both of those things had previously seemed out of character for her.

That left them where they were right now. Sitting side by side, so close yet so far...

He went to the window, staring blankly at the street as questions continued to circle in his mind. What would it mean in the coming days? The wedding? The children? Fortunately, the kids were out of town. With her "husband" dead, she was now free to marry, but should he move forward with it?

Logan sat down next to her again.

"Listen, Jenessa," he turned toward her, resting his arm on the back of the sofa behind her, "I honestly don't know how I feel about everything you just said. I'll need some time to process it all."

"I get it," she responded softly, worry darkening her features.

"But there are some things I need to share with you too. Things I've never told anyone before."

She wasn't the only one with dark secrets.

Jenessa shifted her body to face him, tears glistening in her eyes. The sad expression on her face was twisting his insides like a vise.

"There are so many things, Jenessa. I don't even know where to begin." His chest tightened at what he was about to disclose.

Her lips trembled as she said, "I'm listening."

Logan's arm slipped down from the back of the sofa and he took her hand. He drew in a deep breath, hoping it would steady his nerves so he could calmly tell her everything. "Last night I told you we needed to talk."

She swallowed down the lump in her throat as she gave him a subtle bob of her head.

"Do you remember the picture of that diamond ring I showed you online? The one I said looked so much like my grandmother's?"

She nodded, and her shoulders appeared to relax a little.

"Well, there's a reason I don't have it to give to you, as I'd wanted to—"

"A reason?" She wiped at a stray tear on her cheek.

"It's the thread that connected me to this dreadful situation with—what's his name again?"

"Rafe," Jenessa said. "Rafe Santiago."

"That's right. How could I forget?" He paused for a moment. "Anyway, yesterday I received a call from Mrs. Dobson."

"Your father's housekeeper?"

"Yes, she asked me to come by the estate, so of course I went. But before I headed into the house, I saw my dad coming out of the gatehouse. I was totally taken by surprise to see him out of prison."

"You had no idea he was being released?"

"No. Not a clue," he said.

But Jenessa had known, and she'd failed to tell him. *Why?*

She squeezed his hand lightly. Her touch was comforting but the idea that she had kept this information from him was puzzling. "So, needless to say," Logan continued, "I was pretty stunned to see him at all, but to see him skulking away from the gatehouse, well..." he paused before continuing, the words not easy to say, "it brought back memories..."

"What kind of memories?" She seemed hesitant to ask, almost fearful.

He swallowed hard before he could go on. "Some awful...painful memories...from my childhood."

"Oh, Logan," she sighed.

"It was where my father went to have private space. Where he took his lovers, where he sometimes conducted business, where he..."

Logan closed his eyes and was overcome with a rush of emotions—fear, shame, guilt, panic. It was almost more than he could bear. His lips trembled just thinking about telling her, telling anyone, about the violence he endured at the hand of his father.

She clutched his hand more firmly. "You can tell me, Logan. You can say anything."

Okay, I can do this. No matter what ugly thoughts were coursing through his brain right then, he did love this woman. And, in spite of things appearing otherwise, they would work this out. They had to.

He placed his hand over hers, gazed deeply into her soft green eyes. A ragged sigh escaped him. "He beat me."

"Oh, Logan." She leaned closer. "I'm so sorry. I had no idea."

A wave of nausea washed over him. How could he admit that he had allowed this behavior to continue? That, as a grown man—literally just the day prior—he had failed to stand up to his abusive father? Myriad emotions flooded him. Mostly shame. What kind of man doesn't stand up for himself?

"It...this...is so hard to talk about. It didn't stop back then, when I was a kid. Even after I became an adult...my father..."

Jenessa's face went slack, her eyes wide. "What?"

"I...he...just yesterday, Jenessa, he hit me."

She gently touched the side of his mouth, still bruised from the day before. "This, it was his doing?" Anger flared in her eyes. "Your father did this?"

He bobbed his head sullenly, unable to look at her.

"Did your mother know?"

He shrugged. "She never acted like she did. I'm not sure."

"You should talk to her. Get it all out. It might be cathartic."

"Maybe." His mother wasn't known for wanting to share her feelings or talk about difficult subjects.

"Whether she did or not, your father is not going to get away with this," she said with resolve. "This is assault."

Sensing Jenessa's body move, he raised his head to look at her.

Her back stiffened and her face took on the intense, serious look she always got when she was preparing for a battle, usually with his father. And in that moment, he loved her for that.

How could he have thought anything negative about this beautiful, sympathetic woman? She was a loving, caring soul, and fiercely loyal and protective, like a mother lion. She had to be giving him the unvarnished truth, with a good reason for not telling him about what had happened in Las Vegas.

He raised her hand to his lips, holding her piercing gaze. "I love you, babe." He kissed the back of it lightly and her expression softened.

Yes, they would work this out. Together. One way or another.

CHAPTER 16

JENESSA LEFT LOGAN SITTING IN HER living room, appearing emotionally exhausted, and went to the kitchen to make coffee. As she filled the dispenser with water, she went over all the things he had confessed to her. Her initial response was shock at hearing how Grey Alexander had beat his son, but as she thought more about it, it made sense.

She'd always known Grey to be psychologically controlling, manipulative, insulting, and just plain mean. But physically abusive? How had she missed that? Now Logan's admissions made a lot of things from their past much clearer to her.

She remembered a few times when he had shown up for a date with bruises or a black eye, or maybe having trouble with an arm or shoulder injury. He'd always played it off as the results of playing football.

But she'd seen him play. He was the quarterback, the team's golden boy, and his offensive linemen had been very good at protecting their quarterback. Logan rarely got sacked, but there were times. Still, she'd always bought his explanation.

Now, in retrospect, it just made so much sense, having this piece of the Logan puzzle fall into place. It helped explain some of Logan's character flaws too.

She scooped the coffee into the drip basket and left the coffee machine to do its work. When she sat down beside Logan again, he was deep in thought. "So, Logan, do you think your father is guilty?"

"Of killing this *Rafe* you mean?"

"Yes. Do you think he could have done it?"

Logan shrugged. "Could have. I mean, look at his past…murdering some guy in a fit of rage isn't a big jump, considering the other things we *know* he's guilty of, not to even mention the things he's managed to get away with."

His expression dropped. "I'm sorry, Jenessa."

"What for?"

"I wasn't thinking. Rafe was more than just 'some guy' to you. He was…your husband."

Logan seemed to almost choke on that last word, *husband*. Jenessa couldn't blame him. After all, she was still reeling from seeing Rafe here in Hidden Valley and finding out they were still very much married, at least technically. She could only guess at how it affected Logan.

She shrugged a shoulder. "It's okay. He was a virtual stranger to me, really."

Logan's eyes brightened at that.

"I only knew him for less than twenty-four hours, years ago, and I never even considered that I'd see him again. Actually, it's me who is sorry, Logan." Jenessa cupped his jaw and met his gaze. "I should have told you about it."

As her hand moved away, he nodded but said nothing.

The truth was, she hadn't even remotely thought of telling Logan. It wasn't even something that occurred to her from time to time. She'd forgotten it as if Rafe had just been some man that she'd had one date with and moved on. For Jenessa, that's all it was.

When the coffee was ready, they sat at the breakfast bar and drank, mostly in silence. Each seemed to have a lot on their minds, occasionally exchanging a loving glance and a few casual words.

Halfway through his cup, Logan stood and said he needed to leave. He had some work to take care of, but he would be back later, and they could have dinner together.

She offered him a little smile of understanding. They each needed time to process all that had been said. At least they seemed to be in agreement that their love was strong enough to overcome the obstacles.

She walked him to the door and opened it. "I love you, Logan."

His hands snaked around her waist and he pulled her close. "I love you too. We'll get through this. After all, we have a wedding this Saturday and nothing or no one is going to stop you from becoming my wife."

Her heart swelled as his lips found hers, giving her a soft kiss that deepened into a passionate one, bringing warmth swirling through her body.

When they parted, she could hardly catch her breath. "I...I like the sound of that, sweetheart...becoming your wife."

He smiled widely, and his eyes sparkled with affection, then he stepped through the doorway.

Jenessa watched him go down the walkway and out to his car, still heady from his kiss. He turned and waved before ducking inside. Hope rang in her heart for the first time in days. Come Saturday, they would be married and have their precious family...if nothing else surfaced to stop them.

She closed the door and leaned her back against it, once again alone with her thoughts. His kiss still tingled on her lips.

She phoned Ramey as promised.

"How did it go?" Ramey asked.

"We talked it all out." Though she would keep Logan's confession confidential. "He said he'd be back for dinner."

"So the wedding is still on?"

"Looks that way." Jenessa smiled to herself.

"*Whew*. That's good to hear. You almost lost it all."

"I know. It was a stupid mistake. That crazy night in Las Vegas nearly ruined everything with Logan, which is ironic because I had mostly avoided relationships with men after I had to give my baby away."

"I can't even imagine how hard that would be, Jenessa."

"Incredibly hard. I focused on getting my college degree, then working at the newspapers in Sacramento, as you know. I made my work the center of my life."

"Tell me again how you hooked up with Rafe."

"It was a fluke, really. I met him at Evangeline's wedding. We were both commiserating over lost loves, trying to drown our sorrows with alcohol. I told Logan that Rafe and I had been partying too much, but it was actually more of a pity party."

She *had* been such a loner back then...it made some sense she would jump into something with a sexy stranger after denying herself human—male human—companionship for so long.

When Jenessa had come home to Hidden Valley, not much more than a year ago, that's when men and serious relationships had come into play. Between quickly falling for the kind and handsome Michael Baxter, and pretending she despised her past love, Logan—it had all messed with her head. But none of it had ever brought to mind the subject of her erroneous nuptials.

"I screwed up royally, Ramey."

"Stop kicking yourself for forgetting to tell Logan."

"I need to own my mistake, and the marriage."

"Although," Ramey said, "with Rafe turning up dead, it hardly matters anymore. At least from a legal standpoint. Right?"

"A man is dead, Ramey. A decent man, for all I know."

"Though you really knew very little about him, did you?"

"Still," Jenessa said, "he had been somebody's son, maybe somebody's brother."

"And definitely somebody's husband," Ramey added.

~*~

It was getting to be late evening, and Jenessa hadn't been able to eat, waiting for Logan to return. The two of them were both emotionally drained after the stressful discourse earlier and she was grateful for the time apart to think things through.

Finally she heard his car pull up and then the door close.

She opened the front door before he could knock and greeted him with a warm kiss. She pulled him inside, asking, "Are you hungry?"

"Starving." He sniffed the air. "Did you cook?"

"No, but I can order pizza with the best of them."

He chuckled. "Yes, you can."

Her heart melted at the sweet sound of his laugh. He gently pulled her into his arms and looked into her eyes. There was hesitation in his gaze. With a couple of fingers under her chin, he lifted her face to his. "I'm so sorry, Jenessa."

"What are you sorry for?" It was she who should be apologizing.

He caressed her cheek. "I'm just...I'm sorry my father is such an—"

"Such an incredibly different man than you, my love. It's not your fault, and it's not your problem anymore. We don't need that man."

"No, we don't." His lips tugged into a smile as he said it. "But with all this other drama, I forgot to tell you about the board meeting."

"That's right. Tell me now. I'm all ears."

He opened his mouth to speak but his cell rang. Logan pulled it from his pocket and looked at the display. "It's my mother," he said. "I better take it."

Jenessa nodded and went to the kitchen, both to give him privacy and to get the pizza menu for Mario's House of Pizza. They made the best pies in all of Hidden Valley. As she fumbled around in the junk drawer, Logan walked in, the phone still in his hand but dropped by his side. His face was again blank and unreadable.

"I don't think she knows," he said.

She closed the drawer and faced him. "Knows what?"

Surely he couldn't mean he'd told his mother that Jenessa was already married. Elizabeth Alexander wasn't her greatest nemesis—that spot was reserved solely for her ex-husband, Grey—but hearing that Jenessa had a secret marriage wouldn't make the woman her biggest fan either.

"About the murder," he replied, shoving his phone back into his pocket.

That was a relief.

"Anyway," Logan went on, "I couldn't break the news over the phone. She asked about meeting with us to finalize the details of the rehearsal dinner. I told her we'd get back to her."

"So you never mentioned I was married, am married, to the murder victim in your father's gatehouse?"

"Of course not. And with Rafe being dead, you're not married to him anymore." He came and held her close again, this time resting his lips gently on hers and kissing her softly.

"Are we going to be okay?" she asked, her voice barely above a whisper.

He nodded. "Yeah, babe, we're going to be just fine."

Jenessa hoped he was right.

CHAPTER 17

JENESSA AWOKE AT THE CRACK OF DAWN, still feeling bloated from all the pizza she ate so late in the evening. She had wanted to fall back asleep, but between her brain jumping immediately to her crazy life and her stomach criticizing her for eating so many carbs, she'd given up and gotten out of bed.

Her forty-eight hours was practically up, but what did it matter at this point? Logan now knew about her past indiscretion, and that was what Grey Alexander had used as leverage against her. And with Rafe being dead, she was free to marry Logan without the annulment.

Still, what would the town think when all of this came out, as it surely would.

Jenessa opened her laptop at the kitchen table and made notes of all she knew so far on Rafe's murder, which wasn't much. She had filled Charles in on the identity of the victim as soon as the detectives finished questioning her, but there was so much more to learn.

Charles would want to run a front-page story on this murder, so she had better start chasing down witnesses and potential suspects.

Had the police located Grey Alexander yet? Would he let her interview him?

Her phone beeped a text notification. The screen read that the text was from her lawyer, that he got her message and would be in the office later in the day if she needed to see him.

Jenessa texted back that she had straightened things out herself, though she really had nothing to do with working it out. But he didn't need to know that.

She returned to her computer and her list of potential suspects. Was she on the detective's list? Was Logan?

She needed time—and space—to think. That meant that heading to The Sweet Spot for a latté and a cinnamon roll was out of the question. So, full of restless energy, and in spite of feeling exhausted, Jenessa opted for the gym.

Checking the time, she found it was close to nine. The gym would be almost deserted at this time of day…she hoped.

Driving up to the facility, she scanned the parking lot, which was, as she expected, fairly empty. Good. She could go in, hit the treadmill, and blast out her stress, maybe bring it down to a manageable level.

Jenessa parked, tugged her gym bag from the car, and entered the state-of-the-art fitness center. She didn't go nearly as often as she should, but she was here now, and with only days until she had to zip into her wedding gown, this was definitely the right choice over coffee and a high-calorie pastry.

After scanning her membership card at the front desk, Jenessa headed toward the back. She passed complicated machines that she had no idea what they were, let alone how to use them. They appeared more like instruments of torture, rather than health-promoting apparatuses.

But the treadmill she could figure out, and a good sweat seemed superior to ruminating about her current situation. So, she entered the ladies changing room to get into her workout gear.

~*~

Jenessa slung her towel over the handrails, set her water bottle in the drink holder, dropped her phone and iPod into the accessory tray, and hopped on deck. She studied the instructions for a moment, then simply pressed the *Quick Start* button. All those programs and options were intimidating. Besides, Jenessa liked having the control herself. It was easier when she was at the helm of her own destiny, both in fitness and in life. In a world filled with surprises, it was a nice change to know what to expect.

She started out at a moderate, carefree walk and quickly accelerated to a slow jog. With her headphones in and listening to a high-energy playlist that she had made strictly for exercising, she quickly lost herself in the zone.

Finally, she slowed her pace a little to take a swig from her water bottle without pouring its contents all over herself. As she screwed the cap back on the plastic bottle, she glanced in the wall-to-wall mirrors two rows ahead, in front of the bikes and elliptical trainers. That was when she saw him, looking at her. It was Michael.

Now that was awkward. Her first time here since she had broken up with him, and who should she run into but Michael. And there was no going back. He had seen her see him too.

What was the proper protocol in this type of situation? You know, when you run into your ex at the gym after having an awkward Q&A over your dead husband the day before…that protocol.

Never mind. He was coming over.

She tugged her earbuds out and slowed her pace, but she did not turn off the machine. She needed a buffer, and the treadmill was it. "Oh, hey, Michael."

"Jenessa."

He hopped on the treadmill beside her, set the incline, and started out at a brisk stroll. Apparently, he wanted a buffer too.

"So, have you got any new information on the case?" she asked.

"Are you asking as a reporter or a grieving widow?"

Ouch. That was a little harsh. Even for him. "Michael, I'm not—"

"Never mind, I take the question back. It wasn't fair of me." He wiped at his forehead with the small towel he had draped around his neck. "You explained the situation, and, while I don't understand, exactly—it just doesn't seem like you—I do accept it. And, besides, it's not any of my business anymore."

There was still pain in his voice.

"I've said it before, Michael, but it bears repeating. It wasn't as though I didn't love you. I know you're a wonderful man, truly, and you'll make some woman very happy one day. But, you know, I gave my heart to Logan when we were teenagers, and I suppose I never really got it back. You deserve someone who can give you their whole heart, someone who will love you unreservedly and never have any doubts about it."

"I loved you too, Jenessa."

"I know." A pang of guilt stabbed at her.

"But, to be honest," he paused as if to measure his words, "my time away from you these last few months has made me realize I was more in love with the idea of you."

That was news. Was it true? "I don't follow."

Michael shrugged. "I had such a huge crush on you in high school—"

"That's sweet, Michael."

He shook his head sadly. "But I guess, back then, I knew you'd never return my feelings. I was so gangly and awkward, and you were dating the great Logan Alexander."

"I never knew you felt that way."

"I never wanted you to know." He wiped his brow again. "And I know I've changed since then—"

"A lot."

"Maybe, but sometimes I still feel like the pimply teenager with a mouth full of braces. When you rolled into town last year and seemed to take a romantic interest in me, I could hardly believe my good luck."

She hit *Stop* on the treadmill's dashboard and turned to look him in the eye. "Well, you're a great guy, Michael. Why wouldn't I take an interest? What girl in her right mind wouldn't?"

He stopped his machine as well. "I was so psyched," he blushed at the throwback, teenage word, "that someone like you wanted to go out with me. And then the way you and little Jake hit it off. He was heartbroken you know, when I told him we weren't together anymore."

He bobbed his head toward a row of weight-lifting benches, and the two went to sit down.

"I am sorry about that, Michael. Really. I fell in love with him too, not just his father. He's such a sweet little boy, and I miss him. We can still be friends, can't we?"

Michael lifted his shoulders in a shrug. "I suppose we should, for his sake. After all, I'm sure we'll be running into you a lot since The Sweet Spot is his favorite place to go."

"And this town is pretty small." She dabbed her forehead with her towel, then draped it around her neck like Michael had.

He took her hand, and Jenessa's heart leapt into her throat. Oh, God, was he going to tell her he still loved her? That he wanted her back? Surely not. He knew she was with Logan. Unless he hoped maybe Logan would walk away from her, knowing about her past transgression with Rafe Santiago.

"Jenessa, I've given our break up a lot of thought, and it's time I moved on."

It was, right? Before she and Logan had gotten back together, when Jenessa was still with Michael, Ramey had told her she was hogging all the available men in town. She wasn't still trying to do that, was she? No, Jenessa was fully committed to Logan, and all she wanted was for Michael to be happy. He deserved it.

"That's good to hear. And I'm sure there's a wonderful woman out there just perfect for you, Michael."

She thought of Sara and recalled how her sister had been interested in Michael before Jenessa returned to Hidden Valley last year.

"Perfect, huh?" His brows raised a bit as he said it.

She rested a hand on his arm. "Why don't you ask my sister out for coffee some time? Like I suggested yesterday."

"Your sister, again? Are you certain you wouldn't mind?"

"It might sting a little at first, I won't lie, but I think you two might be good together. And besides, she adores little Jake." Jenessa crossed her arms. "Yes, I'd totally be okay with it, Michael."

Eventually.

And why not? With Jenessa marrying Logan, she *would* be happy to see her sister settle down with someone as kind and loving as Michael.

He appeared to consider it. "But then you and I would run into each other even more often, you know. And you're really sure you're okay with that?"

"Like I said, it might be a little uncomfortable at first." If Michael and Sara's relationship turned into something real, something long term, he might even become part of her family. Her ex would become her brother-in-law…family dinners might be awkward, at first. But no, her sister deserved this. And so did Michael. "But, it's not about me. Sara's a great girl and you're a wonderful man."

"Just not wonderful enough for you?" There was an unmistakable glint of pain in his eyes.

"That's not true. We were good together, overall, and it wasn't that you weren't the right man for me. It's just that Logan is the father of my child, and I've always loved him."

She detected a slight nod. Perhaps he was finally accepting it.

"You and Sara both deserve to be happy too, Michael. You deserve to be with the right people for you." She looked for a genuine nod of agreement, but his face had turned indecipherable.

She stood up, preparing to leave. "Take her out, Michael, see if she's the right one for you. What have you got to lose?"

CHAPTER 18

LOGAN PULLED UP IN FRONT OF his mother's house. While she no longer lived in a sprawling mansion on the Alexander estate, her home was far from modest. It was a symmetrical, two-story white brick colonial, with the roof, window shutters, and front door all accented in black.

Today, he was here under the guise of discussing the wedding rehearsal dinner. In her phone call the night before, his mother had given no indication that she knew anything about the murder at the gatehouse.

He hadn't heard from the police again since they'd questioned him, but he assumed his father had been tracked down and interrogated by now.

Logan climbed the front steps and rang the bell. After a brief moment, Helga, his mother's housekeeper, answered the door, and ushered him inside.

As he stepped into the foyer, his mother called down from upstairs. "Logan dear, is that you?" Then, before he could answer, she sang out, "I'll be down momentarily."

Helga showed him to the sitting room, where a silver tray was set with cups and a steaming teapot on the circular gold-and-glass table. He perched on the edge of the tufted, oatmeal-colored sofa that was nearest the unlit fireplace, facing two cream-colored wingback chairs.

The room—the entire house, really—was, like his mother, refined, elegant, and a little bit stiff. Still, Logan felt more "at home" here than he did at his father's estate. Not that that was saying much. But this was the closest he came to comfort and a safe place.

After his parents had divorced he could come here to lick his wounds and hide out. His mother didn't really bother him much when he was younger. He supposed she had her own crosses to bear where his father was concerned, and she mostly kept busy with her various charities and clubs, lunching with the ladies, and playing tennis from time to time.

He figured the latter served to release his mother's years of pent-up stress after living with his father and all his "quirks." It wasn't easy being the son of the great Grey Alexander, and it most certainly could not have been any easier being the man's wife.

Had his mother known his father beat him? She had never let on, but maybe. He had made a promise to himself to ask her about it today. Point blank. Jenessa had convinced him it would be cathartic for him.

"Logan darling." His mother sashayed into the room, wearing tailored navy dress slacks and a white, pressed blouse, with a single string of pearls at her neck.

She approached him, and he stood to embrace her and receive a formal kiss on the cheek.

"Hello, Mother."

She pulled back a little. "Oh, dear, Logan. Did you get into a fight?"

He touched his lip. "It's nothing."

"You always were getting into scrapes as a child. I would have thought you'd outgrown it."

Maybe she didn't know.

His mother sat in the chair across from him and poured the tea, which surprised him. He had expected her to call Helga to the room just to do it. Maybe his mother was softening up in her old age. Not that she was old—and don't anyone dare call her that—but everyone matures over the years. Although, she hadn't seemed to age at all, physically, since Logan was a teenager. The woman probably had regular spa treatments, and maybe even Botox for all he knew.

Whatever it was, Elizabeth Alexander had aged gracefully.

She seemed rather relaxed today. Too relaxed. It appeared she was still in the dark. The police must not have found any need to question her.

Oh well, no time like the present to enlighten the woman.

"Mother, did you hear about the murder at the gatehouse?"

~*~

"Ramey, is Selena here yet?" Jenessa asked as she strolled, out of breath, into The Sweet Spot. "She's supposed to be meeting us here to look at the cakes you made, but we were planning to have an early lunch first."

"Relax," Ramey said as she stepped around the counter to give Jenessa a hug, before ushering her to a couple of tables that had been pushed together in the corner. "Why are you breathing so hard?"

Jenessa hung her purse on the back of a chair and sat. "I hurried over from the paper. I didn't want to be late."

"Then I'm sure your cousin will be here soon."

Jenessa nodded, relaxing back in the chair.

Ramey dashed off. "Be right back," she called over her shoulder as a customer entered the shop.

Thankfully the café wasn't very busy late on a Monday morning. She could take her time looking at Ramey's creative confections before making a decision on which would end up being her wedding cake. That was, of course, assuming there would still be a wedding.

Jenessa shook that notion away. She and Logan had left things on pretty good terms, in spite of all that had come out in the last couple of days. She touched a finger to her lips, remembering the passionate kiss he had left her with the night before.

Ramey returned, setting a cup of coffee in front of her before dropping into the closest chair. "Any news on the murder case?"

"Truthfully, Ramey, I have almost nothing. I feel so out of the loop on this one." She wasn't used to that.

"Guess Michael's not keeping you up to date? Now that you two are not an item anymore."

"That's true. Now my only hope is George."

"Isn't he retiring soon?" Ramey questioned.

"Supposedly. This might even be his last case."

"I've got to get back to the counter," Ramey said as another customer walked in. "I'll bring the cakes out after Selena gets here." And off she went.

A few moments later, someone tapped Jenessa on the shoulder and she looked up to see Selena standing beside her.

"Have you been waiting long?" Selena pulled out the chair across the table and sat down.

"Not long," Jenessa replied, taking a sip of her coffee.

"What's going on? Are you having pre-wedding jitters yet?" Selena removed the light jacket that she had draped over her shoulders.

"Not exactly. I was just lost in thought." Jenessa stared at her coffee a moment as she decided just how much she should say to her cousin. "That man I talked about? The one from Evangeline's wedding in Las Vegas?"

"You mean your husband?"

Jenessa gritted her teeth at that comment. Selena was probably trying to lighten the mood with an attempt at humor, but Jenessa wasn't feeling it.

"I'm so sorry," Selena was quick to correct. "That was insensitive of me. I realize his showing up here right before your wedding is a real challenge for you. How did Logan take the news?"

Jenessa steeled herself. "The phone call I got the last time we were together?"

"When you dashed off without an explanation? Yeah, what was that about?"

"I told you it was my editor, but I didn't say what he was calling about."

"No. Was it important?"

"I get the feeling you haven't heard the news yet."

"News?"

"Rafe Santiago was found dead in Grey Alexander's gatehouse."

Selena's brown eyes grew round. "He was what?" Her coffee spoon clanked to the table, and her face went stark white, like she'd seen a ghost. It seemed to Jenessa like too strong a reaction from someone over the death of a mere stranger.

She studied Selena for a moment, trying to get a read on the situation before speaking. But she didn't have to, for Selena reached across the table and took Jenessa's hand. "I have a confession to make."

A confession? Surely Selena wasn't going to cop to murdering Rafe. Jenessa held her breath and waited.

Selena pushed her long dark hair back over one shoulder and stared into her cup of coffee. "After talking to you the last time, I remembered meeting him, Rafe, in Spain a few years ago, when I worked at the TV station."

"Wait. You knew Rafe Santiago? But you—"

Selena waved her hand dismissively, then raised her eyes to meet her cousin's. "I said we met. It's not like we were dating or anything. He was handsome, I remember that, but he was a little too rough around the edges for me. And he was always on the move, not the settling down type."

Jenessa became immediately suspicious. "Your eyes say you did more than just meet him."

Selena held eye contact for a moment, then glanced

toward the window. "Okay, maybe it was a little more than just meeting him."

"You and he dated?" Jenessa couldn't believe it. She could accept her sister going out with the same men Jenessa had, Hidden Valley was not a sprawling metropolis, after all. But to have her own cousin, halfway around the world mind you, date the man that Jenessa had accidentally remained married to all these years, well, that was almost too much.

"No, no, it's not like that." Selena wagged her hand. "I mean, not exactly. We did spend some time together, but then he stole my—he stole something from me and just disappeared. And now he's dead. It's all so hard to—"

"Stole something?"

"Can we please change the subject?" Selena looked toward the coffee counter. "Where is Ramey with those cakes?"

CHAPTER 19

AFTER TELLING HIS MOTHER ABOUT the murder at the gatehouse the night before—though, he hadn't mentioned anything about Jenessa's relationship to the dead guy and wasn't certain he would—Logan felt uncomfortable confronting her about her knowledge of his father's abuse. He had promised Jenessa he would, but his mother had seemed quite shaken up when he'd told her what he'd walked in on at the gatehouse, and that the police had been looking for his father for questioning.

Plus, the original intent of his visit was supposed to be to talk about the wedding rehearsal dinner, and that subject never came up either. So where did that leave him? Should he jump in with both feet and just say it, or should he wait until later that night, when he and Jenessa were scheduled to have dinner with her?

Fine, he would just ask her if she knew. She was already upset, or appeared to be, though he didn't know why. It wasn't as though she had ever met this Rafe Santiago.

"I have a question for you, Mother."

She looked at him curiously, as though she wondered what on earth he might ask after the grisly things he had just told her. "A question? What type of question, dear?"

Then, just as Logan opened his mouth to blurt it out, Helga walked into the room, carrying the cordless phone in her hand. "Mrs. Alexander," she handed it to his mother, "the phone is for you. A Detective Baxter."

What on earth did Baxter want with his mother? Surely she couldn't be considered a suspect. She'd had no idea anyone was even staying at his father's gatehouse, let alone that a murder had taken place.

Logan would only hear one side of the conversation, but he decided to try to listen anyway.

His mother took the phone. "Hello, this is Elizabeth Alexander...Yes, Detective Baxter, how may I help you?"

The rest of the brief conversation basically consisted of "Yes, mm-hmm, I see," followed by his mother rising to her feet and calmly announcing, "I need to go down to the police station. Can you drive me, Logan?"

Was Baxter just exercising his authority, and torturing Logan's mother to get at Logan? Or did he actually consider her a suspect? How could that even be possible? The more he thought about it, the angrier Logan became. He would drive his mother down to the station, and he would give Michael Baxter a piece of his mind.

He stood. "Of course I'll drive you." He took the phone from her hand and handed it to a waiting Helga on his way out of the sitting room. He turned back to see if his mother was following. She wasn't.

"Mother?"

She had sat down on the edge of one of the chairs. "Yes, dear, I'm coming."

Her hand went to her forehead and her gaze dropped to the floor, appearing shaken up again.

What was going on with her? From the look of her, her emotions were running the gamut it seemed, and none of it made sense to Logan. She had acted so calm while on the phone with Michael, but before, when Logan told her about the murder, and then now, she seemed a complete wreck.

He knelt in front of her. "What's wrong, Mother?"

"The police are looking for your father."

"Why do they want to question you?"

"I suppose they think I'm still in contact with him, that I know something about what goes on at the estate."

Did she know where the man was? Why would the police think she did? Did they know something Logan didn't?

His mother appeared so shaken. She couldn't be that concerned for his father in this matter, could she? Was she secretly holding out hope that she'd end up with him? He was still married to his second wife, Lauren, as far as Logan knew. However, his stepmother had received a longer prison sentence than his father for her part in their crime. Had his father managed to orchestrate divorce proceedings while incarcerated?

No, she wouldn't want his father back, would she? Although, Logan hadn't really seen his mother dating anyone since their divorce. His father had always had a bevy of women strutting around him, even before the divorce and remarriage, but his mother had always seemed content with her clubs and charities.

"Do you know where he is?" Logan asked, getting to his feet.

"My heaven's no. Although I had heard he was back in town." She rose to leave.

Maybe there was a whole side to his mother he never knew existed. A side that was foolish enough to think his father would not only want her back, but that he would be monogamous—that is, if he was even free from his second wife.

He'd have to nip that in the bud right quick. And Logan knew just how to do that. "Dad was beating me, you know."

She froze in her tracks but said nothing.

"My father, all those years while I was growing up, he was beating me. Did you know that?" Information like that had to snap her back to reality, and she turned back to face him. "I was just a kid, Mom."

"Oh, Logan." She dropped back into the chair she'd been occupying moments ago.

"You knew, didn't you?" He could see it in her face. "Mother, how could you?"

She immediately jumped back to her feet, though she made the move so abruptly she swayed where she stood, as though the blood had suddenly rushed from her head. She reached out to him, then collapsed in a heap on the floor.

Logan ran to her but couldn't get there in time. He knelt beside her and felt at her neck. There was still a strong pulse. He was glad for that. "Helga," he shouted. "Call nine-one-one!"

~*~

"Okay." Ramey approached the table, effectively saving Selena from Jenessa's further questioning. "I've made six different cakes. I know you and Logan already chose the size and layer flavors, Jenessa, so what I have here are all different colors and styles. You'll be able to see what the top layer of your wedding cake will look like."

Aunt Renee came out from the back, rolling a dessert cart.

"Aunt Renee," Jenessa said, "when did you get here?"

Jenessa's aunt walked up to her and placed a hand on her shoulder. "I came in with Selena. I was on the phone, so I went into the back to finish up. Did you girls order lunch yet?"

"Not yet," Selena said. "Since you have the cakes here, maybe after."

"So, six cakes, huh?" Jenessa's stomach rumbled with hunger. "Show me what you've come up with."

Ramey beamed as if she were in cake heaven. "You're going to love them."

She had always loved to bake and cook. That's why, when Jenessa's mother was thinking of opening The Sweet Spot, she had looked to Ramey as a partner, rather than Jenessa or Sara, neither of which had the passion for food that Ramey and Lydia Jones had shared so deeply.

Ramey gestured toward the dessert cart as though she were a TV gameshow spokesmodel. "As I said, the inside is the same, but the outside represents different styles, colors…moods, if you will. We have chic, floral, boxy, sophisticated, traditional, and, of course, a playful one."

"I like this one." Sara, having just strode through the door fashionably late and wearing a gigantic smile, pointed at the playful one. She took one of the lattés that Ramey had set on the table and stirred a packet of sugar into it.

"You know those have vanilla syrup in them," Ramey told her. "They're already sweetened."

"I know," Sara answered, her smile not faltering even slightly. "I'm just feeling like something extra sweet today." She took a tentative sip, then, realizing the coffee had cooled a little, took a longer draw.

"What is up with you today?" Selena asked Sara.

"Well, since you asked…" She looked to Jenessa, a cautious expression on her face. "I was invited on a date today."

There was a bit of speculation dashed around by each of the women, but Jenessa had a feeling she knew who the lucky fellow was.

"Yes, Jenessa, it was Michael. But he said we had your blessing." Sara plopped into a chair and swiped some of the frosting off the playful cake with her finger, then stuck it into her mouth. "Yup. Called it. This is delish, Ramey."

Wow. That was quick. Michael wasted no time asking her sister out on a date. Of course, Jenessa had nothing she could say about that. She had, after all, told him to do it. She just hadn't thought he'd do it so…immediately.

The women each piped in, briefly, about Sara, Michael, and his *potential*, then moved on to give their individual opinions of which cake Jenessa should choose.

"Well, Jenessa," Ramey said, arching a brow at her. "Which one will it be? And remember, it is your decision. It doesn't matter what we all think. It's your day, your choice."

Jenessa looked to Aunt Renee, to get her take, but she had wandered off, and was, again, talking on her cell phone in the corner, probably finalizing the details with the caterer and florist, since she was acting as their wedding planner. Aunt Renee was thrilled to do it, so Jenessa let her be, and made the decision on her own.

"I'll take that one." Jenessa pointed. "It will be perfect."

CHAPTER 20

JENESSA SAT AT THE DESK in her little cubicle at the newspaper, doing her best to focus on the stories she had to finish for the next edition. She had attempted to call Logan a couple of times, but he had not answered. In fact, his phone had gone straight to voicemail and, after the third try, she was getting worried.

There had already been one murder in town, and it remained unsolved, which meant the killer was still out there. And he, or she, could be waiting to strike again. That thought didn't sit well with Jenessa. Not even a little bit. Especially now that she couldn't reach Logan.

The last she knew, he was going to see his mother, to confront her about whether she had known of his father's abuse or not. She picked up the phone and dialed Elizabeth Alexander. Maybe she knew where Logan was, and why he wasn't answering his phone.

When it rang and rang, Jenessa got even more concerned. Why hadn't her housekeeper answered? She tried Elizabeth's cell. That went straight to voicemail, just like Logan's had. What was going on? Jenessa's reporter's mind couldn't let it go. Neither could her anxious bride-to-be's mind.

If she couldn't reach Logan or his mother, at least she could go down to the station and see how the investigation was coming along, and whether they had any leads...or if she should officially worry about her husband-to-be...

She slung a light jacket on and grabbed her purse, ready to walk down to the station, but as she was heading toward the front, Charles poked his head out of his door and motioned for her to join him. She stopped and turned into his office.

"Hey, Boss, what's up?"

"Sit down, Jenessa, please." He gestured toward the armchair in front of his desk for her, and then sat down in his own.

Jenessa was anxious to go but took a seat.

"Have you got anything on the gatehouse murder?"

She shook her head. "No, not yet. I haven't heard anything since they questioned me, but I was about to head down there and—"

Charles stood from his chair, and it rolled backward. "They questioned you? Like a suspect?"

"No. Well, yes, sort of. But I'm sure it was simply routine." Should she tell her boss that the man that was killed was married—technically—to his star reporter? No, that was probably not such a good idea.

"Why would they question you? Were you there when it happened? You didn't say any—"

Shoot. Now what choice did she have? Besides, Ramey would probably spill her guts to Charles later that night anyway.

"You might want to sit down again, Charles."

"Sit down? What? Why?"

"Just trust me."

He slid his chair back up to the desk and sat down, folding his hands on the surface and looking none too pleased with her. "Well?"

"Um, well…" Jenessa began, "I was sort of married to the victim."

~*~

Logan checked his cell phone again, as if somehow, this time, the battery would have miraculously recharged on its own. But it hadn't, of course. Jenessa must be worried about him. He was sure she would have tried to call him, she always did on her lunch. At least she did when she wasn't off tracking down a hot story for the paper. It was midafternoon now, meaning she wouldn't have been able to reach him for the last couple of hours.

He shoved it back in his pocket and resumed pacing outside his mother's hospital room. He would have gone to a payphone to call Jenessa if he wasn't so darn curious about what was happening on the other side of that door.

The doctor had said his mother had simply fainted, thankfully. Logan had been worried it was a stroke or something. God knows his mother had been under enough stress in her life, especially lately. No one in town ever liked finding out there had been a murder.

Even if the murdered person was an out-of-towner. And knowing the killer was still out there somewhere, well, that complicated it even more. Add to that the murder happening on your ex-husband's estate, and his mother had an extra dose of worry.

And then Logan had to go and amp things up, asking her about—no, accusing her of—knowing about his childhood abuse. *Stupid, stupid, stupid.* Why didn't he ever know when to quit?

And now, his mother lay in a hospital bed—for observation, the doctor had said—and she was being interrogated by Michael Baxter and his partner, Detective Provenza. And what's worse…they wouldn't allow him to stay. So, all he could do was pace and wonder how Jenessa was handling all of this.

~*~

Charles had ordered her off the gatehouse story. It was a conflict of interest, he had said, with her potentially being treated as a suspect. Never mind that she had simply been asked a few routine questions and released. No, he was going to give the story to the new guy. How was some young naïve newcomer going to be able to get to the crux of a breaking news story the way Jenessa knew she could?

And where was Logan? Why hadn't she been able to reach him? Perhaps he was in a closed-room meeting with the board and had to keep his phone off.

She went back to her desk to try to work on the "boring" stories she'd been allowed to keep working, but her mind was not in the game. She typed a few lines, then her mind would wander. Why was she just sitting around? Even though Charles had taken her off the story, the police didn't know that. Maybe she could still use her credentials, and her relationship to Baxter and Provenza, to get some information out of them about the investigation.

Couldn't hurt to try. Jenessa closed her laptop and grabbed her purse, intent on heading down to the station to see what she could find out. Her desk phone rang, and she snatched it up to answer it. "Jenessa Jones."

She should have let it ring.

"Miss Jones, long time, no talk. Your time is more than up. When I am done with you, you are going to regret ever crossing my path."

Grey Alexander.

Heat rose up her neck at the sound of his voice, but no fear stiffened her back, only resolve. "On the contrary. It is you who will have regrets. Logan knows all about my marriage."

"So, the wedding is off?" He sounded hopeful.

Jenessa smiled to herself. "No, he still wants to marry me."

"He won't want anything to do with you by the time I'm done talking to him."

"Oh, get over yourself. You've got nothing left, Mr. Alexander."

"Listen here—"

"Since my so-called husband has turned up dead in your gatehouse, you really have no leverage over me. In fact, I dare say, you have done me a favor by killing him. So, as awful as it is that an innocent man had to lose his life, now Logan and I can get married as planned."

She thought she heard what sounded like the pound of his fist on his desk. "Why, you little...How dare you speak to me that way?"

It seemed Jenessa had poked a sleeping bear. Grey Alexander clearly did not like to lose—especially to her. While she felt good that she was able to thwart his scheme, Jenessa couldn't relax. What would Grey try to pull next? She'd never known him to give up easily on anything.

"I'm not through with you, Miss Jones. Not by a long shot."

And with that, Grey Alexander slammed down the phone.

CHAPTER 21

"I APPRECIATE YOUR TAKING ME OUT to dinner, Logan." Jenessa sighed deeply, seated beside her fiancé in his car as he drove toward the home her parents had left to her. "Although, I probably wasn't the best company tonight."

He took one hand off the steering wheel and placed it over top of Jenessa's hands, which were clasped tightly in her lap. "I'm sure I wasn't either." He squeezed lightly, letting his grip linger there.

"Are you thinking about your mother?" she asked.

"Yes." He glanced over at her. "If I would've had any idea that asking her about what my father did to me would have caused her to collapse like that, I never would have brought it up."

"You feel guilty," she said. "I understand that, but you shouldn't, Logan. It's your father who should be riddled with remorse. Though I doubt he is at all familiar with that emotion."

Grey Alexander had done a lot of wicked things in his life, but Jenessa didn't think he'd ever had any regrets. At least none she had ever witnessed.

While his second wife was lingering in prison for her part in their crime, Grey was a free man. Still, rather than act humble and be grateful for his freedom, he had immediately started his campaign to break Jenessa and Logan apart. And, he had likely killed the very man that he'd brought to town to facilitate that breakup.

No, Grey Alexander was the epitome of a calculated sociopath. Jenessa was quite certain there was not a single remorseful bone in that man's entire body.

"And yet it is my mother who seems to be on the Hidden Valley Police Department's radar screen right now."

"Why?" Jenessa asked.

"I have no idea. The detectives wouldn't let me be in her room while they questioned her, and she wouldn't tell me after they left."

"And she was okay when you left her?"

Logan shrugged. "I guess." He put his hand back on the steering wheel, focused his eyes straight ahead.

Jenessa sensed he was trying to be strong. Elizabeth Alexander hadn't exactly been the model mother and homemaker, but she was the closest thing to love that Logan had had growing up. Jenessa felt sorry for that. At least she had a loving family…for the most part anyway, until the aftermath from her decision to give herself to Logan on that fateful night so many years ago.

And even though her father had sided with the Alexanders in sending her away and asking her give up her child, she supposed he'd had somewhat more altruistic motives than Grey had had. Plus, she knew from experience how hard it could be to stand up to the man who owned this town, not to mention the man who paid the bulk of her father's salary.

She could never regret coming back here to live though. If she hadn't returned, if she had only come for her father's funeral and then left again, she probably would never have found her son. Or her way back to the love of her life.

Sometimes bad things—like being fired from her job in Sacramento—led to good things.

This too shall pass, Jenessa reminded herself. Maybe all this was another bad thing that would open the doors to something better.

Jenessa clung to that hope. And, as they pulled up to her house, it was time to change the subject. "So, I'm really looking forward to our honeymoon."

Logan dashed her a quick smile as they came to a stop.

"And then you and the kids moving in here with me after that," she continued.

Logan turned off the car and faced Jenessa, his azure-blue eyes brimming with love. "Me too."

A warmth engulfed her. Her heart was full.

His gaze was riveted on hers as he raised her hand to his lips and placed a kiss on the back of it. "I can't wait."

Neither could she. She pressed a soft kiss to his lips.

"What was that for?" he asked.

"I just love you so much I had to kiss you. That's okay, isn't it?"

"It's more than okay." He offered her a sexy half-smile. "I wish we could shut all this drama out and run off and get married tonight."

"Elope?" Ramey and Aunt Renee would kill them, not to mention Selena and the other out-of-town guests, like her cousin Isabel. "What about your mother? We couldn't do that to her, not with all she's dealing with."

"I know. Just wishful thinking." He quirked the side of his mouth. "The doctor said my mother will be released from the hospital tomorrow. They want to keep her overnight for observation they said. So, if your Aunt Renee takes the kids for the first part of our honeymoon, and Mother doesn't take them until the second part, it'll give her more time to deal with all of…" Logan waved his hand about, "this."

This murder, this deception, this abusive father, this dirty little secret. It seemed they all had to deal with "this."

They were talking about and planning their wedding and honeymoon as though the town was not smack dab in the middle of a scandalous murder investigation. But it was. She was. And she had no outlet. She was taken off the story, and had no "in," at least no legitimate one, with the police, nor did she have a juicy story to write.

Logan's expression turned serious, his lips drawing tight. "I don't want my father coming to the wedding."

That both surprised her and didn't at the same time. She could understand where he was coming from, but had Logan considered the repercussions of forbidding his father from attending?

"Aren't you worried that people will ask why he's not there?"

Logan looked away for a moment, staring out the side window toward the street as if searching for a suitable reply. "I think everyone will just be glad he didn't come."

"Maybe," Jenessa agreed. "But they will still murmur about it."

Should she tell Logan about his father's phone call earlier? About his most recent threats? She wanted to, but she didn't want to cause Logan any further stress. He already had enough on his mind.

She placed her hand on his cheek to turn his face toward her for another kiss. A spike of anger stabbed at her heart when she saw the faint traces of his father's explosive temper still lingering beside his mouth.

Jenessa stroked her thumb gently over the area, then she leaned over and placed a soft kiss there. "I love you, Logan."

He smiled. "I love you too." His fingers wove through her dark tresses, to the back of her neck, and he pulled her close. "I've always loved you." His lips slanted over hers and he kissed her with a thoroughness that left her breathless.

~*~

Somehow, though she wasn't sure how, Jenessa had managed to have a decent sleep, even with the plethora of thoughts dancing through her mind, including the vivid memory of Logan's passionate kisses still vibrating on her lips.

She'd gotten up on time, showered, had a coffee, and was about to head out the door to work, finding Logan had texted her while she was in the shower. His text was short, reading, "I love you, babe," which put a smile on her face. *I love you too, my sweet darling Logan*, she texted back. Too much? No, he would love it.

With only boring "fluff" pieces to work on for the newspaper, Jenessa swore she was going to find a way to go down to the police station this morning and see what info she might be able to finagle out of the detectives.

She grabbed her handbag and her keys and flung the front door open.

But instead of being greeted with a lovely sunrise, she was met with the scowling face of Grey Alexander. "What are you—? Get off my doorstep!"

"I'll do no such thing." He crossed his arms and planted his feet. "I made you a promise last night, and I intend to follow through, Miss Jones."

CHAPTER 22

WHAT WAS GREY ALEXANDER going to threaten Jenessa with now? Was he going to say he'd tell people she was married before, to Rafe? Was he going to remind her that he could have her fired if he wanted? Not only fired but destroy her reputation with lies.

Briefly, Jenessa envisioned the concrete porch crumbling, sucking this vile man into a deep dark hole, never to be heard from again. As entertaining as the notion was, she knew it would take a lot more than that to kill the devil.

"You're full of talk, Mr. Alexander." She raised her chin in defiance. "You've got nothing on me anymore. You shot yourself in the foot when you eliminated the only card you held over me."

He grinned at her, malice seeping from every pore. "Oh, so you think I killed Rafe Santiago?" A chuckle. "Nice try, Miss Jones, but the police don't seem to agree with you. You see, they questioned me—as they did you, I'm sure—and then they sent me on my merry way."

Oh, how Jenessa wanted to reach out and wipe that smug look off his face. What if she told him that he has forever ruined his relationship with his son? No, she should leave that for Logan to do. Or would Grey even care?

"And don't think it was an oversight, that your boyfriend and his partner let me go."

"Ex-boyfriend," she reminded him.

"Whatever." He waved a dismissive hand in the air. "Seems you have lovers everywhere. Boyfriends on the police force, husbands coming out of the woodwork. It's only a matter of time before my son sees you for the conniving tramp that you are."

Jenessa was fuming now, fighting to control her hands as they balled into tight fists. How dare he talk to her like that? What gave him the right to judge her? She wanted to scream.

That man was so infuriating. Even if she and Logan managed to get married as planned, and he moved into her house with the children, would they ever truly have peace with this despicable human being in their lives? Could they ever live happily ever after here?

She attempted to push past him to go to her car, but he moved to block her.

Jenessa stopped dead in her tracks. She pinched her lips together and glared at him. "You are the meanest man I've ever met."

"That's all you've got?"

It was all she could come up with, being so totally flustered by this man's presence. If she and Logan were to have that happy life, to live unobstructed by the overbearing existence of Grey Alexander, they would have to do something drastic. And since she didn't approve of coldblooded murder, maybe they would have to consider moving away from Hidden Valley—far away.

He stood his ground, and Jenessa stood hers.

He shook his head slowly. "Tsk, tsk, Miss Jones. Is that really the best you can do? Sticks and stones and all that." He laughed in her face.

"Get out!" she shouted.

"Oh, but I can't. At least not yet. I didn't think it would come to this, but it has, and I have more."

"More? More what?"

He leaned forward, his angry face hovering mere inches from her own, and he spoke with certainty. "That lovely aunt of yours…"

"What about Aunt Renee?"

He stroked his chin. "Yes, the lovely Renee Giraldy. I had my investigator do a little digging."

Oh, how she wanted to reach out and shove him down the steps right then. But Jenessa held back her hostility, at least as much as she could. "Leave my aunt out of this! This fight is between you and me."

He didn't even falter a bit in the face of her rage. "Wouldn't it be a shame if I leaked what I found? She might find herself in a world of trouble."

"You're bluffing. You don't have anything on Aunt Renee."

At least, Jenessa hoped he was bluffing.

"Let's just say the death of her second husband may not have been from natural causes, as it had been written on the death certificate. My man has dug up some evidence that might point the authorities more toward foul play than natural causes."

He stepped aside, finally allowing her to pass.

"You're a...a...an insufferable jerk!"

"Such big words for such a scared little mouse of a girl."

She reached the bottom step and turned back to him. "You don't scare me."

"Are you certain? I wonder what might happen in this investigation of Rafe Santiago's murder if the police find out your aunt has a history of killing men to get what she wants."

Jenessa couldn't take anymore. As a reporter, she'd often said that everyone has the potential to kill someone if cornered, and she didn't want to find out if this was her limit or not. She scurried to the car, hit the unlock button on her key fob, and climbed in, closing the door so she didn't have to hear another wicked word come out of that man's mouth.

~*~

As if Jenessa didn't have enough to worry about, now she had her aunt to be concerned with. Aunt Renee had been like a mother to her since her mom passed away. How could she sit idly by and let Grey Alexander destroy her aunt's life too?

She started the car and pushed the gas pedal hard, peeling away from the curb, wishing Logan had heard what his father had said to her. She had him on speed dial. Why hadn't she had her wits about her enough to press 1 and let him listen in? But no, she acted like a scared little rabbit—again.

All Jenessa wanted right then was to get this wedding over with—and the murder investigation—and just move on with her life already. And poor Aunt Renee had suffered a heart attack a few months ago…having Grey instigate an investigation to be opened, insinuating she murdered her second husband—and Rafe Santiago too—could very well send her into another cardiac arrest. Even if it all proved untrue.

If?

Jenessa chastised herself. Of course it was untrue. Her aunt wouldn't hurt a fly. Sure, she would fight for her family the way any matriarch would, but to insinuate Renee Giraldy would kill anyone? That was preposterous.

Halfway to the newspaper, Jenessa veered off and headed to Aunt Renee's instead. As much as she did not want to give this news, it would be worse to hear about Grey's threats some other way. Like the police showing up at her door, for instance.

No, it would be far better coming from Jenessa. At least then she could prepare her aunt for the news, give her a chance to absorb it slowly, so as to not affect her heart condition.

It was a short few blocks to Aunt Renee's, and Jenessa slowed her pace. She had rushed off half-cocked, as she often did, and realized she didn't have a plan. She needed one.

She didn't know if her aunt was alone at home, or if her cousin Selena was around. Sara and Ramey would be at work at this time of day on a Tuesday, but Selena had no other obligations here that Jenessa knew of, besides the wedding. She could very well be at the house. Did Jenessa want to deliver this news in front of her cousin?

Though Aunt Renee had offered to let Selena stay with her, the two were not related by blood. So it was probably best if Selena were not around.

She pulled over a block from her aunt's house and contemplated what to do.

Jenessa phoned Ramey for help, then drove into a nearby alley and waited a few minutes for Selena to leave her aunt's house. In the face of Ramey's questions, Jenessa had convinced her friend to call Selena and have her come to The Sweet Spot under the guise of talking about wedding issues.

Jenessa had to promise to answer all of Ramey's questions later, but it was worth it, to have Aunt Renee alone when she mentioned Grey's newest threats.

When she received the text from Ramey saying that Selena's rental car had just pulled up in front of the café, Jenessa proceeded to her aunt's house. She rang the doorbell, and Aunt Renee answered the door immediately.

"Oh, hello, dear. I was just walking by the door on my way to the kitchen for some tea. Care to join me?"

Jenessa agreed, and followed her aunt, taking a seat at the breakfast bar while Aunt Renee put the kettle on.

"So, what brings you here today, Jenessa? I would think you'd be too busy to stop and visit your old aunt."

"Don't call yourself old," Jenessa reprimanded, wagging her finger. "Haven't you heard? Oprah Winfrey says that fifty is the new thirty, so sixty must be the new forty."

Renee laughed at that.

"So, see, you are the perfect age. Besides, the doctor has given you a clean bill of health, hasn't he?"

Jenessa was prying a little, trying to get heath information out of her aunt before delivering the potentially bad news.

"Well, not squeaky clean," her aunt said. "But mostly so. As long as I continue to follow this horribly bland diet they sent me home with, and I keep up with the exercise routine I've been assigned." She pulled two mugs from the overhead cabinet. "Oh, and limit my stress of course."

Stress. There, she had said it. Now how the heck was Jenessa going to drop this bomb without causing any fallout?

The kettle began to whistle, and Jenessa was relieved when Aunt Renee opened a bag of decaf chamomile tea for herself.

"I'll have the same," Jenessa said. She'd let Aunt Renee take a few sips of the calming tea blend, and then segue into her warning her about what Grey Alexander might have in store.

They took their tea to the living room and made themselves comfortable. After a few moments of chitchat, Jenessa began. "Listen, Aunt Renee—"

"That doesn't sound like a promising start to a conversation, Jenessa. Just cut to it. I may be old, but

I'm not senile and I can tell when someone has something to say." She took a sip of tea.

"Oh, my gosh, Aunt Renee. Stop saying you're old. You and supermodel Christy Brinkley are the same age."

"It's just that sometimes you and the others try to handle me with kid gloves. I'm not as fragile as everyone wants to believe. Now, go ahead, just tell me what you came to say."

Renee Giraldy was one smart cookie, Jenessa had to give her that. There was no fooling her. She took a sip of her own tea, lowered the cup, and looked her aunt in the eye.

"Fine. You got me," Jenessa admitted. "I did come here to tell you something...and it might not be good."

"So, bad news, then."

"Well, *potentially* bad news."

"Let me guess...this has something to do with Grey Alexander?"

CHAPTER 23

DIDN'T EVERY BAD THING in this town have to do with Grey Alexander?

"So, I'm right," Aunt Renee said. "Grey is up to something."

"Yes, Aunt Renee, he is," Jenessa said. "But it's not about me this time. Not exactly."

"That's rather vague, dear."

"Well, it is about me in that he's using it to try to get me to end things with Logan. Again. Or still. Whatever. Anyway, this time—how can I say this?—this time he's trying to use you to get to me."

"Me? How so? What could that man have to say about me?"

"He's—okay there is no delicate way to say this. Are you sure you're up to hearing it?"

Her aunt nodded. "Just spit it out."

"Okay. Fine. He says he's dug up some dirt on you, Aunt Renee. About your second husband, and the conditions, um, surrounding his death."

There. She said it.

"What on earth is that man talking about? Why, I think he's the senile one. He's delusional in his old age."

That was a relief.

"Good grief, Phillip died of complications from his diabetes!"

~*~

Jenessa was relieved to know that Grey Alexander was just blowing smoke out his rear end, implying that her Aunt Renee had killed her second husband, and worse, that she could be considered a suspect in the murder of Rafe Santiago. Her "Uncle" Phillip—her aunt had been married multiple times, so Jenessa never really got close enough to any of them to truly consider them family—had died from health complications.

While she wouldn't wish diabetes on anyone, the death was as natural as it could be, Aunt Renee explained.

So, now Jenessa had freed her mind to get some work done. Rather than go to the office as she had planned, before taking her impromptu detour to Aunt Renee's, she would meet up with Logan's mother to discuss the story Jenessa had been assigned covering her annual Garden Club flower show. And, while she was there, it wouldn't hurt to finalize the details of their rehearsal dinner.

She knew from Logan that his mother had been released from the hospital and was feeling better, resting at home, so she drove over, straight from Aunt Renee's.

As she pulled up in front of the white two-story colonial, she contemplated Logan's upbringing. She was glad they would be raising their kids in her more modest family home. It was a large, older Tudor in a well-established neighborhood, but nothing as grand as what Logan had been used to. Growing up in the lap of luxury had not had any visual benefit on Logan and his life. If anything, it had seemed to make life harder for him growing up.

She wouldn't wish his childhood on anyone, certainly not on Grayson and Lily.

Jenessa approached the door and rang the bell. After a few brief moments, Elizabeth's housekeeper, Helga, answered. "Hello, Miss Jones."

"I'm here to see Mrs. Alexander. Is she up to company?"

"I believe so. Please, come in. I'll let her know you're here."

Jenessa stepped inside as Helga climbed the staircase.

When she returned, she said, "Mrs. Alexander is just freshening up and will be down shortly."

Helga escorted her to the sitting room. Jenessa stood by the mantle, studying the family photos Elizabeth had displayed there. Surprisingly, there was still one with Logan's father in it. The family was on a beach—it looked like the Cape Cod area or maybe Martha's Vineyard.

Who took the photo? In it, a young Logan was filling a plastic bucket with sand, sitting beside what looked like his "Sand Empire." Several two-story sand castles were already in place. Yes, Logan had always dreamed big.

Beside him in the picture, on a chaise, was a younger, though not much different looking, Elizabeth Alexander. She had her face bent down, sunglasses on, reading a paperback novel of some kind—perhaps a romance.

Had Elizabeth believed in romance at one time? Surely a marriage to Grey had put the kibosh on those ideals. What kind of woman could continue to believe in "happily ever after" being married to a despicable philanderer like Grey Alexander?

Her eyes went to Grey in the photo. He was in the chair beside his wife, talking on an oversized cell phone, one of the first she figured. Always tending to business, even on vacation with his family. And yet he claimed to want what was best for Logan. Apparently, he didn't consider fatherly love and attention in Logan's best interest.

"Jenessa." Elizabeth sashayed into the room, looking none the worse for wear after having spent a night in the hospital. "I see you've spotted our summer vacation at Martha's Vineyard."

Jenessa hadn't been too far off in her guess of the location. But, in retrospect, Martha's Vineyard did seem a more likely choice than Cape Cod, knowing what she did about the Alexander clan.

Logan's mother sighed loudly. "Ah, how I wish I could go there again before summer is completely over."

"Why can't you go?"

"You know I absolutely couldn't leave before the wedding," Elizabeth said, as she fingered the pearls at her neck.

"Of course. And the fact that you are watching our children part of the time we're on our honeymoon."

"Oh, yes, yes, of course." She seemed to have forgotten that. "Besides, Detective Provenza, and your ex-boyfriend, Detective Baxter, have *requested* that I stay in town for the time being. At least until they catch whoever killed—"

The woman's face clouded over and Jenessa sensed a conflict brewing beneath the surface of Elizabeth's polished exterior. Did she know something about the murder? And why had the police asked her not to leave town? Jenessa knew *why*, it meant they considered Logan's mother a viable suspect, but what she didn't know was why they saw her as that.

It really prickled at her, not having better access to this investigation. Was this how things were going to be from now on? Now that she and Michael were no longer a couple. What fun would it be trying to report on major crimes in this town without having inside access?

As much as Jenessa wanted to pursue questions regarding the murder and what Elizabeth might know, she thought better of it. Instead she took a seat on the sofa beside the fireplace, just as Helga entered the room, carrying a silver service.

"Coffee or tea, Jenessa?" Elizabeth asked. "Normally at this time of day I'd fancy a cup of Darjeeling, but today, after all this rigmarole, I need coffee."

"I'll have the tea," Jenessa replied. The last thing *she* needed was too much caffeine.

Helga stepped up and poured coffee from one pot, and tea from another, leaving the two women alone to talk.

Mrs. Alexander sat across from Jenessa, in one of the matching wingback chairs. She sipped her coffee, then sat back, crossing her legs. "I'm quite pleased to have you joining our family, Jenessa, after all these years."

Jenessa smiled. "Yes, I am too." Though, on many levels, that was a lie. Jenessa *was* pleased to become Logan's wife, but she was far from pleased to become Grey Alexander's daughter-in-law. Her feelings about Logan's mother fell somewhere in the middle.

Did Elizabeth know about Grayson, that the boy was her and Logan's son? It was possible. All those years ago, Elizabeth would have been akin to a puppet on Grey Alexander's strings, playing the dutiful wife, agreeing with her husband when he was pressuring Jenessa to give the baby up for adoption.

"You and my son will have a ready-made family, it seems. Tragic about Summer, though."

"Yes, tragic." Jenessa nodded. "I didn't know her too well, but she seemed like she really loved those kids."

"That no-good husband of hers was a different story." Elizabeth brought her cup to her lips. "Had I known…"

Had she known? Was the woman hinting that she knew Grayson was Logan and Jenessa's son? Was she trying to let Jenessa know that she too had suspected that

Chet Monahan was abusing the children, and Summer too? Did she know about Grayson, and was she regretting her part in the charade?

Thank God, Chet had finally been put in prison for his crimes against that family.

Had Grey known what an animal Chet could be when he let his temper get the best of him? Maybe, in some sick way, Grey had felt a sense of comradery with Chet Monahan.

Jenessa gave her head a shake, then took a sip of her tea. "Thank you for agreeing to let me interview you for the story on the Garden Club flower show, Mrs. Alexander."

"Please, dear, call me Elizabeth. We're almost family for goodness sakes."

"Yes, thank you, Elizabeth." She pulled out her recording device. "Do you mind if I record our interview?"

"Not at all."

"Great. So, tell me, what is new this year? What makes this year's flower show worth seeing?"

The interview took about twenty minutes. As much as Elizabeth liked to gush about the Garden Club and the details of the flower show, really, there was only so much to be said about an annual event, such as this, in a town as small as Hidden Valley was.

Though, now, with a fresh murder investigation in progress, Jenessa could almost feel like Hidden Valley was bigger than it actually was, that she could get her hands on a juicy story once in a while. Except that she couldn't get her hands on this one. Her boss, Charles, had taken her off the salacious story, with good reason.

She had to admit, from the outside looking in, Jenessa did have the most to lose by Rafe being in town. Grey had orchestrated this rather well, hadn't he? He had to be the real killer. Not Jenessa. Not Elizabeth Alexander. And, most certainly not her Aunt Renee.

Was that the entire suspect pool? Oh, no. There was one more. Logan had been questioned too. But she didn't think for a second that he could have done it. And, perhaps, the police had questioned Mrs. Dobson and the rest of the staff at the Alexander Estate, as well. Purely perfunctory, she assumed.

"Would you like more tea, Jenessa? We can discuss the rehearsal dinner."

Jenessa popped her recorder into her purse, then stood to leave. "Actually, Mrs.—Elizabeth—I need to be somewhere. I hope you don't mind. I'm sure whatever you have planned will be perfect." Jenessa took in the décor of the room. "You have exemplary taste."

Jenessa pulled up in front of the police station to see what she could get out of Provenza and Michael. She didn't have high hopes, so any amount of information would exceed her expectations. The only card she had to play was her reporter's card, that was, assuming neither of them knew she had been taken off the story.

As she tugged open the glass door, Jenessa remembered her recent talks with Michael, relieved they had cleared the air between them—or at least they agreed to make an effort toward that. There was still the issue of him dating her sister, but Jenessa had been the one to recommend it, so she had no room to judge.

She approached the receptionist, and the woman gave her a surprisingly friendly smile. Did Ruby know that Jenessa and Michael were no longer seeing each other?

"Perfect timing, Miss Jones," Ruby said.

What did she mean by that?

CHAPTER 24

JENESSA STOOD IN THE RECEPTION AREA of the Hidden Valley police station, confused by what the receptionist had just said. *Perfect timing?*

Just then, Michael and George stepped out from the back of the station. "That was quick," Provenza said to Michael.

Why was everyone acting as though she had been expected here?

"Come on back," Provenza said, gesturing to the door that led to the interrogation rooms, giving away nothing in his expression or tone.

Okay. This was too easy. Either something was up or, for some strange reason, these two wanted to give her the story on the investigation. Jenessa hoped the latter was true, but feared the former was a more likely scenario.

With an uneasy feeling bubbling in her gut, she followed the two detectives to the interrogation room. Normally, if she were lucky that is, she would find herself on the other side of the two-way mirrors, watching Provenza and Michael question a perp, but today she didn't feel so fortunate.

No. It felt a whole lot more like she was the one about to be questioned. Again.

Michael went in first, then George ushered her through the door, and brought up the rear, closing the door behind them. "Take a seat." George gestured toward the perp side of the table.

"What's going on here?" she asked.

"Just have a seat." Michael pulled out the chair for her. A memory popped into her head, an image of him doing this for her at Antonio's Italian Ristorante when they were first dating—but this felt far removed from that.

She almost felt like a criminal. Were they going to question her again in Rafe's death?

"Nothing to worry about, Miss Jones," Provenza said. "We just have a few more questions for you."

"Okay," she said with a bit of trepidation as she sat. The metal chair was cold. She scooched it closer to the table, as if that would make her feel more comfortable. Right now, though, nothing seemed like it could do that.

George took the chair across from her and opened a file folder, but Michael chose to remain standing. He spread his legs, taking a wide stance, crossing his arms over his muscular chest, sending the message that they meant business.

"So, tell us again," Provenza said, "how exactly did you know Rafe Santiago?"

~*~

An hour or more had passed, Jenessa was exhausted.

"You do have the most to gain by his death," George had said.

It seemed like she had reiterated a thousand times what little she knew about Rafe, and it was beginning to feel as though they saw her as a feasible suspect in this investigation. Had she done enough to persuade them of her innocence?

Even if George could be convinced, could Michael? Surely he couldn't actually think she had anything to do with Rafe's murder.

"Listen, now that we're done—we are done here, right?" She glanced between the men for their agreement.

Michael shrugged and looked to his partner. Provenza nodded.

A small sigh of relief slipped through her lips. "Okay, now that we're done, can I ask you a few questions?"

Dual nods in her direction were a good start.

"Okay, first things first. Neither of you actually believe that I killed a man, do you?"

Both Michael and Provenza remained silent, disquieting her.

"Oh, come on—really?" Jenessa resisted the urge to leap out of her chair, outraged that neither man could give an instant affirmation of her innocence. She looked to Michael with raised brows. He offered her nothing in return. "Michael? You know me." She turned to the older detective. "George?"

Jenessa raised her shaking hands in frustration. "Seriously, guys?"

"Look, Miss Jones," Detective Provenza began, "we want to believe you. We really do." He glanced to Michael, who nodded. "But you know how these things go. Remember back when we arrested Logan for Lucy St. John's murder last year?"

She did, but she didn't want to think about that right now…or talk about it. It might give the detectives the bright idea to arrest Logan for Rafe Santiago's murder too, like she and Logan had colluded. So, she ignored the question and changed the subject instead.

"You guys promised I could ask some questions."

"Stop right there." Detective Provenza raised his pointer finger in the air. "I said you could ask. I never promised to answer."

"Duly noted," she said. And pretty much what she expected. "Here goes. Has the ME determined the cause of death yet?"

Provenza paused before replying. "I guess it couldn't hurt to tell you that he's still waiting on test results."

"There was evidence of blunt force trauma to the back of the head," Michael said, "but not enough to kill the victim."

"But that's not for publication," George quickly added.

"I understand." Waiting for tests, huh? Now that would make it harder to pinpoint the murderer. "Obviously then it wasn't a stabbing or a gunshot wound."

"Yes," George said, "it appears that way. But I'm not confirming that."

"That's odd, isn't it?"

They did not respond.

"How do you suppose Rafe died, then?"

"Like I said," George replied, "the ME is waiting on test re—"

"Couldn't have been strangulation, or there would have been evidence of that," Jenessa said. "Poison maybe, or electrocution. Although, if he had been electrocuted, there would be burns."

"That's enough, Miss Jones."

"Maybe someone was able to stop his heart," she muttered under her breath. "Is there any security camera footage recording people's comings and goings from the Alexander gatehouse?"

"Michael and I asked Grey," Provenza replied, "and he said there was a camera in the eaves that faces the front door. He promised to get us a copy, but we haven't received one yet."

"That's great. If it, in fact, exists." Jenessa leaned back in her chair. "But the fact that he hasn't turned it over to you yet, well, that suggests that maybe he already knows what it will show."

Michael remained stoic, arms crossed. "You mean it'll show him?"

CHAPTER 25

AS SHE WAS LEAVING the police station, Jenessa thought of Logan. What was he thinking right then? Did he have any idea that she was being considered a real suspect in this investigation? And what was up with his mother? She had acted strange on a few different levels.

One thing was certain, Jenessa had to solve this murder. It was more than just a juicy story now—it was her future. Could she end up taking the fall for this crime? Had Grey been so desperate to get her out of Logan's life that he would kill a man and frame her for it?

She wouldn't put anything past him.

Her phone rang in her pocket. It was a generic ringtone, so she glanced at the display. Evangeline. She clicked *Accept*.

"Hey, Evangeline." Jenessa hoped that her friend was not calling to say she couldn't make the wedding at all. Too many things were going in the wrong direction. Too many pointing toward this marriage not happening. How happy would that make Grey Alexander?

Over-the-moon happy.

"Jenessa, good news."

Thank God. Jenessa could use some of that right about now. "What's up?"

"I'm rolling into town a day early. In fact, I'll be there before long. Where should we meet? Should I go straight to the bridal shop?"

The bridesmaid dress fitting was the last thing on Jenessa's mind right now, but the wedding was only days away.

Hopefully.

"That is good news," Jenessa said, doing her best to sound cheerful. "Let me call the bridal shop and see if they have an opening. I'll get right back to you."

Jenessa hung up the phone and dialed the shop.

"Hello. This is Jenessa Jones calling," she said when a woman picked up. "My other bridesmaid, the one who didn't make it to the fitting the other day, is on her way into town. Is there any chance we can come in for a fitting in around…" Jenessa glanced at her watch, "thirty minutes, at two thirty?"

The woman put her on hold for a moment, saying she needed to check with the seamstress. Just two minutes later she was back. "You're in luck, Miss Jones. Mrs. Meyers said she is available. Come right over as soon as your other party arrives."

"Perfect. Thank you so much."

Jenessa disconnected the call and texted Evangeline the address.

Now all she had to do was get her mind off her dead husband and onto her husband-to-be.

~*~

Sitting in her car, down the street from the bridal shop, Jenessa was restless as she waited for Evangeline to arrive. She had too many thoughts spinning through her mind to deal with the chance she'd run into people on the street who would ply her with questions. Ditto as far as going to The Sweet Spot to grab a drink and have Ramey interrogate her. No, she should lay low until she had a better sense of how this thing was going to play out.

A silver sedan drove by a couple of times. On the third go around, she wondered if that could be Evangeline.

Jenessa got out and waited beside her car. When the car approached again, and she saw it was her friend, she waved frantically.

Evangeline pulled her sedan into the diagonal parking spot two cars down from Jenessa's. The two women were out of their vehicles, and they stepped onto the sidewalk, giving each other a warm embrace.

"You look beautiful," Evangeline said, leaning back to gaze at Jenessa. "Marriage is going to suit you. I can tell."

"Thanks, Ev. You look great too." She always did. Evangeline's light brown hair cascaded in loose curls around her shoulders, her makeup perfect, her business suit fitted to her tall and slim physique. "I'm so glad you could make it here earlier than you thought."

Relief lifted a weight from Jenessa's shoulders. Finally, she had her entire bridal party present and accounted for. "Shall we?" Jenessa swept her hand toward the door to the bridal shop.

"That's what I'm here for," Evangeline responded, linking her arm with Jenessa's and moving into the shop.

The sales lady stepped up to greet them, leading them directly back to begin Evangeline's fitting.

Thankfully, it didn't take long.

Evangeline had suggested Jenessa try on her gown again, so she could see it, but she declined. She just wasn't up to all those buttons and layers of white. As much as Jenessa wanted to be in that starry-eyed mood, the fairytale feeling every bride is supposed to have leading up to the big day, Jenessa just didn't have it in her today.

So, before long, the two women left the shop and stood outside, deciding what to do next. They picked up a couple of cold drinks at the burger joint and found a park bench on Main Street where they could sit and talk.

Jenessa took a sip of her iced tea, then let the warmth of the afternoon sun drench her. It almost made her forget the present turmoil in her life.

Almost.

"Maybe it's just my journalistic senses, but I get the feeling something is bothering you, Jenessa," Evangeline said. "You didn't seem to be fully present back there at the bridal shop, like I would have expected of a bride-to-be, especially so close to the wedding. You didn't even want to try on your wedding gown for me. What's going on?"

"Pre-wedding jitters, I guess." Should she mention Rafe's murder? They had been old friends.

"Seems like more than that."

Jenessa turned to her friend, took her hand. "I have some awful news, Ev."

Evangeline's emerald eyes went wide. "What? What is it, Jen? Is everything all right with you?"

"Look, I'm just going to say it. There's no way to sugar coat this."

Worry seemed to color Evangeline's expression.

"It's Rafe."

"Rafe?" Her eyes rounded with surprise as she said it. "What about him?"

"It turns out it was him I saw the other day, and, well, he was found...he's dead, Ev. They say he was murdered."

Evangeline pulled her hand away from Jen's, and it flew to her chest as she gasped. "He was what?" Her surprise turned to sadness. Her eyes misted, as the reality dawned on her. "How awful." Her gaze dropped to her lap. "I wish I had come earlier, when I was supposed to. Maybe then I could have seen him one last time."

Jenessa handed her friend a tissue from her purse. "Did you guys keep in contact over the years?"

"Oh, heavens no. We wanted to." Evangeline dabbed at her cheeks with the tissue. "It's like I said before, we haven't seen him in years. A few times, after we got back from our honeymoon when he was back from an assignment we did, but then it was like he fell off the map."

Did Evangeline know Rafe had been in a foreign prison for a few years? How much did Evangeline and Rudy really know about Rafe? Especially since it seemed he hadn't been completely honest with Jenessa about what his job entailed.

Had he been keeping secrets from all of them, or just Jenessa?

"Rafe and Rudy were pretty close, weren't they?" Jenessa asked.

Evangeline took a deep breath. "Yes, at one time, they were. That's why he was Rudy's best man. But it's hard to keep a friendship going when the other one disappears. You know how you and I have had to work at it to stay in touch, at least once in a while."

Jenessa nodded. That was true. It had been more than six months since they had spoken to each other when Jenessa had phoned Evangeline to ask her to be in the wedding party. Their friendship could easily have fallen by the wayside too.

Evangeline looked into the distance. "Rudy will be so sad to hear his friend is dead."

She remained quiet for a bit, and Jenessa wanted to give her time to process the news. Finally, she turned back to Jenessa. "Did you talk to him before he died?"

"Only briefly. As you might remember, I didn't know him before your wedding and then he flew out the next morning. I never saw him again after that."

Did Evangeline know about what had happened between her and Rafe after their wedding? Had Rafe mentioned to Rudy that he had married Jenessa in Las Vegas in one of the few conversations they had had? Her friend didn't seem to register any knowledge of it. It was probably best to keep it to herself, at least for now.

Evangeline put her hand on Jenessa's shoulder. "It must have been quite a surprise to see him here after all these years."

"Yes, it was." That was an understatement if ever there were one. "But truthfully, I hadn't thought of him again once I left Las Vegas."

"So what was he doing in this little town?" Evangeline seemed to have composed herself. "I mean, no offense, Jen, this seems like a charming place to live, but it doesn't look like the kind of place Rafe would hang out or be doing a story."

Jenessa shrugged. "I'm not really sure."

How could she tell Evangeline that her fiancé's father had brought Rafe to town to blackmail her and force her to stop the wedding? "Like I said, we only spoke briefly."

Evangeline certainly didn't seem to know that Jenessa and Rafe had gotten married that night, or that the marriage had never been annulled. It was probably best to keep it that way. The less people that knew those details, the better it was for Jenessa.

Evangeline shook her head sadly. "Such a shame. How did he die?"

"The medical examiner hasn't made a definitive statement yet, so I can't say."

Her friend perked up a little. "Maybe I can do a story on Rafe's murder for my newspaper. He led a pretty incredible life, working in exotic and dangerous places all over the world."

Jenessa smiled to herself. Just like Jenessa, Evangeline was a reporter to her core. Why was it people like them went straight to a story angle? It wasn't as though they didn't have compassion…but there was just something about a juicy story that really got the wheels turning. It was no wonder the two had become friends—birds of a feather. "I can let you know when I hear what the ME determines."

That is, after the Herald got this story out first—even if it wasn't Jenessa writing it—but after that, what would it hurt to give her friend the scoop?

"Hey, where are you staying while you're in town?" Perhaps she and Logan could take Evangeline to dinner while she was there, running it by Logan first, of course.

"I'm sorry, Jen, I can't stay. My editor only gave me the afternoon off. I'm working on that important story in Sacramento that I need to get back to."

"You came all this way for a couple of hours?"

Evangeline stood up from the bench. "Sacramento is only two hours away. I'll return on Friday afternoon for the rehearsal dinner. Hopefully Rudy can come with me this time. I'd better get on the road or Jack will have my job."

"I miss Jack. Tell him hi for me." Jenessa rose. "I'd better get going, too."

She watched Evangeline drive away, a sinking feeling washing over her. With a big, hot story to cover, would Evangeline really be able to make it back?

CHAPTER 26

"I'M HERE TO SEE DETECTIVE PROVENZA...and *Baxter*." The name of his fiancée's ex-boyfriend caught in Logan's throat as he said it.

The middle-aged receptionist at the police station ran a hand over her red hair before gesturing to the row of chairs against the far wall. "Have a seat, Mr. Alexander." She smiled at him. "I'll let them know you are here."

"Thanks, Ruby." He wanted to tell her to call him Logan. She had known him most of his life, as did the majority of townspeople who had been here for a long time. *Mr. Alexander* reminded him of his father, and he was the last person Logan wanted to think of right then.

He took a seat and pulled out his cell phone to text Jenessa while he was waiting.

"Mr. Alexander?" Ruby said.

Logan.

He glanced up. "Yes?"

"The detectives will be with you shortly. They are just finishing up with something."

He nodded.

How nice of them to call him in and then keep him waiting. Another of Baxter's power trips? Logan's attention went back to his text message screen. He typed.

Hey, Jenessa. Hope your day is going better than mine. Just got called back into HVPD. Not sure why. Anyway, looking forward to seeing you tonight! Love you.

He added a heart emoji and hit *Send.*

Just then he heard voices booming from down the hall. It sounded like his father. Great. That would be the cherry on this sundae from he—

"Logan. How nice to see you." His father's gaze swept around the area. "The venue could have been better chosen but—"

"Hello, Father," Logan said coolly.

Grey seemed to chafe at the formal greeting but then hid it with practiced ease.

"Thanks for coming in," Detective Provenza said to Logan's father, shaking his hand.

"You've been a great help." Baxter actually patted the man on the back as he spoke his appreciation for the senior Alexander's visit.

Before Logan could utter another word, his father sailed out of the police station as though he hadn't a care in the world.

Was that whistling Logan heard as the old man strolled away?

"Come on in, Logan," Baxter said.

He stood and followed the two detectives to the back room, all the while trying to figure out why his father had the appearance of the cat that ate the canary after being questioned in a murder investigation that happened on his own property. Something wasn't right.

How could the police let his father go, let alone believe for even one second that the man was innocent?

~*~

Logan had texted Jenessa saying that he had been called back into the police department for a second round of questioning too, so she decided to stop by Aunt Renee's house to try to get her mind back onto the wedding and off Rafe Santiago's murder.

She'd had a brief respite while at the bridal boutique with Evangeline, but afterward, conversation had gone back to the topic of Rafe, and now Jenessa found herself brooding again.

Aunt Renee was so gung-ho about planning the wedding, and she was a naturally positive person, so if anyone could detour Jenessa's mind back to more pleasant things, it was her aunt.

She pulled her sportscar into her aunt's driveway and got out. Her gaze traveled over the Mercedes Roadster from hood to trunk. The exhilaration of driving that car had always been a source of distraction for her, but today, not even the purr of the engine had switched Jenessa's gears. She sighed and tossed the keys into her purse, then made her way up to the entrance, rapping her knuckles on the door before letting herself in.

"Hello? Aunt Renee?" she called out as she set her purse on the console table and wandered through the hallway toward the kitchen. "It's me, Aunt Renee. Jenessa."

The house was eerily quiet, and the hairs stood up on the back of her neck. What if something had happened to Aunt Renee?

Any number of things could have gone wrong and they all swept through Jenessa's worried mind in a matter of seconds. Grey's threats could have somehow panned out and maybe Aunt Renee had been arrested. Or her heart could have started acting up again with all the stress. Maybe her aunt was collapsed on her bedroom floor.

"Stop it, Jenessa," she chastised herself. "You're always making mountains out of molehills."

Giving her head a shake, she climbed the stairs to her aunt's bedroom, calling out her name again. She was probably just having a relaxing bath or shower. Maybe she was drying her hair and hadn't heard Jenessa announcing her arrival.

There. That was better. No need to go jumping to such awful conclusions.

But as Jenessa searched through the entire second floor, there was no sign of Aunt Renee.

Her heart began to again pound in her chest and her breathing quickened. "Aunt Renee," she called out again. "Are you here?"

Her aunt's car had been in the driveway when she had pulled up. Where would she go on foot? Not far, that was for sure.

Jenessa stepped up her pace and ran back down to the first floor, where she heard voices coming from the patio area at the back of the house. She scurried through the french doors, out to the patio, to discover her cousin Selena sitting in a chaise, poolside, sipping iced tea with Aunt Renee.

"Jenessa dear, what's the matter?" her aunt asked as Jenessa stumbled, practically out of breath, onto the patio.

"Oh my gosh," Jenessa gasped, as she pulled up a patio chair. "I thought...never mind what I thought. I'm just glad to find you out here." She poured herself a glass of tea from the pitcher sitting on the glass table.

Selena rose from her chaise. "I'd love to stay and chat," she swallowed the last of her drink, "but I have to step out for a bit." She leaned down to give Jenessa a hug, then Aunt Renee.

Where would she be off to?

Selena must have read the curiosity in Jenessa's eyes. "Don't worry, I'll be back before dinner."

And with that, she was gone.

Jenessa turned to her aunt. "I wonder what that was about. Did I chase her away or something?"

"Of course not, Jenessa. Don't be so dramatic." Aunt Renee took a sip of her iced tea. "I'm sure she just had something to do."

But what could Selena have to do in sleepy little Hidden Valley? She didn't know anyone besides the family, as far as Jenessa knew. And Rafe, apparently. But he was dead.

And there it was. She had circled back to Rafe. Poor, dead Rafe.

"Okay," Aunt Renee started, "now I know something is bothering you. You have that little furrow between your brows that you always get when you are stressing about something."

Jenessa rubbed her frown lines.

"What's on your mind, my dear?"

Aunt Renee was right. What she wanted was a distraction, but what Jenessa *needed* was to talk it out with someone she trusted.

"Fine. You're right. I do have something weighing on me."

Her aunt took another sip of her iced tea. She looked to Jenessa's glass. "You want a splash of vodka in that? I can go in the house and find some."

"No. That's the last thing I need. That's how I got into this whole mess."

When Jenessa glanced back at Aunt Renee, she was grinning, just teasing her. That made more sense, since she knew Jenessa's nearly teetotaling ways quite well.

"It's this thing with Rafe." Jenessa sighed. "It all came out of nowhere—thanks to Grey Alexander—and now an innocent man is dead, because of me."

"Now, now. Not because of you, Jenessa. Because of that vile Grey Alexander. This was his doing. Even if he wasn't the one that killed that poor man, and I'm not saying he wasn't, he certainly was the one responsible for him coming to town. Grey Alexander started all this mess. Not you."

Jenessa swiped at the tears that had found their way down her cheek. Her chest was heavy with emotion, hot tears burning for release, but now was not the time to break down and cry.

Aunt Renee handed her a napkin. "Dry your eyes, dear. Don't let Grey win."

"You're right. I know you're right, Aunt Renee." She breathed in deeply and dabbed at her tears. "But he sees me as a gold digger and thinks that Logan will be taken in by my so-called extravagant tastes. That is just completely garbage."

Aunt Renee nodded. "Aside from that sportscar of your father's that you drive, there isn't an extravagant bone in your body."

"Maybe if I came from a rich family, if I had gone to an ivy-league college…"

"It's not about you, Jenessa. It's about that conniving Grey Alexander."

Jenessa raised her eyes. "But would he go so far as to kill a man, one that he brought to town, to end my chances of marrying his son? That doesn't make sense, even for him."

"Well, you do have a point there. It's like he bought a new pair of shoes just so he could shoot himself in the foot."

"Huh?" Jenessa huffed.

"Bringing Rafe to town is the new pair of shoes, and killing Rafe is shooting himself in the foot, while wearing the new shoes."

Jenessa stared blankly at her aunt, having no idea what she was talking about.

"What I mean to say is—"

Jenessa waved her hand in the air. "Never mind. I think I get the gist of it. If Rafe was the thing he was holding over me, then killing him takes all the cards out of Grey's hand. Unless…"

Aunt Renee poured more iced tea. "Unless what?"

"Unless," Jenessa straightened her shoulders, as if she were sloughing off a heavy jacket, "since he discovered that his plan had failed—Logan did not break up with me—he decided to kill Rafe and try to pin it on me. I've been questioned twice, you know."

Aunt Renee looked stunned. "Twice? Really? They've only questioned me once so far."

"So far?"

"Well, George—Detective Provenza—did say he might be back. And I don't think he was referring to being my plus-one for the wedding."

CHAPTER 27

THOUGH EXHAUSTED AFTER THE LONG CHAT she'd had with Aunt Renee, Jenessa was still no further ahead in figuring out who killed Rafe. It truly did not make sense that Grey would kill the man. Unless, as she had said, he hoped to pin it on her or her aunt in order to get her away from Logan for good.

That didn't really add up either, but it was all she had.

Her phone call with Logan a moment ago had not cleared up anything. He had told her about his interrogation with George and Michael, which was uneventful he'd said, but he had said one thing that piqued her interest.

He'd told her that his father had been on the way out of the police station as Logan had come in. That he'd been certain he had heard the man whistling a jaunty tune as he left. Not the sign of a man who feared going to jail for murder.

She had asked him if he'd mind her staying at Aunt Renee's to eat, since Sara and Ramey had just popped in with fixings for dinner. He'd agreed—reluctantly—and told her he would stop by her place for dessert later.

Jenessa wandered into the kitchen where Ramey was helping Sara make dinner, a grilled chicken salad.

"Looks delicious," Jenessa said. "Do you need any help in here?"

Ramey smiled. "No. Thank you. We're almost done."

Sara was at the stovetop, grilling the chicken breasts. "Go relax, Jen."

Ramey was tossing the romaine lettuce with sourdough croutons, dressing, and parmesan cheese. "You could set the table."

"I'm on it." Jenessa went to the dining room but found Selena already covering the task. When had she come back in? *Odd she hadn't noticed.* So, instead, Jenessa brought a pitcher of lemon water and glasses to the table, placing them in the center.

Aunt Renee came and took her seat at the head of the table, followed by Selena and Sara. Ramey carried the salad and grilled chicken platter to the table but did not pull out a chair for herself.

"Aren't you staying?" Jenessa asked.

Ramey beamed from ear to ear. "I can't tonight. I have a date with Charles." Ramey's rosy cheeks went a deeper shade of pink. "I think he's close to popping the question. He says Charlie is coming around. Hopefully that hasn't changed this week while he's been at camp."

"That's awesome," Jenessa said. "What's different?"

"Charlie. Can you believe it?" She giggled. "He and Grayson have been so good for each other since they became friends."

It made sense, since they had both lost their mothers.

"Is Charlie helping Grayson deal with losing his mom?" Aunt Renee asked.

Ramey's face brightened with a small smile, placing her hand on Jenessa's shoulder. "Yes, and Grayson—I hope—will show Charlie how great it is to have another mother in his life."

Jenessa nodded. She hoped so too, for her own sake. And for Ramey's sake. Sweet and nurturing, Ramey would make a wonderful mother, given the chance. If only there was such a friend to help Lily through. But friend or not, Jenessa would do her best to be a comfort to that sweet little girl.

"I can't imagine myself having children," Selena piped in.

"Because of your career?" Ramey asked.

"No, because I can't seem to find a man I want to spend the rest of my life with, let alone soon enough that I'm not too old to have kids."

A melancholy look clouded her lovely features. "I thought I'd found Mr. Right once...a long time ago, but..."

Surely she couldn't be referring to Rafe, could she? There still seemed to be more to her cousin's relationship with Rafe than Selena was letting on.

"You'll find someone," Sara added. "First of all, you're gorgeous, Selena. And secondly, I believe there's someone out there for everyone."

"A lid for every pot, they say," Aunt Renee added.

"Sometimes we just have to be patient and wait." Sara was glowing almost as much as Ramey had been a moment ago.

Had Michael made a move? Maybe there was more there than Jenessa knew.

Her aunt leaned in and whispered in Jenessa's ear. "Are you sure you're okay with this whole Sara and Michael thing?"

Jenessa shrugged. "Why not? Michael's great, and I only want the best for my sister." She would just have to deal with her own awkwardness in their presence.

"That's the right spirit," Aunt Renee whispered, with a bob of her head.

Yes, why not? After the loser Sara married years ago, and then Michael's cousin Luke breaking her heart last year, Sara was due for a good man she could build a life with. How could Jenessa stand in the way of that?

Later that evening, at the sound of her doorbell ringing, Jenessa rushed to the door to meet Logan. She eagerly flung it wide, and he scooped her into his arms the second he stepped inside. He swung her around as though he had just come back from a stint in the army—and she loved it.

228

After he set her down, he raised her chin so she was looking at him. She was drawn into the beckoning azure blue of his eyes. "Jenessa Jones, I love you."

The words were like warm honey pouring over her pounding heart.

"Nothing, not my father, not some secret dead husband, nothing or no one will ever make me stop loving you." And with that, he planted a kiss on her pleasantly surprised mouth, a kiss so full of passion and emotion that she melted against him.

When, finally, he released her, she staggered back a bit, gasping for air and feeling weak in the knees. "Wow." She raised a finger to touch her lips, which were positively vibrating from the kiss. "Wow," she said again, sliding her hands up his chest and around the back of his neck. "I love you too, Logan, and I cannot wait to be your wife."

"I was hoping you would say that." He smiled at her as he put a hand on her arm, sliding it down gently as he stepped back. "Come with me." He took her hand and led her to the living room.

What was he up to? Her heart pulsed with anticipation.

They sat together on the sofa and Logan reached into his pocket. He stared into her eyes. "Now, don't get too excited."

How could she not?

He pulled out a red velvet ring box. "Now, I know this looks like it's simply a box, but it's not just any box. It's the one from my grandmother's ring." He opened it, the small hinges squeaking a bit from age. "And I know it might be empty right now, but that is just temporary. I am going to find the perfect ring for you, Jenessa. One that is as beautiful and cherished as you are."

"Oh, Logan," she sighed, beaming a smile at him, her lips trembling with emotion. She reached out to softly stroke his cheek. "You have no idea what those words mean to me, sweetheart."

Jenessa couldn't imagine being any happier than she was in that moment. She had the man she loved sitting in front of her. She had her son back—or would as soon as he came home from camp. And she would have a daughter, too. Life couldn't be more perfect. And no one, not even that miserable Grey Alexander and his odious threats were going to change that.

Logan found her lips again, and she wove her fingers through his thick blond waves. He pulled her close and her soft curves fit perfectly against his firm body. The kiss lasted until Jenessa felt as though she would be totally overcome with her passion for this man.

She pulled back and got lost, again, in Logan's baby blues. In her mind she was swimming in a deep blue infinity pool, the water so warm and still that every ripple found its way back to her heart. This was her life now. Nothing else mattered. Grey Alexander was but a blip on the radar. A speedbump in the road of life.

In Logan's arms, she knew that they would ride this wave to shore and be stronger for it. Together they could handle anything, weather any storm.

~*~

"I think that's your phone," Jenessa said, slowly pulling out of Logan's embrace so he could grab his cell phone from the coffee table and answer it.

He glanced at the display. "It's my father's house phone." His eyes returned to Jenessa's. "I don't want to answer it."

He and Jenessa had connected so deeply a moment ago, Logan didn't want anything to take away from that—especially not his father.

"Go on, answer it." Jenessa spoke the words with her mouth, but her eyes said even more. There was a strength and resolve in them that told Logan they would survive this little hiccup. Yes, a hiccup was all it was. He held her gaze for a moment longer because there he could see a confidence that said they would be together forever, that not even his father could tear them apart.

"Okay," he said, trusting her, and hit the *Talk* button. "Yes, Father, what do you want?"

"It's not your father, Logan."

It was Mrs. Dobson, his father's housekeeper.

"I'm sorry for snapping, Mrs. Dobson, I thought—"

"Don't worry, Logan. I know what you thought, and I don't blame you one bit. I'm calling because I have good news."

Good news for a change? That was a welcome relief. "What is it?"

"I've got your grandmother's ring, dear."

"My what?" Logan looked to Jenessa, who was perched beside him with anticipation written all over her face.

"Your grandmother's engagement ring. The one you dreamed of giving to your lovely bride someday."

"You do? But how?"

"I'll explain when you get here. I've got it stashed in a secret safe place, waiting for you."

Excitement lit him up and he could hardly hold on to the phone. "That's amazing. Thank you so much, Mrs. Dobson. I don't know how I'll ever be able to repay you."

He covered the bottom of his phone and turned to Jenessa. "It's Mrs. Dobson. She's got my grandmother's ring."

"Now, don't get too carried away, Logan," Mrs. Dobson said. "I've also got a bit of bad news."

Logan felt his face drop. "I'm ready. What is it?"

"I'm afraid there is no easy way to tell you this, Logan. It's your mother…"

"My mother? Did she collapse again?"

"No. I just heard from Helga, her housekeeper. Your mother has been arrested."

CHAPTER 28

LOGAN GOT OFF THE PHONE and turned to face Jenessa. His appearance went ashen.

"What is it, Logan? What did she tell you?"

"They've arrested my mother in the death of Rafe Santiago."

Logan's mother? How in the world had they tied her to Rafe? To his murder?

Suddenly the news of the found ring didn't seem as important. This had to be Grey's doing. Who else could be so wicked as to make it seem as though his ex-wife had killed the man? No wonder Logan had heard him whistling his way out of the police station earlier.

And, after all, he had let his second wife go to prison for their crime, hadn't he? But in that case, she had been there, had done the deed. But there was no way

Elizabeth Alexander would have, could have, killed Rafe Santiago.

Was there?

Logan shot to his feet. "I have to go."

"Of course, I'll go with you."

"No, I think it's better if I go alone. My mother would be mortified if—"

"Say no more. Go. Be with your mom."

"I need to find out what the heck is going on here. It should be my father sitting in jail, waiting for an attorney—not my mother."

And with that, Logan grabbed his phone, shoved it in his pocket, and hastily slipped his shoes on. They both went to the entry. He started to open the door, but paused, pulling Jenessa toward him and planting a firm but quick kiss on her lips.

He released her and pulled the door all the way open. "I'm beginning to think this town is cursed for me." He stepped through and dashed toward his car.

Jenessa's heart was heavy as she closed the door and went to the window to watch Logan drive away. If Hidden Valley was cursed for him, it was cursed for her too. Maybe everything that was going on was happening for a reason. Maybe life was telling them to take their children and move on from Hidden Valley.

Logan marched through the narrow glass doors to the Hidden Valley jail, where his mother was being held.

He approached the desk to check in with jail lobby staff. A stern-looking woman sat at the counter, reading a magazine. She glanced up when Logan neared. "Good evening, sir. How may I help you?"

"I'm here to see my mother. Elizabeth Alexander. I'm not too late, am I?"

The woman looked at the clock on the wall. "It's nine PM, you've got half an hour."

That was a relief. Logan had been worried they would deny him visitation until morning. Thirty minutes wasn't much, but it would have to do.

"I'll need to see some ID." The woman held out her hand, waiting.

Logan pulled out his driver's license and extended it to her.

She examined it as though she believed it might be fake. Surely, she recognized his name. Though, perhaps, having Grey for a father worked against him in this scenario.

The woman handed back his ID, then looked at a piece of paper. "I see you are on the list of allowed visitors." Then she went on to recite all the rules and what he could and couldn't take into the visitor's area before visually scanning Logan from head to toe. "Since you have no containers—that is to say, bags, cases, or backpacks—please empty your pockets and then kindly walk through the metal detector, sir."

Logan placed the items from his pockets into a plastic tray and stepped through the detector. On the other side, the woman handed him back his items.

"What about my cell phone?" he asked.

"I'm sorry, sir, no cell phones are allowed during visitation. There are lockers available for you to store personal items." She gestured to a nearby wall. "You may retrieve it on the way out."

"Okay," Logan said, placing his phone into one of the lockers. He turned the lock and pocketed the key.

"Sign here."

Logan signed a piece of paper which said the jail was not responsible for lost items and the woman pressed a buzzer underneath her desk.

A burly, stone-faced man opened the door and stepped into the lobby. The woman behind the counter nodded to him. "This is Logan Alexander. He is here to see the new prisoner, Elizabeth Alexander."

Those words gave Logan chills.

"Please take him to the visiting area, Officer Carlson."

The blocky guard nodded and opened the door. "Right this way, Mr. Alexander."

Carlson directed Logan to a visiting area, which was coldly sterile looking. It was empty, except for a young woman and a small child sitting at a table with a tattooed, shaggy-haired man.

His insides twisted in worry over how his mother was handling this. He had been briefly incarcerated at this very jail, not that long ago, yet it felt like forever. So much had changed in his life since then. Logan recalled how that case turned out. It ended with his father and stepmother being arrested.

The guard gestured to a table on the far side. "The jail reserves the right to video-record any visit as a part of normal jail security procedures. This visit is subject to audio recording also for security reasons."

Logan glanced at the upper corners of the room where the cameras were mounted. "I know the drill."

"Let me finish, I have a whole thing," the guard chided. "While visiting, if an inmate says or implies anything about committing suicide or doing other self-harm or harm to others, or of being a victim of physical or sexual assault or knowing of another inmate who is, please contact jail staff immediately."

It was a rote speech—that the guard seemed to enjoy sharing a little too much—but, still, his mother must be terrified in this place.

"Duly noted," Logan said, and let the guard leave to bring his mother to the room.

About five minutes later, his mother was escorted in, thankfully unshackled, but definitely not wearing a Michael Kors pantsuit any longer.

"Oh, Logan." She reached out to embrace him.

Logan looked to the guard for permission. He nodded, and Logan and his mother hugged. Sadly, it held more emotion than Logan could remember feeling from his mother in recent years.

She released him, and they both took a seat opposite each other at one of the worn, plastic tables. The chairs were mounted to the tables and the floor with square metal poles.

"Mother, what happened? How could they arrest you for the murder of someone you never even met?"

His mother's eyes, which had been staring deeply into Logan's, suddenly darted away, then they dropped down to fix on her hands, fidgeting on the tabletop. "Well…"

Well? Was his mother hiding something from him? Did she know Rafe Santiago? How?

The twisting in Logan's stomach turned to full-on writhing. First, he finds out his fiancée is married—correction, was married—to the man, then he finds out his father brought him to town to end his wedding, and now this. Had his mother somehow known this guy too?

Boy, did Logan feel like a mushroom…hidden in the dark and fed a bunch of—

"Listen, Logan," her gaze slid back to him, "I can't really say anything right now. Your father's lawyers have advised me not to talk about any of this, not even to you." She leaned closer and whispered, "This place is bugged, you know." Then she sat up and plastered her special brand of "smile" across her face, as if to make him feel better.

It did not.

If anything, it made him more afraid of what was hiding behind that forced veil of pleasantry.

Oh, Mother, what have you done?

CHAPTER 29

JENESSA HAD TOSSED AND TURNED the entire night, her mind filled with nightmares of all kinds. She'd had one where Logan's father had turned into a two-headed serpent who had tried to eat her, and one where his mother was a secret agent sent from the Middle East to kill Rafe. She'd even had one where her own mother and father were both alive, and they were chastising her for getting married to Rafe and not inviting them.

She'd gone to bed without hearing from Logan after he'd left to go see his mother in jail. It was no wonder she'd had such an awful, fitful sleep. Still, life went on, and today she had much to do. On top of planning a wedding and trying to solve a murder, Jenessa had actual work to do for the paper.

Charles was a great boss, but in the newspaper game, deadlines were standard operating procedures, and to be heeded at all costs. Even if it was just a society-page story. Plus, she was hoping to make a quick stop at the police station before heading in to work. She may not be writing the story in this murder, but she definitely had a personal investment in solving the crime.

In spite of having sworn off high-calorie treats— *sort of*—until after her wedding, Jenessa planned to make her usual stop at The Sweet Spot to get her coffee buzz. At least she knew Ramey's smiling face would lift her spirits, and an extra shot or two of espresso in her mocha would wake her up.

She texted Logan a quick good morning, hoping his ringer was turned off and she wouldn't wake him in case he hadn't slept last night either. Then she tucked her blouse into her skinny jeans and dashed off to discover what the day had in store for her.

The bells on the door to The Sweet Spot jingled their familiar greeting and the aromas of freshly baked muffins, cookies, and cinnamon rolls drew Jenessa in to the warm environment of the café/bakery. Ramey's smiling face was simply icing on the cake, so to speak.

Jenessa waved at her friend and took her place in the line. Her mouth began to water, and her stomach to rumble, as she eyed the glass bakery case, filled with delicious pastries and baked goods that Ramey had no doubt been up since five AM creating. She loved that about Ramey.

In this way, her friend was so much like Jenessa's mother had been. She took great pride in perfecting recipes of all kinds, not just baking, and her face lit up with delight as she watched people enjoy what she had created.

The cinnamon rolls were calling Jenessa's name. Should she give in? Or resist? Tiny little fingers of guilt crept into her mind, knowing she had a very fitted wedding dress to squeeze into in a few short days. She didn't have time for the gym this morning, so she had better pass.

The customers in front of her filtered to tables or out the door, and Jenessa reached the counter. "Hey, Ramey." Judging by the smells wafting out from the kitchen area, Ramey already had the second batch in the ovens.

"The usual?" Ramey asked with a broad smile. "Or are you sticking to your guns on the whole eating light thing?"

"What guns?" Jenessa replied, only somewhat sheepishly. Her friend knew her too well. How could Jenessa deny herself a treat after walking into the café, with its glorious smells and delectable treats all visible in the fully stocked display case?

"You don't make it easy on a girl."

Ramey stepped over to the case and pulled out the last roll with a pair of tongs, setting it on a plate. "There you go." She placed it on the counter and turned to the espresso machine.

Jenessa leaned closer. Her resolve was disintegrating. "Make it a double shot today, please." Then she pulled a piece off the forbidden cinnamon roll and popped it into her mouth while she waited. "Mmm, that's good."

The cinnamon and sugar formed a perfect duet on her tongue and the bread positively melted in her mouth. "So good." She tugged off another bite, as Ramey worked on her drink order.

"If I can't fit into my dress, I'm blaming you, my friend."

Jenessa sighed with anticipation, and her shoulders dropped from where they had been hunched up, practically to her ears, without her even realizing it. She loved everything about coming to The Sweet Spot.

Although there was a part of her that was thinking about leaving Hidden Valley, there was also a part that would miss this place, and the people she loved, very much. Really, it all came down to Grey Alexander, didn't it? Everything, all the bad stuff anyway, was either directly or indirectly related to him.

Ramey set the cup on the counter in front of Jenessa with a proud smile. "Mocha perfection," she announced.

Jenessa inhaled deeply and closed her eyes. "Yes it is."

Ramey snatched the cinnamon roll away and hid it.

Jenessa was surprised by that. "What are you doing?"

"I'm not going to take the blame when you can't fit into that gorgeous gown." Ramey sounded serious.

"Okay." Jenessa lowered her head in mock shame. "Two bites were better than none."

Ramey frowned at her, looked at the missing portion of cinnamon roll, then snatched it up and took a bite. "Mine now." She grinned.

Jenessa couldn't help but smile back. Ramey was a good friend. Jenessa's best friend. And she was a truly good person—one of the best. "Hey, that reminds me, how did your evening go with Charles last night?"

"Well, he didn't propose." Ramey fake pouted. "But, soon, he said. He's hoping after being gone to camp all week, Charlie will be more open to the idea."

"Be patient." Jenessa gave her an encouraging smile. "I know Charles loves you, and Charlie will too."

"I hope you're right, but I'm not getting any younger. Tick tock."

Jenessa smiled and took her cup to a table in the corner. With her marriage only days away, she no longer needed to worry about her own so-called biological clock winding down. Though coming to new motherhood with children who were already half-grown, and already at least partially molded into the people they would become, was its own kind of challenge, wasn't it. Ramey was going to face that challenge with Charlie too, just like Jenessa would with Grayson and Lily.

When she sat down at her table and glanced back at Ramey, her friend was already smiling again and helping the next customer in line. In that moment, Jenessa was so grateful for Ramey's cheerful outlook on life. She had helped Jenessa through more than her share of ups and downs.

Still, she was truly blessed. While Hidden Valley had had its share of bad times for her—really bad times—she couldn't deny the good that she'd found there. The man of her dreams. A best friend she could always count on. A loving aunt, and, despite her and Sara's occasional squabbling, a sister she could rely on too.

And the children...

So very blessed.

It was just a matter of time before they would finally be a happy family—one that knew they belonged with each other. Even precious little Lily. In spite of her not being blood related to any of them, Jenessa would love that little girl as if she were her own.

Logan rolled over and looked at the clock. Almost eight thirty in the morning. He hadn't slept past seven in a long time. Of course, he hadn't actually fallen asleep until a couple of hours before.

How could he sleep, knowing his mother was locked up in jail? The woman wasn't built for tough times. Not that she wasn't strong in her own way, but his mother had lived a pretty charmed and sheltered life.

He couldn't imagine her doing menial work of any kind. If she was convicted of this crime and sent to prison, how would she survive?

A vision of his mother wearing prison scrubs and ladling out watery mashed potatoes to hardened female inmates flashed through Logan's mind. He shuddered. That was not the image of her that he was used to seeing.

What evidence did the police have on her? What was she hiding? Had Rafe's cause of death even been determined yet? Maybe Jenessa knew by now.

He checked his phone, which he had put on vibrate so he could sleep. There was a sweet text from Jenessa, hoping to hear from him this morning. He'd give her a call, but right now his mind was spinning with questions.

If he was going to accomplish anything today, he needed to get up and get dressed.

The lawyers would be at the office by this time, hopefully working on getting his mother out of jail. But if his father was behind his mother's arrest, how hard would his dad's attorneys try to get her out? Probably not too hard if it kept his father out of jail. No, Logan would need to find an unbiased lawyer to fight for her freedom. And he knew just who to call.

CHAPTER 30

JENESSA HAD DRAINED EVERY LAST DROP of mocha from her mug. Was she stalling? Perhaps. She relished the comfort of this place, but once she got up from her table and headed out, she would be forced to deal with the real world.

As if on cue, the bells tinkled as the door shot open. In walked her cousin Selena. She made a direct beeline for Jenessa's corner table. *Hello, real world. Good-bye, utopia.*

Selena's lithe body sashayed up and slunk into the chair opposite Jenessa, wearing a tight sheath. "I saw that sweet little sportscar of yours parked outside and knew I'd find you in here."

Jenessa offered up a smile. Forced.

Not that she didn't love her cousin, for she did. It was just that Selena reminded Jenessa of Rafe, and the awful end to his short life, and she had wanted to at least make it out of the café before having the truth thrust in her face.

"So, have you heard anything else about the murder case?" Selena asked.

And there it was. Was she asking out of personal curiosity or professional?

Should Jenessa mention that Logan's mother had been arrested? On a personal level, she didn't mind telling her, but if Selena was building a story for her own news station back home, then Jenessa had to keep Logan's family out of it. Correction, the decent members of his family. That did not include Grey.

Jenessa shrugged. "I don't think they've found the killer, if that's what you mean."

That was true. Detectives Baxter and Provenza only thought they found the murderer. That was an omission, sure, but not an outright lie. Jenessa was okay with that, under the circumstances.

"Hmm." Selena stood, adjusting her fitted dress. "I'm going to grab a coffee. Do you want anything else?"

What Jenessa wanted was to be back in her little bubble of solitude. But, since that was not about to happen, "No, I'm good."

~*~

Logan hung up the phone, feeling better now about his mother's situation. He had had the bright idea to call on one of his friends from college. Jonathan Goldman had been his dormmate while he'd been getting his BA in Political Science, before going to law school. Now he was a bigshot criminal attorney in San Francisco, and he was the perfect person to get Logan's mother off these ridiculous charges.

Rather than call his mother at the jail, he would get cleaned up and head over there to tell her about hiring Jonathan. But first, he needed to grab a bite to eat and something to wake him up, since he'd only had about two hours of sleep. He definitely needed a jolt.

He shot Jenessa a quick text, saying he would call her later on, and was heading off now to see his mother. Then he grabbed a cold slice of pizza from the fridge and shoved part of it in his mouth as he cracked open a Red Bull. After choking down a huge bite, he guzzled back almost the entire can of energy drink.

Logan dropped the rest of his slice on a paper towel, then sat at the breakfast bar and flipped open his laptop to read a few business headlines online while he ate. There was one headline in particular that caught his eye and made him bolt to the door to retrieve the local paper.

He snatched it from the floor and closed the condo door with dread. Logan tucked the folded paper under his arm as he walked back to the breakfast bar and hopped on his stool. He squeezed his eyes shut, briefly, afraid that when he opened the paper his fears would be confirmed.

Reluctantly, he opened his eyes, flipped open the paper too. And, yes, it was true. Front-page headlines announced his mother had been arrested for the murder of Rafe Santiago. She would be completely humiliated if she saw it.

Since Jenessa had been pulled off the story, she would have had nothing to do with this. If she had still been working on it, there was no way this information would have been plastered on the first page of the paper for all to see. Although, she did not have the last word on what was published—that was Charles.

And, while he respected Charles McAllister well enough, he questioned how the man could have allowed this to go to print.

Then, it all became clear to him. Crystal clear.

His father.

While, at first glance, it might seem like the paper was giving its owner a black eye, it all made perfect sense. His father clearly was setting up his mother to take the fall for this murder. Logan supposed his father couldn't get enough on Jenessa to frame her for it. For that matter, Logan himself had been called in twice for questioning too.

Anger spiked at Logan's temples, rage spurred him forward. He would go see his mother at the jail to let her know he had a new lawyer to represent her, but first, he was going to have a few words with his father.

Jenessa had left her car parked in front of The Sweet Spot while she and Selena walked through town and chatted. Her cousin seemed to want to stick to Jenessa like glue today.

She had purposely failed to mention to Selena she was on her way to the police station, hoping to avoid another barrage of questions, but the time had come.

"This is me," Jenessa said as they came to a stop in front of the Hidden Valley Police Department.

"Wait, Jen." Selena reached for Jenessa's arm as she looked over the building. "I want to go in with you. May I?"

Was that a good idea? Aside from wondering why Selena *wanted* to go in—for her story most likely—how would Provenza and Michael take it? But, on second thought, it couldn't hurt, she decided, and her cousin might even be an asset.

What would her tack be to get them to talk about the case? Selena might be helpful in that regard. Two sharp reporters were better than one.

"All right." Jenessa flung the door wide. "After you." She stood back and let Selena enter first.

"Hello, Miss Jones," the receptionist said as the two women entered the police station. She glanced down at her desk calendar. "I don't see your name on the list. Were Detectives Baxter and Provenza expecting you?"

It was definitely better that they hadn't been, after her last trip here had turned into an interrogation. "No. They're not expecting me, but I'm hoping they can see us. Do you think that might be possible, Ruby?"

The woman raised a pointer finger. "Let me check."

Jenessa strolled to the front windows and glanced out as Ruby called to see if they could go back. Selena joined her there.

"Crazy how the simplest things can turn so complicated, isn't it?" Selena commented.

Jenessa pulled her attention away from the cars passing by and focused on her cousin. What exactly did she mean by that? "A little too crazy, if you ask me." It seemed like a safe reply.

Selena nodded her agreement, just as George Provenza wandered out to greet them. "Hello, Miss Jones." He turned to Selena, his eyes sparkling as he took in her natural beauty. "And who is this?"

"This is my cousin, Selena. She's a television reporter from San Diego, here for my wedding. Do you mind if we go back to your office and talk about the Rafe Santiago case for a few minutes?"

"San Diego, huh?" Provenza seemed to consider it a moment, then, finally he shrugged. "Baxter is probably going to curse at me for it, but you know me, Miss Jones…a sucker for a pretty face. How can I resist two?"

Jenessa smiled and touched George on the arm. "Thank you, Detective. You know I appreciate any help you can give."

Michael glanced up from the papers on his desk as Jenessa, Selena, and George entered the office the two men shared. "Jenessa." He appeared a bit surprised.

"Hello, Michael."

She had wondered if he would be in. With what George had said, she assumed Michael might have stepped out for a while, but that clearly wasn't the case. So, time to improvise, make the best of the situation, and hope Michael didn't cop-block Jenessa where Provenza was concerned.

"Nice to see you." Was it Jenessa's hopeful imagination, or were things with Michael a little less awkward than last time? That was progress at least.

Jenessa looked to George. "Thanks for agreeing to see us." Then she shifted her focus back to Michael again. "Michael, this is my cousin Selena. She's here for the wedding, but since she is also a TV news reporter—"

"From San Diego," Provenza interjected.

"That's right." Jenessa paused, hoping to impress them with Selena's credentials. "We were hoping we might ask a few questions about the case."

Michael may be contemplating a relationship with Jenessa's sister, but that didn't stop his eyes from traveling to her voluptuous cousin and lingering there momentarily. *Men.*

Jenessa seized the opportunity to try to convince Provenza to share some information, saying the public wanted to know. Michael snapped out of his temporary Selena-induced trance and tried to put the kibosh on her attempts.

"I don't think that's a good idea, George."

Provenza looked to Michael. Jenessa watched the exchange.

"You know," Selena began in her light Spanish accent, "if you give me the interview, people all over San Diego will be hearing your name. Maybe the station will even send a camera crew out this way."

Perfect timing. Jenessa was impressed with her cousin's quick thinking. Michael might not be swayed by the limelight, but George was another story. This was likely going to be his last big case before retirement, and wouldn't it be nice for him to go out with a bang?

George lifted his eyebrows and cocked his head, continuing his silent pleading with Michael. Finally, a look of resignation flashed across Michael's face and he shrugged. "Fine." He pinched his lips together for a moment. "But I want it on record that I object."

Selena perched on the edge of Provenza's desk and took out her cell phone, as George sat down. "I'd prefer Jenessa ask the questions, if you don't mind, since she is more familiar with the details of the case."

Provenza nodded.

"Mind if I record the interview, Detective?" Selena held out her phone.

George seemed positively smitten with Jenessa's cousin. It could have been her beauty, or the fifteen minutes of fame she had offered him, but either way, it worked.

"So, George," Jenessa said, bringing his focus in her direction, "have you got the security footage yet?"

He shook his head. "Nope. Mr. Alexander seems to be dragging his feet on that one."

"All right. Well then, what can you tell me—us?"

Provenza crossed his hands on his desk. "The vic— *ahem*, Mr. Santiago—had some bruising on his face and right hand, in fact, there were some open cuts on his knuckles too. He had apparently gotten into a fight with someone, though we haven't confirmed with whom. Yet."

"Yet?" What was taking so long?

"Well, the ME was having the lab test the blood for cross contamination with other DNA," Provenza replied. "As well, there were fingernail scrapings to test for DNA. That all takes time."

"We do know that Grey Alexander also had a couple of bloody knuckles on his right hand, along with a small cut above his left eye," Michael added. "Put two and two together and we figured Grey was the one who had gotten in a fight with Santiago. That, together with the housekeeper telling us she thought she heard fighting but hadn't seen who was in the gatehouse. Just assumed it was Grey and Mr. Santiago."

"Then why has Elizabeth Alexander been arrested for murder?" Jenessa asked.

"I guess you read today's paper," he said.

She shook her head. She hadn't had time.

Michael looked surprised at that. "No?"

Provenza laid a hand on a file on his desk. "Let's just say we have evidence putting Elizabeth Alexander at the gatehouse around the time of Rafe's murder."

Logan's mother had been to the gatehouse? To see Rafe? Why? It made no sense.

"Does that mean you have a time of death?"

"We're not releasing that information," Provenza replied.

Jenessa's gaze caught Selena's. "Why not?"

He ignored the question. "Listen, it doesn't mean we've given up looking at Grey Alexander," Provenza continued. "Elizabeth might be in jail, and yes, we did arrest her for the crime, but, Miss Jones, things are not always what they seem."

Not always what they seem? What did he mean by that?

"We're pretty sure Grey got into it with Rafe, and we know that Grey brought him to town. There was a money transfer in progress the night he was killed, so we also know that Grey was doing some sort of business with Mr. Santiago."

Did they know the "business" had to do with her? Should she tell them?

Not yet. The last thing Jenessa wanted was to be back swimming on top of the suspect pool.

"Can you tell us, George, how Rafe was murdered? Was it the fight that killed him?"

Though, if it were, surely they would not be holding Elizabeth Alexander for the crime. They would have Grey in jail instead. And they wouldn't be running all these tests, unless they were just trying to cover all their bases.

"There were no signs of severe blunt force trauma, at least not sufficient to kill him, unless he hit his head on something and developed inter-cranial bleeding during the fight. The ME won't know until he completes the autopsy."

"Why is the autopsy taking so long?" Jenessa asked.

George shrugged.

Did he not know? Or was he not willing to say? Like he wasn't saying what the time of death was.

"Is there anything else you can tell us?" Selena uncrossed her long, tanned legs then re-crossed them the other way on George's desk, appearing to draw the eyes of both men.

Michael shifted his gaze to Jenessa. "Like I said, the housekeeper at the Alexander estate," he pulled the file from George's desk and looked inside, "a Mrs. Dobson, told us she was bringing fresh towels to the gatehouse the evening before and heard Grey and Rafe Santiago arguing from outside. Or, she assumed it was Grey and Rafe, since she didn't actually see them. Then she heard things breaking like they were fighting, so she rushed off without leaving the towels."

"So, who found him? Who reported it?" Jenessa asked. "Was it Mrs. Dobson when she brought Rafe's breakfast?"

Provenza and Michael shot each other a raw stare. She could tell they were debating whether or not to tell her. Provenza nodded once. Michael returned the gesture.

"It was Elizabeth Alexander."

CHAPTER 31

JENESSA PACED HER SMALL CUBICLE at the paper, trying to keep her temper in check. After she'd left the police station, and Selena had gone her way, she finally read the front-page article about Elizabeth Alexander's arrest, the one Michael had mentioned.

It was awful. How could Charles print such trash!

If she had been the one in charge of the story, there was no way it would have been printed. The new guy in town…was he trying to make a name for himself, or perhaps something more sinister? Maybe he had taken a bribe from Grey Alexander. Or Grey had pressured Charles to run it, full of hyperbole and poorly written as it was.

She marched down to Charles's office, finding him standing behind his desk, staring out the window, deep in thought.

"Got a minute?" she asked, taking a seat before he could reply.

He turned and shifted his gaze to her. "What's up?"

She held up the front page. "Really, Charles? This is rubbish."

He took a seat but said nothing.

"You know this is a pack of lies."

"Elizabeth Alexander was arrested in connection with Rafe Santiago's murder. That is a fact," Charles said. "I'm sorry you don't like it, but—"

"Did Grey put you up to this?" She struggled to keep her temper under control. "He did, didn't he?"

"This subject is closed." Charles crossed his arms over his chest. "Take the rest of the week off. You have a wedding to get ready for, don't you?"

Jenessa shot up from the chair, her eyes riveted on him. Grey had gotten to him, the truth of it was in his eyes. She pinched her lips together, lest she say something she would surely regret.

She stomped back to her cubicle and sat down with a huff. She didn't know how exactly, but she was certain that Elizabeth's arrest had something to do with Grey. It had to.

Had he called her to the gatehouse, knowing she would find Rafe's body and be considered a suspect? She'd probably touched the body and had somehow gotten her DNA on him, dropped a hair or a fiber from her clothing, trying to check for a pulse. Jenessa would have done the same thing. Wouldn't anyone, finding an unresponsive person on the sofa, look for some signs of life before calling the police?

Rafe hadn't been covered in blood when she'd seen his body, so it would not have been immediately obvious that he was dead.

Jenessa's desk phone rang, breaking her out of her thoughts.

"Hello, this is Jenessa Jones."

"Afternoon, Miss Jones."

"Hello, Detective Provenza."

Pleasantries. She'd play along.

"To what do I owe the pleasure of this call?"

George lowered his tone. "I just spoke to the ME."

Was George giving her this information over Michael's objections? Not that Provenza needed Michael's permission to do his job. George was the senior partner. He'd be stepping down soon, but for now, George could still make his own calls. And this one sounded like it might prove fruitful. For Jenessa, that is.

"I'm going to share something with you, Miss Jones, so you can pass it on to that pretty reporter cousin of yours, if you don't mind."

"Sure, sure, George. I'll pass it right along, as soon as you give it to me."

He kept his voice hushed, but she could hear him just fine. "So, the ME said he discovered sleeping pills in Rafe's system, but not an overdose or enough to kill him."

"Someone could have slipped them into a drink. Did the CSIs find any glasses? Wine glasses? Anything like that?"

"That info I'm not free to pass along."

"So, is that it?"

"No, the ME found something else. A drug known

as insulin glargine. Apparently, it is a slow-acting insulin. But…the strangest thing…"

"What, George?"

"The ME did not find any puncture wounds. You'd think the man would be covered in 'em if he was taking insulin regularly. Question for you, Miss Jones."

"Yes?"

"Was your husband a diabetic?"

Her husband. Technically he had been, but in reality, she hardly knew him. She had no idea if Rafe was diabetic.

"George, we were only—never mind, I have no idea if Rafe Santiago was a diabetic."

"Well, the ME said he checked for finger pricks, which is typical for a diabetic to check their blood sugar several times a day, but there was no sign of it. He also checked his blood sugar and it was within normal range. So, I'm guessing not."

"What about his stomach area and inner thighs? Did the ME check for insulin needle marks there?"

"Yes, as a matter of fact, but didn't find any there either."

That was interesting. "George, do you think that giving insulin like that to someone who doesn't have diabetes could have been the way he was killed?"

"Why do you ask?"

"I don't know much about the disease, but it seems like any time you give someone medicine for a condition they don't have, well, that could be dangerous. Right?"

"I would think so."

"And if there was no blunt force trauma severe enough to have killed him…George, do you know if the

ME checked between his toes and fingers for a needle mark? It would be tiny."

"I don't know…never thought to ask. Speaking of which, how do you know to do that?"

"Seriously, George? Don't you watch any of those crime dramas on TV?"

"Not many. They seem too slick and hyped up for my liking. Now, Matlock, there was a show I could sink my teeth into."

George really was a dinosaur. Jenessa had to remind herself of that from time to time.

"Besides having seen it on a crime drama a while back, Selena also told me about it happening in a case she was reporting on."

"What case?" Provenza asked.

"After Selena and I left the police station, she and I were talking about ways someone could die with no outward signs."

"And…"

"She started telling me about a story she had done a number of years ago. It was an investigative piece for the TV station she worked at in Spain, on the murder of a politician in Madrid. That was how the assassin delivered the drug that killed him. Between the man's toes."

"What? I've never heard of such a thing," Provenza said.

"Apparently, it's a thing."

"Hmmm…"

"What's that, George?"

"I was just wondering if Grey Alexander is a diabetic."

Jenessa had to think about that. She couldn't remember it ever coming up. "Not sure, George, but I can ask Logan later tonight."

"Yes, do that," he said, "and make sure you report back to me about it. Not Michael, you hear?"

"Not Michael? Why?" She played along, even though now she knew for sure he was going behind Michael's back in talking to her about this.

"Just because."

"Okay, George. I'll talk only to you."

~*~

"Hello," Logan answered his phone. His deep, rich voice calmed her.

"It's so good to hear your voice, Logan," Jenessa said. "I've had a horrendously busy day."

"You too?"

Sounds of a bustling office with people talking in the background told her he was still at work and not in his private office.

"Listen, I'm almost done here at the newspaper. Do you want to get dinner later?"

"Sure. I'd love that. I'm just waiting for a call back from my old college buddy."

"College buddy?"

"Yeah, Jonathan Goldman."

"Why?"

"He's now a high-priced criminal attorney in San Francisco. He's agreed to help me with Mom's case."

"Speaking of that…"

"Of my mother's murder charges?"

"Yes, that."

His voice became serious. "What about it?"

"Well, I found out something today that might help get her released."

"What is it?" His words came quick.

"I can't give you all the details, but I need to ask you if your father is a diabetic."

"What does this have to do with—"

"Don't worry about that, just trust me. Is he?"

"Yeah, he is. He was diagnosed type two about ten years ago. Why are you asking about that?"

"Like I said, I can't go into it right now. But I need you to promise me you won't say anything to your father about this—or anyone else."

"Okay, I promise." His mind must have been whirling with questions. "I was about to pay him a visit, after I hear from Jonathan, but I can wait. Talking to my father will probably just get my blood boiling anyway."

She could relate. That was usually what happened whenever Jenessa had any interaction with Grey, as well.

"After I speak to Jonathan, I'm free to meet you for dinner."

"I was thinking about Mexican. Sound good?"

Logan agreed.

"Okay. I just have one more thing to wrap up here," Jenessa said, "so call me when you're on your way."

"Let's just say seven, at Chapala's."

She hung up the call and immediately dialed Provenza, hoping that Michael was not around so she could talk freely with George.

"Provenza," the older detective answered.

"George, it's Jenessa."

"Miss Jones. You got something for me?"

"I do. I just found out that Grey Alexander was diagnosed with type two diabetes about ten years ago. I think we got him now, George."

"Well, not sure if we got him—"

"Just wishful thinking."

"But," he continued, "we sure got enough for a search warrant. Thanks a bunch, Miss Jones." And Provenza hung up the phone.

Jenessa practically giggled she was so elated. Even if she wasn't officially working this story, coming up with a solid lead was still exhilarating. And putting Grey back behind bars, where he belonged, well, that was icing on the cake. Hopefully icing that would last twenty-five to life.

CHAPTER 32

LOGAN STEPPED OUT OF THE SHOWER and swiped his hand across the mirror to clear the steam, seeing his reflection. He still looked worn out, which he was, but at least he felt a bit better. He'd needed a quick reboot before dinner with Jenessa, so he took a few minutes to rain some hot water down on himself.

He was grateful that she had talked him out of going to see his dad. Nothing good ever came out of a visit to his father's estate, or, at least, it rarely did.

Logan had tried to visit his mother at the jail earlier in the day, but he'd been informed it was lunchtime and therefore he was not allowed to see her. He had been unable to get back after that, having had to deal with some issues that had arisen at work. Two of the managers had called Logan in a panic. There were problems with one of his father's companies—they wouldn't say which—and they needed a senior member to mitigate things.

Where his father had gotten to, Logan had no clue. The man was acting strange, even by Grey Alexander's standards.

Logan heard his phone buzzing and rushed to the bedroom to fish it out of his pants pocket. "This is Logan Alexander."

"Logan, oh, I'm so glad I reached you." It was Mrs. Dobson. "I tried about fifteen minutes ago and you didn't answer. I was worried."

"I was in the shower. What's going on, Mrs. Dobson?"

"Everything is out of control here, Logan. They have a warrant."

"Who has a warrant? For what?"

"The police. To search the estate, Logan. And your father is not here."

If he wasn't at home, and he wasn't at the office, where on earth could the man be?

"Logan, please, can you come? There are cops all over the house picking through everything. They're making a huge mess. I don't know what to do."

There went dinner with Jenessa. Logan sighed. "Sure, Mrs. Dobson. I'll come. I just have to make a quick call and I'll head right over."

Logan hung up the call and dialed Jenessa.

"Hello, Logan. I'm almost ready. Are you at the restaurant already?"

He pictured Jenessa, putting the final touches on her hair and makeup. Not that she had to. With makeup or without, Logan found Jenessa to be the most stunning woman he had ever met.

"Listen, babe, I've got bad news. Or good news, depending on how you look at it."

"Oh no. Logan, what is it?" Her voice seemed tentative.

"Mrs. Dobson just called me. Apparently, there is a team of cops at my father's estate, and they are tearing the place apart, according to her."

"That sounds like good news to me, Logan."

"That part is good, I agree. Hopefully they find evidence to tie him to this crime, and my mother can be released before spending another night in that awful jail cell."

"So, what is the bad part?"

"I can't meet you for dinner."

"Oh." Disappointment colored her response.

He hated making her sound that way, but it couldn't be helped.

"Mrs. Dobson asked—no begged—me to come over. She sounded really stressed out by all the chaotic activity at the estate."

"No, of course, I understand, sweetheart. Besides, it might be good to have eyes and ears on the situation as it unfolds, someone to make sure we stay in the loop on this investigation. Maybe you can try to get some info out of the police while you're there?"

"I'll see what I can do." Although Logan wasn't Detective Baxter's favorite person.

"Or I can meet you there," Jenessa offered. "But I doubt my presence would be welcome."

"You're probably right." Although Baxter and Provenza might tell her more than they would him. "But we won't know until you try."

"You don't have to tell me twice," she said. "I'll be right over."

Logan smiled at her determination. "Have I told you lately how much I love you?"

~*~

"What the hell is going on here?" Logan's father hollered as he stormed through the front door of his mansion, which was currently swarming with police officers, rifling through every nook and cranny of the place. It was an enormous home, so it was taking them quite a while to make any progress. Still, the place looked like a tornado had blasted through the front door and was making its way around the mansion.

"Who's in charge here?" Grey demanded as his eyes bounced around the room. "Where is your warrant? What on earth are you looking for?" he shouted to whoever would listen.

"Hey!" He marched toward an officer who was picking up a Chinese vase in the living room. "That's a priceless piece of art, you buffoon! Get your grubby paws off—"

Grey Alexander was pissed—and it was clear he was going to make it known to anyone within earshot. The questions and insults were flying without respite. Logan's father wasn't even giving anyone a chance to answer before blasting them with the next outraged iteration.

Fortunately, he hadn't spotted his son yet, who watched from behind another cop in the foyer.

Logan looked around for Baxter. He was not in sight. Neither was his partner. Surely the two detectives must be on the premises somewhere. Logan couldn't imagine either of them leaving this to chance. Not to mention how much Baxter would want to gloat over another Alexander scandal.

Jenessa slipped through the partially open front door. Fortunately, no one but Logan saw her. He motioned for her to come to him.

She nodded and tiptoed across the foyer. "What did I miss?" she whispered.

Somehow, in spite of his father's ranting, Logan heard a shout come from upstairs. It wasn't completely clear, but it had sounded like someone had said, "I got something."

Logan looked at Jenessa. "Stay here."

"But, Logan—" she started to argue.

He checked to make sure the coast was clear. "Please, just stay here, out of sight."

"All right," she reluctantly whispered.

Since he seemed practically invisible to his father in that moment, Logan snuck out and made his way up the stairs. He followed the trail of debris from room to room, until he came to his father's bedroom, where he finally found Detectives Baxter and Provenza.

Logan lingered outside the door, away from sight but able to see in the mirror's reflection, listening to the details of the discovery.

"What is it?" Provenza asked the officer in front of him.

"I found this." The officer held up one of Grey's Lantus insulin pens in his gloved fingers.

"Bag it," Provenza ordered, smiling. "Looks like the same type of insulin found in the vic's system." He turned to Baxter, who was just disconnecting from a phone call. "You got the arrest warrant?"

"In progress as we speak," Baxter replied.

"Perfect. We have witness testimony to Grey's violent fight with the victim, combined with the ME confirming it was Grey Alexander's blood found on Santiago's knuckles, and Santiago's blood on Grey's shirt."

"And now, with the fact that Grey was diabetic, and we have his insulin," Baxter added, "looks like we're good to go, George."

The two men headed toward the door, so Logan ducked into the guest room nearby, allowing them to make their way downstairs, where he could still hear his father screaming at everyone. Hopefully Jenessa would not be discovered.

Once he could overhear the detectives talking to his dad, Logan crept down the stairs too. He glanced around for Jenessa, but there was no sign of her. As he entered the living room, he saw Detective Provenza cuffing his father, while Baxter read him his Miranda rights.

His father might have the right to remain silent, but he sure wasn't exercising it. On the contrary. The man was even more outraged—if that were possible—and he was hurling a litany of vulgar and incendiary threats and insults at basically anyone within earshot.

As the detectives led Grey from the house, he finally seemed to notice Logan standing there. "Logan!

Son. You have to get me out of this. Call my lawyers. This is a mistake!"

Logan did not reply. Rather, he stood in stony silence and stared as the cops marched his father out the door, a barrage of conflicting emotions assaulting him from all sides. He did not move until someone shut the front door. It was Jenessa.

"Where were you?" Logan asked.

"I heard the cops coming down the stairs and I stepped into the coat closet," she explained. "Are you ready to go?"

"I think I need to stay until all the police are gone." He also needed time to settle down his emotions and figure out what his father's arrest would mean to the family and the business. "Why don't you go home, and I'll call you later."

"All right." She gave him a quick kiss before leaving. She looked back as she opened the front door. "I love you, Logan," she said and went out.

I love you too.

The team was wrapping up their search. Mrs. Dobson came to stand beside Logan in the foyer.

"Thank you so much for coming, dear boy. I don't know what I would have done without you here."

Logan put an arm around her and pulled the stocky woman in for a hug. "Do you have any idea how many times you saved me growing up?"

He released her, and she smiled at him, touching him on the cheek, the way she used to when she had comforted him as a youngster. "You're a good boy, Logan—a good man—you always were. You never deserved what that odious man did to you."

"I've always wondered why you stayed working here for so long. My father is a tyrant at the best of times."

"Oh, Logan, don't you know? I stayed here for you."

He looked into her gentle eyes. *For me?*

"Come." She took his hand, leading him to the sofa in the now quiet living room. She sat down and patted the space beside her. "Here. Have a seat."

He did, and Mrs. Dobson—Logan's savior so many times—reached into her dress pocket and pulled out something small, which she held tightly in her closed hand.

"Put your hand out," she directed softly. When he complied, palm up, she dropped something into it. He looked down and sucked in a sharp breath at the sight. His heart swelled with excitement. "I'd forgotten you said...with everything that's happened these last couple of days. Where did you—?"

"Let's just say I rescued it when your father went to jail, and I've held it in safekeeping for you."

"But where did you find it?"

She hesitated for a moment. "In the back of your father's sock drawer. I was putting his laundry away a few days after he left, and I saw something sparkle in the light."

"And he never knew it was missing because he wasn't here. I get it."

"No more talking, Logan. Just get in that shiny red car of yours and drive over to your fiancée's house and put that thing on her finger."

He grabbed Mrs. Dobson and gave her a squeeze. "You are amazing, you know that?"

The woman's cheeks grew pink as she blushed.

"Thank you." Logan stood to leave. "You're an angel, Mrs. Dobson."

~*~

Was that the doorbell Jenessa just heard? It was after ten and she had been brushing her teeth. She turned off the water tap and listened again. Yes. It was the front door, and now someone was knocking wildly. She opened the blinds in the bathroom and peeked down to her front walkway. Logan's car was in her driveway.

Something must be wrong.

CHAPTER 33

THE DOORBELL RANG A FEW TIMES in rapid succession. Jenessa looked at the clock on the bathroom wall, which read ten twenty. She hadn't expected to hear from Logan this late. She spit out the toothpaste she still had in her mouth and took a quick swish of water, expelling it in the sink before scurrying down the stairs in her pajamas and flinging open the front door.

But when she did, Logan was not standing there. She glanced side to side, then back to his car in the driveway, before looking down, realizing he was on one knee on her front porch. "Logan, what are you—?"

"Shhh," he said, his face plastered with the biggest smile she had ever seen him wear. He took her left hand and reached into his pocket with his free hand, fumbling for something.

Then, his eyes flashed up to hers, glinting with emotion, the porch light's reflection quivering in his gaze. "Jenessa Jones, will you marry me?"

Jenessa's own eyes were filling with tears of joy as she saw the beautiful diamond ring in his hand. "Oh, Logan. You got it? How?"

The grin remained firm on his face. "Answer my question, woman."

Jenessa began to laugh and cry, all at the same time. She stuck out her trembling naked ring finger. "Yes, Logan, a million times yes!" She began to vibrate with excitement. "Put it on, put it on!"

He slid the ring on her finger, then stood to meet her gaze. Cupping her face in his hands, he kissed her long and hard, his hands moving down her back as she clung to him.

When she pulled back for air, he smiled at her. "You have no idea how much I love you."

"I love you too, Logan," she managed to get out before his lips were on hers again.

Finally, he released her, and she tugged him into the house, closing the door behind him.

She stuck her hand out and admired the dazzling diamond. "Oh, Logan. It's beautiful," she cried. "It's perfect."

He slipped his arms around her again. "Just like you."

The ring was almost the same as the one they had seen on the computer, only this one was even more stunning. "With everything else going on," she said, "I had completely forgotten about Mrs. Dobson finding the ring."

"Me too." Logan beamed at her. "What a night!"

They went into the living room and snuggled together on the sofa, Jenessa staring at the gorgeous diamond ring on her finger, and Logan staring at her.

She looked up at him, sure that nothing but love was shimmering in her eyes. For the first time since all this recent drama began, pure joy filled her heart. "It's really going to work out, isn't it?"

He nodded as he put an arm around her, then took her hand to examine the diamond ring. "It suits you, babe—beautiful and classy, made more brilliant under pressure."

Her lips spread into a smile at the sweet compliment, unable to take her eyes off the dazzling jewel. It did suit her. Perfectly sized, the ring looked like it belonged there, like it had been made just for her.

"I can't wait to make you my wife."

She laid her head against his chest and a lovely vision formed in her mind. She and Logan were picnicking in the meadow near the lake, with the kids—their kids—playing in the field nearby. She sighed. It was merely a dream now, but soon, soon it would be her reality.

~*~

Jenessa brought two cups of decaf to the living room and handed one to Logan, then she slowly sat down on the sofa beside him, curling her legs up under her.

"What a crazy night this has been," she said.

Logan blew on his coffee, then took a sip. "Well, it was absolute chaos when I arrived at my father's place. Mrs. Dobson was beside herself. There had to be at least a dozen police officers on the main floor alone."

Jenessa blew on her own coffee. "They must have had the entire Hidden Valley police force there." She took a drink.

"And probably half the force from a neighboring town too," Logan added. "You didn't go upstairs, but the upper floor was also crawling with cops."

"I'm surprised your father didn't have a heart attack, as furious as he was."

"Before you got there, he came blustering into the house, screaming bloody murder, or, to be more precise, that he was going to bloody murder someone if they didn't get everyone off his property."

Jenessa bobbed her head. Yes, that sounded like Grey. Full of threats and raging violence.

"Do you think your father could have killed Rafe?"

"Don't you?" Logan asked.

"It seems the most likely…"

"But?"

"But the method of this murder seems a little too soft for the Grey Alexander I know. He seems more like a crime-of-passion sort of guy."

"Maybe after the fistfight the two had, Dad had the night to come to his senses—and to do some research on how to kill a man with insulin—"

"Yeah, hoping our small town medical examiner would miss it." She took another sip.

"Probably."

"Did he see you there?"

"That's right, you were in the closet. He did notice me after they were cuffing him and reading him his rights."

"I would have liked to have seen that."

"Of course, he denied it all." Logan rolled his eyes. "I wouldn't expect any less from the man."

Jenessa agreed. "Anything else?"

"Well, let's just say I got an earful upstairs when they found the insulin pen in my father's room. Your ex and his partner practically jumped for joy when the officer brought the pen out and dropped it in an evidence bag."

That could be big.

She set her cup on the coffee table. "So, they found it, huh…do you know if it was the same kind that killed Rafe?"

"That's what Provenza said," Logan replied. "That's why you were asking me about my dad having diabetes, wasn't it?"

"Sorry for not telling you. I swore to George that it would stay between us."

"It's all right. I'm glad you asked. If my father killed that man, no matter who he was, he deserves to be in prison. Using insulin like that shows that he had to have planned it out carefully. He must've assumed he wouldn't get caught."

"Yeah." Jenessa nodded slightly. "And he still took out an insurance policy by framing your mother for it." She leaned back against the sofa. "Did you know he was even trying to pin it on Aunt Renee?"

Logan shook his head in disbelief. "Man, he was covering all his bases, wasn't he?" He set his cup down on the table beside hers. "You, me, your aunt, my mother…he must have thought he had it made when they arrested my mom."

"Not anymore," Jenessa said.

Logan put his arm around her and she leaned in to him. "You're right about that," he said. "He was absolutely livid as they shoved him out the front door."

"Why don't we change the subject?" She stuck her hand out to admire the sparkling ring again.

"What would you like to talk about?" Logan asked, with a little mischief in his voice.

Jenessa raised her eyes to his, shifting her body toward him. She ran her fingertip gently over his bottom lip. "I'd rather talk about our honeymoon."

CHAPTER 34

LOGAN WOKE UP FEELING ON TOP of the world. Jenessa had his grandmother's ring on her finger, his father was in jail for murder, and his mother should be released soon, if not already. The upside-down reality of his life had righted itself...he hoped.

Though Logan wouldn't wish jail on anyone, most assuredly not his mother, his father was a different story. The man was evil, seeming to grow more so as he got older. Logan could testify to that.

Grey Alexander had a violent and unpredictable temper, but he wasn't stupid. Would he use his own insulin to commit murder?

Logan showered and shaved, then popped a couple slices of bread into the toaster for breakfast. After downing a coffee and spreading almond butter on his toast, he headed to the jail to see his dear old dad.

~*~

"Ah, Mr. Alexander, you again." The desk officer at the jail recognized Logan from his visit the other evening. "I'm sorry but your mother has been released. I just started on day shift today, and she was gone when I arrived."

"Thanks, but I'm not here to see my mother. I'm here to see Grey Alexander. My father."

"Your father this time, huh?" She scanned her computer.

Logan could guess what the woman was thinking, though she said nothing further about it.

"Oh, yes. I see he was brought in last night."

"I should be on his list," Logan said. "Can you look?"

Logan began emptying his pockets as she checked for his name.

He waited for her to confirm it. She waved him through, then he stepped between the two detectors.

As Logan was ushered to the visiting area, he saw that his father was already there waiting at a table. "About time you showed up."

That was his father. No loving hug. No pleasant words of greeting or thanks for coming. Straight to the gut punch. Before anything else had transpired, Logan's father had already managed to let Logan know just how much of a disappointment he was.

"I got here as soon as I could, *Dad*."

Logan bit back *It's good to see you too*, and he took a seat across from his father. The visiting area was slightly more populated than it had been the other evening when he'd come to see his mother, but it was still rather empty. Logan figured there were not likely many prisoners at the local Hidden Valley jailhouse.

"Where's my lawyer? Did you even bother to call him?"

Logan closed his eyes briefly and took a deep breath. His father could have called his lawyer himself too. Logan was pretty sure he had been offered his one phone call. Regardless, he had promised himself that he wouldn't let his father get to him today. It was too perfect a day.

"Yes, Dad, I called. He's out of town on vacation, and we need to call in another lawyer—a junior partner—if you want someone right away."

His father's face began to turn an angry shade of red. The man looked as if he might have a stroke right then. "I don't want one of the amateurs working on your mother's—" He pounded his fist on the table, and the guard rushed to his side.

"You'd better calm down, inmate, or we'll nip this visit in the bud right quick," the guard said through gritted teeth and a face that was all business. Add to that the fact that the guard had a substantial body that would intimidate most men, and his father would have to be stupid to get on this guy's bad side. "I don't care what your last name is. You're in my jail now."

Logan's father seemed to acquiesce, leaning back in his seat and clasping his hands on the tabletop. "Fine, then. Logan, let's discuss other matters."

What other matters could there be?

"Tell me you've finally come to your senses and called off this farce of a wedding to that gold-digging bi—"

"No, Father," Logan interrupted before his dad could say the ugly word he was about to. "I have not—and will not—call off my wedding to Jenessa. In fact..."

Grey sat forward quickly. "What?"

"In fact, she is now proudly wearing Grandmother's diamond engagement ring."

Logan sat back and waited for his father to blow another gasket. He didn't. Instead a cold, much more frightening kind of malice washed over him. Was that the sound of his father's teeth grinding from across the table?

Finally, from between those teeth, his father said, "I don't think I heard you correctly, *Son*. It sounded like you said you gave that woman my mother's diamond ring."

Logan remained silent, held his father's gaze without flinching.

"Now, Son," he tapped a beat on the table, "I don't see how that is even possible, since that ring has been missing ever since I—"

Ever since you beat me over it, Dad? That's what Logan wanted to say. What he did say was "Ever since it went missing all those years ago...yes, Dad. It seems to have turned up after all this time."

Logan was not about to give up the fact that Mrs. Dobson had been the one to find it and hand it over to Logan. The woman had done too much for Logan over the years for him to throw her under the bus like that.

Somehow steam managed *not* to come billowing out of his's father's ears, though Logan wasn't quite sure how.

"Why do you hate her so much? Jenessa is a beautiful person, Dad, inside and out."

"Dammit, Logan, think with your brain, not your— the woman has been out for our family's money ever since she rolled into town. First, she tried to ruin your life by getting pregnant. Probably thought you'd do the so-called right thing and marry her." He shook his head with contempt. "She isn't good enough to marry into the Alexander family. She's just someone who wants to marry into money. Trust me, Son, I know the type."

His father probably did know the type. The man had certainly had his share of affairs over the years, and many, if not all, of those women were likely of the gold-digging variety. But not his Jenessa. He knew her better than that.

Logan leaned forward, as close as he figured the guard would allow, and stared into his father's flaring eyes. "You want to know something, Dad?" Logan didn't wait for a response. "I would have married her sooner, if you hadn't pressured her to give our child up for adoption. What you did to us, to our son, was unconscionable."

His father stared blankly back, as though he were innocent of the accusations Logan was making. "You think we don't know? Did you really believe that what you did would never come out?"

Logan's father didn't blink an eye. The man was clearly well-practiced in the art of denial.

"We know, Dad. We know Grayson is our son, and that you secretly orchestrated his adoption by my own cousin, without disclosing to her the baby was mine."

With that, Logan did detect the slightest flinch in his father's poker-face façade, but the man's lips remained unmoved.

"That's right. It's good you're not denying it. It would be pointless anyway. We've done the DNA tests. I know. Jenessa knows. And soon," Logan stood from the table, "soon Grayson and this whole town will know!"

Then, Logan did something he should have had the guts to do years ago. He walked out on his father. Not so much as a look back in his direction. Logan just strode out, knowing that his father was, for perhaps the first time in his entire life, rendered speechless.

Logan was done with Grey Alexander and his narcissistic ways. He was going to leave this jail as fast as he could. Let his father rot, for all he cared.

Just as Logan slid into the driver's seat of his car, his cell phone rang. It was a number he didn't recognize. He hit the *Talk* button. "Hello, this is Logan Alexander."

"You have a call from an inmate at Hidden Valley Correctional Center. Do you accept the charges?"

What? His father must have sprinted to the payphone to call him. As much as Logan wanted to decline, he accepted. Part of him wanted to hear how his father was going to try to weasel out of this one.

"What do you want?"

"Logan? Son? I didn't do it. I didn't kill that man. Sure, I lost my temper, we fought, but I didn't kill him."

"So you say."

"You can't believe I would beat that man to death," Grey blustered over the jailhouse phone.

CHAPTER 35

"NO," GREY SHOUTED into the jailhouse phone. "Rafe Santiago was very much alive when I left him that night! Sure we fought, but I didn't kill him."

Logan was regretting accepting the call from his father. "We both know how brutal you can be, Dad."

"I did not do this, Logan! I swear it."

Something was niggling at Logan. His father didn't seem to have any clue that Rafe had actually been killed by an injection of insulin. It meant that there was a chance, however small, that his father did not commit this murder.

"I'm listening."

"Good, Logan, that's good. I need your help, Son. I'm sure the cops won't be looking for evidence against anyone else, so we need to hire a top-notch private investigator—"

That comment sent a flash of anger through Logan. "You mean like the one you hired to dig up dirt on my fiancée?"

Grey was silent on the other end of the call. Logan had made his father speechless twice in one day. Twice in less than an hour even. "Yeah, I know about that. Did you think she wasn't going to tell me? That I wouldn't understand? It was a mistake for you to bring Rafe to town."

"I just thought—"

"Sure, Jenessa made a stupid mistake too, an uncharacteristic mistake, all those years ago, but it's over now. The man is dead, and that's on you, Dad, one way or another."

"See, Logan, see. That's how you know I didn't kill him. He was more useful to me alive. Dead, the man is worthless."

Wow, his father really had a way with words, didn't he?

"Listen, Dad, I have to go." Logan looked at his watch. "I have an appointment."

"Logan? Wait! Don't hang—"

But he did—and it felt good. He turned the key in the ignition of his shiny red BMW and sped out of the parking lot.

~*~

Logan was on his way to his appointment with the Board of Directors to discuss his father's recent arrest and the impact it would have on the company again, but he hoped to see Jenessa first. He shot her a quick text but, to save time, decided to head to the paper without waiting for a response.

He pulled up, parked in his father's spot—the man had a named parking stall at all his companies—and then hurried into the building.

"Oh, hello, Mr. Alexander." Alice, the elderly receptionist, swooned at him.

He leaned down on the counter and smiled at her. "I'm here to see Jenessa. Is she available?"

"Oh my, yes, I believe she is," Alice sweetly replied. "Let me buzz her for you."

Logan gave her a nod and went to take a seat along the row of windows, facing the street. Moments later, Charles McAllister came out to the waiting area. He approached Logan, extending his hand. "Logan. Great to see you."

Logan stood and pumped the man's hand.

"Why don't you come back to my office while you wait for Jenessa?"

"Sure." Why not. He followed Charles down the hall.

McAllister gestured to the chair in front of his desk. "Have a seat, Logan. I have something I'd like to say."

That was odd. What could Charles McAllister have to say to him?

Logan sat, while Charles took his desk chair on the opposite side. "Listen, Logan," he looked down at his hands, folded on the desktop, "about that story. The one about your mother." He raised his eyes to meet Logan's. "It wasn't up to me. Your father…"

Logan bobbed his head in recognition. He had wondered about that himself. It didn't seem like a

Charles McAllister move to publish that story on his mother. It was a Grey Alexander tack if it was anything.

"I want to apologize—"

"I understand," Logan interrupted, raising a hand. "No hard feelings."

"I heard they released her. Locked up your old man instead."

Logan nodded. Yes, they had locked his father up, and he had been sure it was the right action, but now…now he wasn't so certain. Had his father just been playing him, pretending not to know about the insulin connection, or had he really not murdered Rafe Santiago?

"I'm sure Grey's arrest would make a terrific front-page story," Charles said, "but you know your father would have my head…not to mention my job."

As Jenessa walked past her boss's office, she heard Logan's voice trailing into the hallway. She stopped in the doorway. "Logan. What are you doing here?"

He stood up and went over to her, giving her a quick kiss on the cheek. "Didn't you get my text? Or the call from Alice saying I was here?"

"Text? No, sorry, I was in the copy room and my phone is in my purse in my cubicle. You want to grab a quick coffee?" She looked to Charles. "That's okay, isn't it? I can bring you back something."

"You go," Charles said with a lift of his chin. "I'll get my own coffee in a bit. Always a good reason to see my little redhead's smiling face."

He was speaking of Ramey, of course. Jenessa was thrilled that Ramey and Charles had hit it off so well. Soon, Ramey had said, Charles would propose to her and before they knew it, both Jenessa and her best friend would be married women with kids.

It was crazy how their lives worked out. When she had first come back to Hidden Valley after her father's passing, a little more than a year ago, Jenessa wouldn't have even imagined things would turn out the way they had.

"Let me just grab my purse, sweetheart. I'll meet you at the front."

Jenessa left Logan in her boss's office and scurried to her cubicle to get her bag, catching up with Logan as he came out of Charles's office.

"We might as well walk over. The weather's perfect," she said. "Unless you prefer to drive?"

"A walk would be nice." Logan took Jenessa's hand and wove their fingers together. "Might as well enjoy what summer we have left."

Logan was right about that. The days were still quite warm, but the mornings and the evenings were beginning to take on the cool of the coming autumn season.

Jenessa loved this time of year, though. That little nip in the morning air, the anticipation of fall and the changing leaves. She always looked forward to the rich reds and golds that the trees turned not long before dropping their leaves.

The couple strolled along Main Street for a few blocks, neither in any hurry to get where they were going, but instead enjoying each step of the journey.

"This is how life should be, isn't it?" Jenessa leaned her head onto Logan's bobbing shoulder.

"What's that?" He placed a soft kiss on the top of her head.

"People are always in such a hurry to get to the finish line that they often forget to pay attention to the race," Jenessa muttered. "I don't want my life with you to be that way."

"What do you mean?" he asked.

"I don't want to wake up one day and realize that life has flown by without our even noticing."

"Yeah, me either."

"Our son is already almost a teenager."

"Wish we hadn't missed the early years," Logan said.

"At least we have him in our lives now, and we have little Lily to watch grow up, too." The idea of it made her smile.

"Are we ready to be Mom and Dad?" he asked, his eyes lit up with joy.

"Absolutely." She gave a little laugh. "Sure, we have some hurdles to help the kids over, but, yeah, I think we're more than ready."

Her life with Logan and the kids was what she wanted to focus on. She drove any thoughts of Grey and Rafe out of her mind, for now. She was going to marry this amazing man and they were going to build a happy life together. They had the complete package. They would be married with two children and living behind the white picket fence of her family home. All they needed was a scruffy mutt to complete their American dream.

Jenessa stopped outside the doors to The Sweet Spot and turned to Logan.

"Something wrong?" He looked a little puzzled by her pause.

She shook her head a little. "No."

"What is it then?"

Her heart was full. How could she explain it? She stared deeply into those gorgeous blue eyes. "It's just...I love you, Logan."

He planted his hands on either side of her face and kissed her softly. "You have to know that I love you...with all my heart."

~*~

The lovebirds got coffees and sat at a table near the windows to soak up the afternoon sun. Logan stirred cream into his coffee, then took a sip. Jenessa sensed something was on his mind. He rarely came to visit her at work in the middle of the day. Plus, she knew he was busy with his own job. The board was likely scrambling now that Grey had been arrested. Again.

That was a good thing, though. That man was where he belonged, as far as Jenessa was concerned. She, for one, was glad he had been caught, and she couldn't deny it gave her some bit of pleasure to have been part of that. Getting the info on his diabetes, which led to his arrest, was one of the high points in Jenessa's stressful week.

"Listen, Jenessa, I have something to say."

So, she had been right. Logan did have something on his mind.

"What is it?" She reached across the table and took his hands in hers.

"So, you know I went to see my father at the jail this morning."

Jenessa nodded. "How did it go?"

Logan shrugged. "Let's just say it didn't go well. He was being his usual antagonistic self, and I got up and walked out on him."

Good for him. She was proud of Logan. It was about time he stood up to that man.

"But here's the thing…"

Thing? What thing?

CHAPTER 36

JENESSA TOOK A SIP from her coffee and waited for Logan to continue his story.

"When I went in there," Logan said, "I was ready to write my father off, but something he said—or rather, something he didn't seem to know—well, it got me thinking."

"Don't tell me he managed to convince you he didn't do this. Surely you can't believe him just because he said he didn't kill Rafe. There's evidence, Logan. Indisputable evidence."

"About that…yes, I know that my father takes the same kind of insulin that killed Rafe, but here's the thing. He didn't seem to know about that being the cause of death."

"Maybe he was lying—"

"He denied killing the man—I knew he would—but he just kept saying that Rafe was alive when he left him, after they had fought. It sounded like my father thinks Rafe was beaten to death. He doesn't seem to know anything about the real cause of death. The insulin."

"Maybe he's just—"

"Yeah. I considered that too. I figured he was just playing me. But there was something in his voice when he was pleading for my help...I don't know. I don't want to believe him. It's easier to just let him hang for this."

That was also her first thought. Let Grey Alexander go to prison—again—and get him out of their lives so he couldn't do any more damage. But she didn't want to be that person, didn't want to let this wicked man turn her into somebody she did not want to be. Besides, if he was innocent of this crime, then it wouldn't be right to let him swing and the real murderer get away. But if Grey didn't do it, then who did? And why?

"Will you help me, Jenessa? Help me prove my father—I don't know—guilty or innocent. Whichever he turns out to be."

She was quiet, thinking over all the ramifications of Grey's potential innocence.

"If you can't do it, I understand." Logan released her hands and sat back in his chair. "That man has caused you a lot of pain in your life, and he probably doesn't deserve our sympathy, but—"

Grey had caused them both a great deal of pain. Logan had suffered considerably, as well. But stronger than her loathing of Grey Alexander was Jenessa's sense of right and wrong. She had become a journalist because of her desire to bring about the truth, not so she could write juicy gossip and get paid to do it. No. Ultimately the truth was what mattered to her.

If Grey had done this, if he did kill Rafe, he deserved to pay for his crimes, but if he didn't...it didn't matter that his heart was evil, and he had done so many other despicable deeds in his life. If Grey did not do this, then that meant there was someone else out there that had done it. A killer could still be on the loose on the streets of Hidden Valley.

Jenessa stayed at the Sweet Spot for another latte after Logan left to get to his board meeting. She needed some time to come to terms with the fact that maybe, only maybe mind you, Grey Alexander did not murder Rafe Santiago.

"There you are!" Selena hurried to Jenessa's table and pulled out the chair that Logan had been sitting in before. "I've been calling you, Jenessa, but all I get is voicemail."

"Sorry, I must have left my ringer turned off." Jenessa dug around in her handbag for her cell phone.

Her cousin waved at Ramey as if Ramey should know what she wanted and just bring it over to the table. Jenessa didn't know how things were done in Spain, but here in sleepy little Hidden Valley, one was still expected to stand in line and place your order when it was your turn.

When Jenessa caught Ramey's attention, Ramey rolled her eyes behind Selena's back and mouthed the word *Americano?* To which, Jenessa shrugged. She leaned toward Selena. "Did you want an Americano?"

"*Sí,* cousin. Please."

Jenessa nodded at Ramey, surprised that Ramey had known that. Though, she supposed, working all these years at the café probably gave her some sort of coffee ninja capabilities. She did always manage to know exactly what Jenessa wanted whenever she came in. Even when Jenessa didn't want to want it.

"Please, Jenessa," Selena begged after Ramey set her coffee down, "please let me shadow you again today. Aunt Renee is dragging me all over town, checking and double-checking on final details of the wedding—she's driving me *loca!* Completely crazy."

If truth be told, she could use Selena's help again, with Michael and Provenza. They would certainly think *she* was the crazy cousin if she showed up telling them she suspected Grey might be innocent. Heck, Jenessa herself thought she sounded crazy too.

"Okay, sure," Jenessa agreed. "Here's what I'm thinking." Jenessa explained what Logan had told her, while the two women drank their coffees.

Detective Provenza had the crime scene photos scattered all over his desk when Jenessa and Selena stepped into the office.

"Thanks for agreeing to see us," Jenessa said.

George gave her a small smile. "I've learned that sometimes your perspective can be helpful." Then his eyes slid to Selena.

Michael stuck a hand in the air. "I want to go on record, again, saying I was not in favor of bringing you back here." He put his hand down. "This is all on Provenza."

"I understand," she said to Michael before letting her gaze travel back to the photos for a moment. "Selena might be helpful as well."

"Of course," Provenza agreed.

Selena took a step toward Provenza. "I also appreciate your allowing us to help, Detective."

Jenessa eyed the scatter of photos again, then gave Selena a meaningful stare, hoping her cousin would pick up on the hint. Selena did, and asked if George would get her a cup of coffee. Of course, he fell all over himself to do it. So, after George left the room, Selena sidled up to Michael and began to talk to him.

Jenessa took advantage of the opportunity to scan over several crime scene photos, grateful for Selena's distraction of him.

A few moments later, Provenza returned with Selena's coffee, which Jenessa knew she didn't truly want. Still, Selena took a significant sip and thanked George for his kindness.

"So, to what do we owe the visit?" Michael asked, always the one to want to get straight to business.

"Listen, guys," Jenessa glanced at both men, but lingered on Provenza, knowing that Michael was no longer under her spell. "You're going to think I'm crazy, I know, but hear me out."

They both remained quiet, but Provenza gestured that she had the floor.

"I have reason to think that maybe, just maybe, Grey Alexander might not be the killer."

There. She had said it out loud.

Michael stared at her in silence, a slight frown giving away his skepticism, but George shot up from his seat, throwing his arms in the air. "Aren't you the one that demanded we arrest him?"

"Yes, but—"

"Don't worry, Miss Jones," he seemed to calm a bit. "It wasn't on your say-so alone." George paced around to her side of his desk. Then, when he caught her staring at the photos strewn about on top of it, he flipped a few upside down to cover the rest.

"Come on, George," Jenessa moaned. "Just let me have a look at them. There might be something there."

He folded his arms over his chest and glared at her.

"Listen, young lady, just because I'm an old guy who happens to be retiring soon, doesn't mean you can jerk me around like that. We've got the right guy in jail for this. We found the evidence. You know that."

"But that's the thing, George." Jenessa turned to Michael. "Michael? You guys know how I feel about that egomaniacal ogre. Why would I even suggest he might not be guilty if I didn't have a good reason to doubt?"

Selena stood from where she had been leaning on Provenza's desk. "She has a point, fellas. Think about it. What if he is innocent?"

"Of this crime, that is," Jenessa added.

"Wouldn't you want to make sure you have the right man?" Selena asked.

George gave Michael a look, then returned his focus to Jenessa. "What is your good reason?"

"Logan went to visit his father in jail this morning. Grey insisted Rafe was alive when he left, that he couldn't have been the one to beat him to death."

"But he wasn't beaten to death," Selena said, "was he?"

George looked to Michael again. "No, he wasn't."

"It seems Grey doesn't yet know the real cause of death," Jenessa said. "So…can I see the photos?"

Michael laced his hands behind his head and leaned back in his chair. "George?"

Provenza muttered and scratched at his grey hair. "Good grief, woman, you infuriate me sometimes. I can't wait to retire." He flopped down into his chair. "Fine. Look at the darn photos. But no taking pictures of them."

She held back her victory smile and nodded.

"And no reporting on any of this, you hear?"

"I hear you, George." Jenessa shot Selena a private grin.

He threw up his hands in dismissal and Jenessa began to dig through the photos, studying the details of the crime scene.

"Oh my gosh! This one." She slid out a photo of the dead body, laying on the sofa. "Here." She pointed at the man. "Rafe's topaz necklace with the thin leather strap." She faced the picture to George. "It's missing from his neck."

"What?" George's brows wrinkled as he said it.

"He was wearing it when I last spoke with him."

"And?" George questioned the significance of that.

"And, he had told me that it contained a secret worth killing over."

Michael stood up and crossed to the desk to have a look. "And you are just mentioning this to us now, why?"

"Because it never crossed my mind until now."

"What could be in a topaz stone that is worth killing a man over?" Michael asked. "How big was it?"

"Well, not in it, more likely behind it," Jenessa replied. "It was about an inch and a half, I'd say. Maybe two. And I remember it had a metal backing that it sat on."

"Still, what could it have been?" Michael asked again.

"I don't know," Jenessa shook her head a little, "but if we find that necklace, I think we find our killer."

She looked to Selena to back her up, but her cousin seemed lost in her own thoughts.

"Do you have it in with Rafe's possessions?"

George shook his head. "I don't recall seeing anything even remotely close to a topaz necklace."

She turned back to Michael. "What about in the search of the Alexander estate?"

"No. Nothing. But," he paused, "the team was focused on the insulin connection. We didn't know to look for jewelry."

"And what about the search of the gatehouse?" Jenessa pressed.

"Don't think so, but we can pull the evidence and check it again. We weren't looking for anything like that before."

Jenessa was certain she was onto something. What—or rather, who—she wasn't sure, but it felt like the right track. Why would Rafe mention the topaz necklace to her if it didn't have meaning or connection? Perhaps he had a sense that his time was almost up, and he wanted someone to be able to find his killer.

"I hope you know I'm not trying to free Grey Alexander, but I do want to get to the truth," Jenessa said.

She didn't care about Grey lingering in jail while this investigation went on, but she did not want this scandalous mystery hanging over her and Logan's wedding day...which now was only two days away.

CHAPTER 37

STANDING OUTSIDE OF THE HIDDEN VALLEY
Police Department with her cousin Selena, Jenessa said,
"That went better than I expected."

"Yes, it did," Selena agreed with a graceful nod. "It
looks like you might have found your smoking gun, so
to speak."

The two had taken no more than a few steps back
toward Main Street when Selena came to a sudden and
complete stop. "Oh no."

"What? What is it?"

"I think I forgot my sunglasses back there," Selena
said, rummaging in her purse. "You go on without me.
I'm just going to pop inside and grab them."

"Oh. Okay," Jenessa agreed. "But I can wait for
you."

"No, no. You've given me enough of your afternoon. Besides, you probably want to find that handsome fiancé of yours and tell him about the news."

That was true. Jenessa did want to let Logan know about the latest development in the case. Hopefully George and Michael would be okay with that.

"All right, then."

Selena tucked her handbag under her arm. "I'll see you later? At Aunt Renee's?"

Not sure she would make it to her aunt's place later, Jenessa agreed anyway, just in case.

Selena gave her a quick one-arm hug, then went back inside the station. Jenessa could see her talking to the receptionist, through the glass door, so she took off down the street at a brisk clip.

Jenessa slowed her gait to check the time on her cell phone. It was just after three. Logan was probably still in his meeting with the board, so she headed to the newspaper to work on her articles…and maybe mention the latest to Charles to see if he might put her back on the story.

~*~

Jenessa's trip to the office got derailed before she'd even reached the front doors. A worrisome thought struck her on her walk back. If she told Charles about the new lead, he might just send that new reporter out on the story. Rather than let him do that, she would go see Grey herself and figure this thing out.

So, when she reached the Hidden Valley Herald, instead of going inside, she went to her car, hopped into it and sped off. As she turned the corner, almost to the jail, her phone rang. It was Ramey. She hit the Bluetooth button on her dash to answer.

"Hey, Ramey. What's going on?"

"You and Selena shot out of here so fast, I couldn't help but think something was up."

How much could she share? There were so many questions churning in her mind, things that still didn't add up.

"I'm on my way to visit Grey in jail."

"Why?" Ramey practically gasped, her tone sounding incredulous. "Did something new turn up?"

"I can't say right now."

"Even if I swear an oath to keep it to myself?" Ramey pressed.

"You can't even tell Charles."

"I swear, Jenessa, I swear. Tell me already."

"Okay, as long as you swear."

"Yes, I swear. Cross my heart, hope to die," Ramey uttered, with impatience.

"Well, remember I told you Grey was trying to blackmail me into calling off the wedding?"

"Yes, that dirty—"

"What if Rafe had also been blackmailing Grey? Or someone else?"

"Blackmailing? Oh no."

Jenessa went on. "Or was this all about a secret Rafe shared with me?"

"What secret?" Ramey questioned.

The topaz necklace. But sharing that might put Ramey in danger.

311

"Something Rafe showed me the day before his body was found," Jenessa said. "He seemed spooked."

"Showed you? I don't get it," Ramey confessed.

Jenessa pulled her sportscar into a parking space in front of the jail. "I've got to go, Ramey. I'll explain more later, when I can."

She pushed the Bluetooth button to hang up and went inside. After she had talked and cajoled them into letting her in to see Grey—her name hadn't been on the list, but she'd managed to use her press badge—she went through the drill, emptying her pockets and such, having left her purse in the car, knowing they would make her dump it in the bin for inspection.

An enormous—the word burly would be an understatement—guard led her to the visiting area. Shortly after, Grey Alexander came scowling into the room.

"What are you doing here?" he spat. "Come to gloat?"

Appearing as though he wasn't going to sit down, the guard *nudged* him down onto the chair.

Grey tightened his lips in an angry visage, but wisely kept his objection to himself.

"Look," Jenessa started, "I don't blame you for being mad. Let's face it, there is no love lost between us. But I do love your son, contrary to what you might believe. And because of that, I am here to help."

"Help?" he snarled. "I don't want your help. You're just trying to convince me to let this whole wedding issue go. You'll never get my blessing if that's what you're after, Miss Jones. Never."

This man was infuriating! Here she was ready to help get him out of prison, and he didn't even have the good sense to shut up and hear her out. Maybe she should tell him just that—or simply get up and leave. She didn't owe him anything.

The only thing stopping her was her love for Logan. So, Jenessa bit her tongue, again—it seemed she was always doing that with Grey Alexander. Still, if he didn't want her help...

"Listen, don't flatter yourself. I'm not here for you. Helping you is just an unfortunate side effect of helping Logan. He feels that you may be telling the truth—and let me emphasize the word *may*—and I agreed to help him find out. That's all."

Plus, she needed to find out if he really did commit the murder or if someone else did. She wasn't investigating this case for Grey's sake. Maybe not even for Logan's. Not really. She needed to uncover the truth to put her own mind at rest.

He crossed his arms and slumped back in the chair. "Do whatever you want, Miss Jones. I can't stop you. But I won't need anyone's help, especially not yours. My attorney is on his way down here. After my hearing in a couple of hours, he will bail me out. Then I'll hire his firm's investigators to get to the bottom of this."

Grey stood up, signaling the visit was over.

"One more thing before I go," Jenessa said. "For Logan."

Grey sat back down, crossing his arms again, his expression revealing his annoyance.

"Before I leave, Logan was wondering how you managed to get out of prison early."

"My son was wondering, huh?" He appeared to be thinking it over for a minute, then opened his mouth to speak. "Since it is for my son's peace of mind, and since you asked so nicely, I'll tell you. Plus, maybe it'll teach you never to underestimate me again."

Grey's words were pleasant enough, but his delivery was laden with sarcasm. "My cell mate turned out to be my ticket out of that place, though he didn't know it."

His expression turned smug.

"How so?" she asked.

He huffed a laugh and appeared proud to have gotten the upper hand. "Fine, Miss Jones, I'll tell you, but this goes no further than you, me, and Logan."

She nodded her agreement.

He glanced around before leaning in. "This guy had cleverly gotten someone to sneak a cell phone in to him."

His voice lowered. "In the middle of the night, when he thought I was asleep, he made phone calls. Even though he kept his voice down, I have excellent hearing. I overheard him on several occasions giving information and ordering things to be done to some very important people."

"To government officials?" Jenessa asked in little more than a whisper.

He shrugged and relaxed back in his chair.

"Like what?" she asked. "Hits?"

"I can't say," he shot forward, "but I got my attorney to make a deal for me."

He puffed out his chest proudly, as though he had come up with a revolutionary idea. "I got early release in return for giving the DA information on this guy and his little *business transactions*."

"Your cell mate must have been someone important."

Grey shook his head no. "No one I've ever heard of."

"But still…"

"He certainly didn't present himself as some sort of crime kingpin. The guy was kind of a weaselly little schmuck, if you ask me. Just a nothing of a man. And his name was Rudy. Ha! What kind of a name is that for a crime lord?"

Rudy? Now he had Jenessa's full interest. "Rudy what?"

"What difference does it make?"

"Rudy what?" she repeated.

"Peters." Grey glared at her. "Why, you think you know him or something?"

Jenessa shook her head no, but the truth was she might. How many men with that name could there be? Probably at least a few. Jenessa let her imagination relax and refocused on the man sitting in front of her. "Won't you have to testify?"

"That's all you're getting out of me." And with that, Grey stood to leave.

CHAPTER 38

SO JENESSA WAS BACK TO PONDERING...

Grey had said the name Rudy Peters. Had she heard him correctly? Evangeline's husband was named Rudy Peters. But, no. No, that couldn't be. Rudy was one of the most mild-mannered men Jenessa had ever met.

Still, Evangeline had been evasive about whether or not he would be coming to the wedding with her. She hadn't elaborated as to why when Jenessa had asked. Of course, there was the chance he just had to work or something. And, really, the odds of Grey's Rudy Peters being Evangeline's Rudy Peters? Miniscule at best, right?

The guard came to Jenessa's table. "Time to leave, miss."

She stood and followed him to the door, questions bombarding her mind with each step she took.

Wouldn't the guy Grey ratted on know it was him? There would have to be a trial for the new crimes at some point, even if the guy was already in prison, and then Grey would have to be put into witness protection. Wouldn't he?

The guard opened the door for her.

She tossed out an absent-minded "Thank you," and kept going, leaving the jail.

Maybe Grey was lying. Making up a story to get her off his back. That wouldn't be totally out of character. In fact, it seemed more in character for Grey to be lying than it was for the Rudy Peters she knew to be a high-level crime boss.

Perhaps Rafe had mentioned his friend's name, that he had met Jenessa at Rudy Peter's wedding, and Grey was using it to twist her around. He didn't seem at all afraid of retribution. And wouldn't he be? If he had just ratted out some mafia guy to save his own hide, wouldn't that come with a certain level of fear?

Or was Grey Alexander just that cocky and arrogant, that he believed he was untouchable? If his cell mate truly did have connections to organized crime, then, in prison or not, Grey might be in a whole mess of trouble once this guy found out who sold him out. And that wouldn't be tough to do. How coincidental was it that Grey was released, all of a sudden, without serving out his entire sentence?

Jenessa reached her car, unlocked it, and climbed in—the questions and possible scenarios still coming at her with rapid-fire speed.

The warden could make it known Grey was simply being transferred to another facility, in order to protect him, maybe even at the DA's request.

Grey's story seemed too unbelievable, though, on many levels. And his mentioning the name Rudy Peters? It was possible there was more than one man by that name in all of California, assuming Grey was telling the truth. She would check the internet when she got home.

But what if it *was* Evangeline's Rudy?

Did Ev know? Of course, she would know he was in prison, assuming it was her Rudy, and she would know what he was arrested for. There would have been a trial. If it were a big deal, wouldn't Jenessa have heard about it?

Maybe he had just been arrested on something like drunk driving, assault, drunk and disorderly, or embezzlement? That could easily have slipped under Jenessa's radar. Grey hadn't said what had landed this particular Rudy in prison with him. It had to have been a minor crime, otherwise the two wouldn't be in the same low security level of lockup.

She wouldn't put it past Grey to be lying to her. But then again…

All Jenessa knew was she needed to find Logan. Now.

~*~

"Logan, I'm glad you could get away." Jenessa smiled as she held the door open wide.

"Anything for my girl." He stepped through her front door and kicked off his shoes in the entry. "I brought Chinese takeout. I know it's early for dinner but since I didn't have lunch…"

"No, it's perfect." Jenessa gave him a hug and a quick kiss. "I didn't eat much either and I'm starving."

Logan took the bag to the living room as Jenessa dashed to the kitchen to grab forks and plates.

When she returned, Logan had made himself comfortable on the sofa. "Is it okay if we eat in here? I've had enough of hard-backed chairs for one day."

"Sounds great." She took a seat beside him and handed him a plate and fork.

They both took a moment to dish some food onto their plates and take a bite or two before resuming their conversation.

"Hard day?" Jenessa asked.

Logan sighed and swallowed down the mouthful of moo shu pork. *Was it that obvious?*

He had had a stressful day, but he didn't want to burden her with the gory details of his board meeting. "Yeah, a lot to work through with the board, but I'd rather hear about your day."

He was hoping she had tracked down some more info on his father's case, because he needed something positive to latch onto right then.

"My day?" Her lovely green eyes drifted upward. "Where do I even start?" She took a bite of food, as if she needed a moment to get her thoughts together. "It was super busy. First, Selena and I went to see Detective Provenza and Michael. As you might imagine, they were resistant when I suggested that it might not have been your father that killed Rafe after all."

That was to be expected.

"But," Jenessa stuck a piece of ginger beef into her mouth and chewed for a moment, "I did manage to convince them to let me look at the crime scene photos."

"They actually allowed you see them? How'd you manage that?"

"I have my ways." She flashed a mischievous smile at him. "I noticed something—something important." She stopped to take a drink of the soda she had brought with her from the kitchen. "I can't tell you what it was, but it was enough to pique Provenza's interest in my theory."

"Something important?" Now his interest was aroused too. "Why can't you tell me?"

"Provenza made me promise. It's a police thing. That's the only way he'd let me look at the pictures."

He nodded his understanding. "Go on."

"Well, next I went to—now don't get mad at me—I went to the jail."

She did what? "To see my father?" Logan couldn't believe Jenessa would do that. That had to be an incredibly difficult thing for her. If this wasn't proof of her love for him, Logan didn't know what was.

"Yes. I went to see your father. He was obstinate and sarcastic, as you might imagine, but he listened to me, and guess what?"

Had his father gotten angry at her? And then that meathead of a guard would have had to assert his authority over him? That was Logan's guess. "What?" Better to just let her tell him.

Jenessa continued, filling him in on how his father had managed to get released early from prison, or at least how he claimed it happened. Logan hadn't figured it was due to good behavior, but he hadn't come up with anything close to that bizarre story either. His father claimed he'd been cell mates with some mafia boss? In a minimum-security prison? Too crazy for Logan to comprehend.

"And don't freak out about what I'm going to say next, because I doubt it's true, but…"

But what?

He steadied himself.

"But…your father's ex-cell mate has the same name as my bridesmaid's husband. I'm sure it's just a coincidence." Jenessa filled her mouth with food again, and Logan chewed on this new bit of information she'd just dished up. "Or it's a lie."

She swallowed and took a drink. "I checked the internet. There are over twenty-five Rudy Peters on Facebook alone."

"So you think he made it up?"

"Probably threw that particular name in purely to upset me."

"How would my father know that name?"

"From conversations with Rafe, I'm assuming. It was at Rudy Peters' wedding that we met."

"Yeah, he easily could be lying, babe." Logan's father was a master manipulator. "Don't let him get to you."

"Lying or not, I have a plan." Jenessa swallowed. "Another one of my cousins—a third cousin really, or my second cousin once removed…I never can figure this stuff out. She's the daughter of one of my mother's cousins. Anyway, she works for the FBI and I—"

"You have a cousin at the FBI?"

"Distant cousin," she pointed out again. "But yeah."

"What's her name?"

"Isabel Martinez."

"I've never heard you talk about her."

"I may never have. We're not as close as we were growing up, as you can imagine, but I did invite her and her husband to the wedding."

Logan looked impressed. "Then I'll get to meet this FBI agent?"

"I got her RSVP, so yeah." She nodded. "I seem to remember she had mentioned once that she has ties to other government agencies too—she used to work in DC—so I'm hoping she can help. I was planning to call her after you leave this evening. If this story your dad told is true, she has to be able to dig something up on his old cell mate. And, fingers crossed, it is not the same Rudy Peters that's married to one of my bridesmaids."

~*~

Logan left shortly after dinner, saying he had to figure out some stuff to do with work, so, Jenessa seized the opportunity to call her cousin Isabel. She rifled through the junk drawer in the kitchen and dug out the old address book that had been her mother's. Jenessa flipped through it until she came to the name Isabel Martinez, showing her husband Alex as well.

Seeing her mother's handwriting made Jenessa's heart briefly twist with sadness, but she pushed it down. No time for that right now. She had a crime to solve.

She took her phone to the couch and dialed the number.

"Hello," a woman answered, with a slight Latin accent.

"Hi, Isabel. This is Jenessa."

"Oh, hi, Jenessa. It's nice to hear from you. How are the wedding plans coming?"

"We've got almost everything buttoned up. Only two more days."

"I have your invitation stuck up on my refrigerator, and I was thinking about your family today."

"That's sweet."

"It must be so sad that your mom and dad won't be there to enjoy your wedding. Lydia was more like an aunt to me than a cousin. I'm sure she would have loved helping to plan it with you."

"Yes, I'm sure she would have." Jenessa took a deep breath to keep her emotions in check. "Anyway, Isabel, the reason I'm calling is…"

CHAPTER 39

JENESSA WENT ON TO EXPLAIN everything she knew to Isabel. Her cousin had kept quiet all through Jenessa's discourse.

"Rafe Santiago, you say?"

"Yes. Why? You've heard of him?"

"I'm not at liberty to say."

"Isabel, I'm not just the press. I'm family. And I'm deeply involved in this case—up to my eyeballs."

"Your eyeballs, huh?" It sounded as if Isabel had stifled a laugh. "As long as I have your solemn word that anything I tell you will be kept in strictest confidence."

"Absolutely. I never reveal my sources," Jenessa assured her.

"Do you have any reason to think your phone is not secure?"

What? "No," Jenessa responded emphatically. "Why?"

Isabel took a long pause to consider it before she responded. "Precautions. We can't be too careful. But maybe you could be of value in this case."

"I can. Trust me."

Isabel paused again. "You're probably not going to believe this, but Rafe Santiago has been on the FBI's radar in a joint effort with the CIA."

"He was?" Why would Rafe have been on their so-called radar? Was he with the CIA? Is that what he meant when he said he didn't work for the news agency?

"Listen, Jenessa, we should talk."

"Okay. Go ahead."

"No, on second thought, I don't want to say anything else over the phone. However, I will be in town soon and we can talk in person."

"When, tomorrow?"

"Late tonight, actually."

"Tonight? Is Alex coming too?" Jenessa had never met Isabel's husband, and she was hoping to see him at the wedding.

"No, he's the lead attorney on a big case and he can't get away. But I'm sitting at the airport right now waiting for my flight to Sacramento, then I'll drive down from there. We can talk in the morning."

Jenessa's mind was swimming. This whole thing was growing bigger by the moment.

First, Grey Alexander brings Rafe to town to try to sabotage her wedding to Logan, then she meets with Rafe and he tells her all this cryptic stuff about his past, and now? Now she finds out Rafe was on the FBI's radar and he may have been in the CIA? What would happen next? Jenessa was almost afraid to find out.

Almost.

Instead, her reporter's juices began flowing full force, and she couldn't wait to find out more.

"But what about—"

"Not now, Jenessa. It's better not to continue discussing it over the phone."

Jenessa understood. Perhaps, hopefully, Isabel would share more in person.

"Like I said, I'm getting in late tonight, and then I will check into my hotel. Let's make plans to meet for breakfast."

"We could meet at The Sweet Spot. It's the best café in town. It's the one my mother opened with my best friend, Ramey St. John. Now my sister Sara helps her run it."

"That sounds good, but…I think it would be better to meet somewhere we can speak privately. What about your house?"

~*~

Jenessa had barely slept, anticipating her cousin Isabel's arrival.

Promptly at seven thirty in the morning, Isabel Martinez arrived on her doorstep. After the cursory greetings and a small bit of chitchat, Jenessa showed her to the living room.

"Can I get you a cup of coffee?"

"Yes, that would be great," Isabel replied, lifting a white paper bag. "I brought muffins and pastries from that café you mentioned. I see what you meant. Everything looked delicious. And that redhead, the one with all the smiles, she's the friend that you mentioned, right?"

Jenessa nodded, glad Isabel saw Ramey as she did.

Isabel followed Jenessa through the house, back to the kitchen at the rear, looking out each window, and glancing around almost suspiciously.

"Is something wrong?" Jenessa asked.

"The children you told me about, are they here?"

"No, they're still living with Logan at his condo. Besides, they've been at camp this week. We'll be picking them up later today."

"And Logan?"

"He didn't stay here last night. I'm sure he's at work."

Isabel looked around again. "So, no one will interrupt us? Or overhear?"

"No, we're alone. Why all the secrecy?" This whole thing was starting to feel surreal. Something in Jenessa's gut told her this thing was bigger than Grey Alexander. Bigger than Rafe Santiago, too.

Despite Jenessa's reassurances, Isabel still seemed uncertain of the house's security.

"Do you have takeout cups for this coffee?"

"I do. But why?"

"You know what, let's take a drive. I'll bring the muffins, you can bring the coffee. Show me where my cousin Lydia was buried."

~*~

Jenessa agreed to show Isabel her mother's gravesite. Did Isabel really care to see where her mother was buried? Or did she think the cemetery would be a place that had no chance of being bugged? She was starting to think the latter was true.

They climbed into Jenessa's car, eating the muffins and drinking their coffees as they drove.

It had been less than a week ago when Jenessa had come to the cemetery to talk to her mother, when she had been confronted by Grey Alexander. That was the moment this entire bizarre nightmare had begun. But Jenessa didn't bring that up. Not yet. First, she wanted to hear what Isabel had to say.

"Listen, Jenessa, I'm going to go out on a limb here and tell you some things I normally wouldn't, because we need your help. But like I said on the phone last night, what I am about to say cannot be repeated...to anyone. Do you understand?"

Jenessa got chills. Why all the secrecy? Still, she promised. "I won't say a word. You can trust me."

"You're a reporter, so I figured you would understand."

"Sure, trust is everything when trying to get a source to open up."

"Exactly right." Isabel was emphatic about that.

As they drove, Isabel shared some very shocking things. She confirmed that Rafe worked for the CIA, that he had reported that he'd discovered some Americans that were helping the Russians, but he never identified them. He spent a few years in Europe and had spent some time in Spain.

"Spain?" Jenessa asked, thinking of Selena.

"Yes. Our records indicate he knew our cousin Selena, and the CIA has kept track of her movements and activities."

"I know there are political dissidents in Spain, but you said Russians."

"Some factions within Spain appear to be connected to Russia, yes."

"Are you saying you think she's one of them?"

This was almost more than even Jenessa's imagination could contain. She was both scared and exhilarated, being a part of this far-reaching investigation.

"An impressionable young woman, just out of college—Selena could have been turned," Isabel said.

"Turned?"

Isabel nodded. "Into an asset."

"And you think Rafe was going to expose her…and the others?"

"He said he had some critical intel, but then he disappeared. Our case went cold for a while."

"Disappeared? He told me he was captured and spent a few years in an Afghan prison."

"He told you about that?"

"Yes."

"He must have trusted you. You never said how you knew him."

Jenessa slowed the car to enter the cemetery parking lot. "We were sort of married."

"What?" Isabel's eye's popped wide and her mouth hung open for a moment, quickly getting control again. "What do you mean, sort of married? How did I not know about that?"

She shrugged. "It didn't amount to much. It was one intoxicated night I spent with him in Las Vegas, and...well, we woke up married."

"When did this happen?"

"Eight years ago." Jenessa pulled into a parking space and shut the engine off. "It was only one night and then he was gone, until this week."

Isabel opened a notebook and wrote something down in it. "That must have been right before he went to Spain and connected with Selena."

"Connected? In what way?"

"You promise this is just between us, right?"

Jenessa nodded. "Of course."

"Okay. Rafe had some information that she might have been involved in something, so he got close to her."

"That's strange."

"How so?"

"Selena did mention to me that she had met him, but said he wasn't her type, that he was too rough around the edges."

Isabel flipped the pages in her notebook. "That's not what the reports say. He got close to her for several months."

"Close? How close?"

"I can't say, Jenessa. I've already said too much. But I can tell you this, she was furious when he disappeared."

Then Jenessa remembered something Selena had said to her. "She told me he took something from her."

"What was it?"

Jenessa shook her head. "She didn't say."

Was it something that proved she was involved in some bad stuff? Did she truly know her cousin Selena at all?

"Did you want to get out and go see where my mother is buried?"

Isabel looked out the window and scanned the landscape. "Maybe later. Honestly, I only wanted to get you out of the house, so we could talk. I just had an uneasy feeling there. It felt too open, too exposed."

That was pretty much what Jenessa had assumed.

"I took a taxi to your place this morning," Isabel said. "I used a rental car to drive here from the airport, but honestly, I don't trust rentals that much." She shrugged. "Job hazard. Can you drop me at the Hidden Valley PD? I have a meeting with," she glanced at her notes, "a Detective Michael Baxter and Detective George Provenza. I need to learn more about this murder case."

"I can tell you that I've already seen the crime scene photos, heard about the ME's report, and talked to all the potential suspects," Jenessa said. "And I was there when they arrested Grey Alexander."

What else would Michael and George tell Isabel? Jenessa was dying to know, but would Isabel share it with her?

"You're pretty thorough, Cousin."

"Thanks." Jenessa felt a little swell of pride.

"I may ask you about that later," Isabel said, "but right now I need to interview the local police, get their take on things."

~*~

With nothing more she could do but wait to reconnect with Isabel, Jenessa went to the newspaper to try to work on her Garden Club story, even though Charles had told her to hand the story to the new guy and take the rest of the week off. She couldn't do that. She needed something to occupy her time between conducting interviews and finding clues, knowing the wedding details were being covered.

She was struggling, though, trying to hold her attention on the trivial Garden Club story and her interview with Elizabeth Alexander before her arrest. Jenessa's mind kept drifting back to this salacious murder mystery unfolding right here in her small hometown.

It was a good thing Aunt Renee was handling all the wedding planning, making it easier for Jenessa to concentrate on the Santiago case. How could she possibly manage the wedding details amidst all this chaos?

Jenessa forced herself to focus and wrap up her story on the Garden Club flower show. She had just emailed it off to Charles when her cell phone beeped a text notification. It was Isabel, and she wanted to get together for lunch.

With her and Selena.

Jenessa agreed and picked up her things to head over to the hotel restaurant where Isabel had suggested they meet.

When she arrived, Isabel and Selena were already seated at a corner booth. They seemed like strangers rather than family, eying each other with suspicion, but not saying much. Did Selena know her every move was being tracked? By the CIA, the FBI, the NSA, or whomever it was that was watching her?

Jenessa approached the table. "Sorry I'm late."

"No, we were early," Isabel said. "Have a seat."

"All right." Jenessa slid into the booth. Her gaze bounced between Isabel and Selena, and suddenly her throat felt terribly dry. She took a sip of the ice water that had already been poured for her.

Selena turned to Jenessa. "So, how is our story on Rafe's murder coming?"

"I'm still gathering facts." Jenessa didn't know how much she should say now that she knew Selena might be working for "the other guys".

"You seem a little sad that he's gone," Isabel said to Selena. "Jenessa tells me you knew him in Spain?"

CHAPTER 40

"RAFE? SURE, I AM A LITTLE SAD he's dead." Melancholy appeared to fill Selena's brown eyes. "What a waste of a promising life."

Jenessa couldn't disagree with that.

Selena took a sip from her coffee cup, turning her attention to Jenessa. "I wrote an outline of the piece on him for my news manager. He said I could do the story if and when I have more information."

"That's good." Jenessa gave a nod.

Or had Selena had been gathering facts with Jenessa purely for her own needs...diabolical needs if she in fact was a spy for the Russians?

"So, Selena," Isabel said, drawing her attention back, "you said you didn't know Rafe very well?"

Selena set her cup down. "Yes, that's right."

Jenessa shot a quick peek at Isabel and a light kick under the table.

Isabel frowned at her.

"But you also said he took something from you," Jenessa went on. "Money? Jewelry?" *A topaz necklace, perhaps? Confidential information?*

Selena's gaze dropped to her lap. "Fine, if you must know, Jenessa. I don't like talking about it, but since you won't let it drop," she lifted her eyes to meet Jenessa's, "I will tell you. The thing Rafe Santiago took from me was my heart. He stole it, broke it, stomped on it, then disappeared."

Isabel piped in now. "So, you're saying you were in love with this Rafe fellow, and he broke your heart? That's what he took?"

"I don't like to admit it, Isabel, but yes." Selena closed her eyes for a moment. When she opened them, they were glistening. "I really thought he loved me, but then he just up and disappeared, and I never saw him again."

"And that's all he took?" Isabel questioned.

"Yes." Selena's brows knit together. "Why? What did you think?"

Selena certainly didn't seem like an international spy. On the other hand...

"It's just that," Isabel appeared to want to push it, "isn't it a bit coincidental that Rafe was here in Hidden Valley at the same time you are here? I mean, after all those years of not seeing each other."

"Yes, coincidental. That's a good word for it."

But was it the right word for it?

Isabel's face grew more serious. "So, you never went to the gatehouse to confront him? Find out why he left without a word?"

Selena turned on Isabel. "Just what are you implying? Are you trying to say you think I was involved in his death somehow?"

Jenessa put her hand on Selena's. "I'm sure Isabel isn't saying that at all."

But that was a bold-faced lie, it was exactly what Isabel was doing.

The dossier on Selena was evidence she and Rafe had been more involved than Selena was willing to admit. Not to mention the fact that it was Selena who had told Jenessa about the Spanish politician being murdered by someone sticking a needle full of slow-acting insulin between his toes. Should Jenessa bring that up in front of Isabel?

Jenessa didn't want to second guess her, but Isabel did seem ready to hit Selena with both barrels—and with good reason.

Evidence was beginning to point at Selena, but what was the honest truth?

After their contentious lunch with Selena, Jenessa and Isabel drove a short distance to Crane Park, at the end of Main Street. Isabel continued to be dead set against talking anywhere that she didn't feel was adequately secure. She wasn't quite ready to trust the situation, or maybe the town...

But, she was finally going to share with Jenessa what she learned when she was with Michael and George earlier, so Jenessa was happy to oblige her and talk in the park. Maybe Isabel was right to be cautious.

After all, Jenessa hadn't any clue how to determine if her phone had been tapped or her home bugged.

The afternoon temperature was pleasant at any rate, a good day to sit in the nearly empty park and chat with her cousin. A family with small children were playing on the swings. They got out of Jenessa's Mercedes and strolled over to a group of vacant picnic tables.

"I meant to say something earlier, Jenessa. That's a pretty sweet car you've got there."

Jenessa glanced back at the sportscar, sparkling a deep blue-gray in the midday sun.

"A Roadster?"

"Yeah," Jenessa replied softly, her gaze still on the car as emotions rose in her. "It was my dad's. I got it when…when he passed away."

"Hey, I'm sorry for bringing it up. First, I suggest visiting your mother's grave, and now the car thing. Sometimes my timing sucks."

Jenessa shrugged and slid her attention back to Isabel. "Don't worry about it. Why don't we sit?"

The pair sat across from each other, rather than side by side. Isabel said she wanted to be able to have eyes on the entire park around them, and it would be better if they could both take in a large area. She also wouldn't let them sit too near the tree line at the table that Jenessa often shared with Logan when they would meet for lunch.

"Before we talk," Isabel reached into her handbag and pulled out a small black device that looked a little like a fancy remote control, "I need to sweep you, your purse, and your cell phone, specifically."

Jenessa was surprised, but also not.

Isabel was a pro, so she must know what she was doing. Jenessa stood and lifted her arms out to the sides, the way she had seen people do on TV. Isabel swept the device around Jenessa, then worked on her purse and cell phone.

"All clear," she said, taking a seat again on the bench. She put the device back in her bag. "It's not foolproof, of course. The bug or tracking device would need to be transmitting for me to get a signal, but at least it helps."

She smiled as Jenessa took her seat again across the table.

"It was in my suitcase," Isabel said.

"What was?"

"The sweeping device."

"Oh."

"I figured you might be wondering why I didn't use it before when we met."

Jenessa had wondered that. "You really are good at reading people, Isabel."

"That's why they pay me the big bucks." Isabel chuckled. "So, what's on your mind, Jenessa?"

"I'm anxious to know," Jenessa began, "did the detectives have any more information on the topaz necklace?"

"No, nothing about the necklace yet," Isabel said.

"What could have been hidden behind the stone that was worth killing for?"

"Something that small, I'm thinking it had to be a microchip with some kind of information. Provenza said Rafe wasn't wearing it when they found him. Lucky you noticed that in the crime scene photos."

"Lucky I got to see them at all. Did the detectives tell you they didn't want to let me see the photos?"

"No, but I'm not surprised. So, you talked them into it?"

"Kind of, after Provenza saw me glancing at them. Selena helped by keeping the men distracted."

Isabel gave a little laugh. "I can imagine. Sounds like Selena. And your keen eye for details certainly came in handy."

Jenessa gave a little nod. "I'm glad I noticed he wasn't wearing the necklace in the pictures, but I wouldn't have picked up on that detail if Rafe hadn't shown it to me, the day I spoke to him."

"When was that?"

"The day before his body was found," Jenessa said.

"You know, Detective Provenza did mention that when you asked them about the necklace, it was the first they'd heard about it."

"Yeah, I figured that at the time."

"Provenza said they looked in the evidence box, but nothing. Maybe you can give him a sketch of it, so they know exactly what to keep an eye out for."

"Sure, I can do that. That's a good idea."

Isabel scanned the park and Jenessa followed suit. Nothing unusual. Maybe Isabel would be able to relax a little now, since nothing appeared to be out of the ordinary.

"The way Rafe was killed," Jenessa mused, "that person had to be very deliberate and calculating."

"Injecting insulin in a hidden spot. A professional job, for sure."

"I really hate telling you this, but it was Selena who told me she had seen that happen before, when a politician in Spain was assassinated that way."

"I'll have to make a note of that. Selena is family, but if it turns out she's the one…"

"I don't even want to think she could do something like that."

"But it's our job to find the truth," Isabel said, "no matter what."

Jenessa traced her fingertip over some random initials that had been carved into the wooden top of the picnic table, thinking. "Whoever killed him, it had to be for the necklace, don't you think?"

"It certainly looks that way. The detectives are sticking by their collar though. They think this Grey Alexander is their man."

Even after Jenessa told them Grey thought Rafe was beaten to death? Maybe they didn't believe him.

"But you don't?" Jenessa asked.

"No. I am leaning toward agreeing with you. It had to be someone from Rafe's past."

"His past. Now that could involve a lot of people from anywhere in the world, if he was working for someone like the CIA. But who?"

Isabel leaned forward. "Now that's the million-dollar question, isn't it?"

Jenessa met her cousin's eyes. "We find that necklace and we find the killer."

"That may be true, but don't be surprised if the chip has already been removed and passed along. Things move quickly in the spook world."

Hearing Isabel talk that way got Jenessa's blood pumping.

"Being an FBI agent must be an exciting life—even more exciting than being an investigative reporter. Chasing bad guys rather than stories."

Maybe, now that they had reconnected, Jenessa might plan a trip to Paradise Valley someday to visit her dear second cousin once removed...or whatever Isabel technically was to her. But first, Jenessa had to get through this investigation and marry her high school sweetheart.

"Well, let's hope we find that necklace," Isabel said, "with the chip, or whatever, still in it."

"The idea that dangerous spies might be lurking in Hidden Valley gives me chills."

"In a good way, right?" Isabel smiled.

Jenessa pinched her fingers almost together. "A little bit." She grinned back.

"Yeah. You seem the type," Isabel said. "Being an investigative reporter takes similar *cojones*."

"Yes, solving a murder case is a special kind of rush," Jenessa agreed. "I wonder how Grey Alexander's private eye got hold of Rafe. It's not like he could just Google him."

Isabel did another quick scan of the park. "From what I've been able to piece together, the man contacted Rafe's last cover employer, a news agency where we have some assets hidden. The PI apparently left a message for Rafe to contact him, that there was an urgent and lucrative job for him."

Jenessa found herself also gazing around the park, looking for any unexpected movement in the trees. "And

Rafe contacted him? Didn't he have to work through his agency?"

Isabel's eyes darted around. "I've already said more than I should have."

"Please, don't start back peddling."

Their eyes met. "I could get myself in hot water with what I've shared."

"My lips are sealed, Isabel," Jenessa promised in her most solemn voice. "I swear. I never reveal my sources."

"I don't know——" Isabel looked away.

"Rafe was my husband, Isabel. Please." If Jenessa had to play up that angle, so be it.

Isabel turned back to Jenessa and leaned in, closer this time, before answering in little more than a whisper. "You didn't hear this from me, and I warn you to keep it to yourself."

"I will."

"When Rafe was arrested in Afghanistan and put in prison, the agency had to disavow any knowledge of him or his operation. When he got out, he went pretty much rogue in trying to solve his case, find his moles, and expose them. My guess is that Grey Alexander's money was an enticement."

"He did say something about taking Grey's money to finish his job."

Isabel glanced behind her before continuing. "Listen, Jenessa, I need to remind you, we never had this conversation, and I don't want to see any of these details in your story. Do I make myself clear?"

Jenessa offered a blank stare. "What conversation? You were never here."

A small smile bloomed on Isabel's face before she got up from the table.

"Before you go, I'd like to invite you to have dinner with us tonight," Jenessa offered.

"Us? You mean you and Logan?"

"No, I mean all of us. The bridesmaids wanted to throw me a bachelorette party, but with the murder and everything, it never happened, so we're doubling up on the rehearsal dinner."

"That sounds nice, but I have a ton of paperwork to do before going to bed. I'll just order room service at the hotel."

Jenessa stood now too. "That doesn't sound like much fun."

"I'm not here for fun," Isabel looked across the park. "I'm on a case."

"Did you forget this is also my wedding?"

Isabel paused, her eyes flicked to Jenessa's. "I'm embarrassed to admit it, but I did forget, but only for a moment."

"Oh my goodness. What time is it?"

Isabel looked at her watch. "It's still early. Why?"

"Because I completely forgot something too. My other bridesmaid, Evangeline, is arriving today."

"She's your bridesmaid and she's only now arriving?"

"She's also a reporter. She's been busy on a big story in the state capitol. Actually, I never mentioned it, but she is the one that introduced me to Rafe. It was at her and Rudy's wedding, where we met."

"That's how you met Rafe?" Isabel muttered, wearing a puzzled expression.

"What is it?"

"Never mind." Isabel said a light shake of her head. "It was nothing. Listen, I'll be at the wedding tomorrow, if I can. But I do have a lot on my plate today, so no promises."

"But Isabel, it's my wedding."

"I know. I said I'd try. Deal?"

"Deal," Jenessa reluctantly agreed. "Assuming our wedding even happens tomorrow, with all the madness going on in this town."

"Say," Isabel paused, "this Grey Alexander, any relation to your fiancé?"

CHAPTER 41

LOGAN'S GROOMSMEN, friends from college, were due to arrive later that afternoon. He had called them and told them not to come any earlier, with everything that had been happening. They had laughed and said they would have his bachelor party without him then. Logan had no doubt they would keep that promise. All three of them were still single, and they hadn't seemed to notice the passage of time, or that they were grown men now, not frat boys.

But Logan didn't care. Bachelor parties were of no consequence to him anymore. All that mattered to him now was picking his kids up from camp later that day and marrying Jenessa. His friends could check in to their hotel on their own, and he would see them at the rehearsal that evening.

He phoned Jenessa.

"Hey, babe, how's your day going?"

"Crazy," she said. "I've been with my cousin Isabel most of the day. She's ridiculously smart. If anyone can solve this mystery, it's her."

"Can't wait to meet her."

"I invited her to the rehearsal dinner, but she said she's busy with the case all night."

"That's too bad."

"You'll meet her tomorrow. She's supposed to be coming to the wedding, assuming everything works out."

"I can't believe I'm getting married with my father in jail."

"Well, we'd expected him to be in prison before. We had no idea he'd even get out in time, let alone get arrested again."

"Yeah, I know, but—"

"Wait a minute. You mean he's not out on bail already?"

"Nope. I think he slept with one too many judge's wives. They denied his request for bail. Said he was a flight risk."

"Wow. I didn't see that one coming," Jenessa said.

"Me either. I've rarely known my father to not get his way."

"Maybe money doesn't buy near as much as it used to, Logan."

He chuckled. "I suppose not."

Logan's call waiting beeped and he checked the display. It was his mother. "Hey, Jen, that's my mom calling on my other line. I'll see you soon to go pick up the kids."

"Okay, see you soon. I can't wait. I love you."

~*~

Jenessa sat in her home office, at her late father's enormous antique oak desk, making notes in her computer of all she knew of Rafe's murder investigation, still hoping Charles would allow her to write the story. Her cell phone rang on the desk. It was Ramey.

"Hello, Ramey."

"This is your reminder to pick up the kids at five today."

"How could I forget?"

"I just thought, with all you've had to deal with this week and the wedding..."

"I would never forget to pick up my children." *My children.* "That has a nice ring to it."

"What?"

"My children," Jenessa said with a sigh.

"Someday I'll say that too." Ramey sounded a little forlorn. "If Charles ever gets around to asking me to marry him."

"I wish this mystery had been solved before the kids got back from camp," Jenessa said. "I worry about them returning in the midst of a murder investigation, but hopefully things will be quiet in Hidden Valley, if just for a couple more days."

"Don't worry," Ramey said. "I'm sure it will all work out. I've got to get back to work. See you at the community center."

After Ramey hung up, Jenessa reflected on what Logan had said. Grey had been denied bail. She was shocked, especially when they were looking into other suspects.

Or were they? Provenza seemed only too happy to send Grey up the river and be done with it all. But Jenessa was all about the justice. It was more than just chasing down suspects in a case. It was about chasing the right ones. And something inside her—as much as she hated to admit it—didn't quite believe Grey Alexander was the right suspect.

Someone could be framing him. But who? Who knew his history with diabetes and knew about his dealings with Rafe? Mrs. Dobson? Elizabeth?

The list was long. The man had made a lot of enemies, stepped on a lot of people as he climbed the ladder of success.

Was it someone he took advantage of in a business deal, trying to set him up? Or a disgruntled employee just waiting for him to get out of prison to frame him? No. That didn't make any sense. It was more likely it had to do first with Rafe, then with Grey.

Someone probably followed Rafe to town, then saw an opportunity to kill him and throw the blame on someone else. Grey Alexander and his legendary temper might have walked straight into that one.

She needed to talk to Isabel, ask these questions, before they drove her crazy. She dialed her number and Isabel picked up.

"What enemies did he have?" Jenessa started with.

"Jenessa?"

"Yes, sorry. I was just thinking of Rafe and all these questions came flying at me, so I hoped you were available to talk."

"I know I swept your phone earlier, but as I said, it isn't foolproof. Your line might not be secure, Jenessa. Let me ask you a few cursory questions."

"Okay."

"Have you noticed any strange sounds coming from your phone? Like unexplained static, scratching or popping? This can be caused by a capacitive discharge when two conductors are connected."

"No. I don't think so."

"What about the battery life? Unchanged lately?"

"I'm not needing to charge it more frequently, if that's what you mean."

"Okay, so far, so good. Now, the area of your phone where the battery is located, has it been getting extra hot?"

Jenessa didn't think it had. "No. I'm pretty sure it's been normal."

"One more thing. Have you noticed any random activity, like your phone acting up, doing strange things like apps opening on their own? Or indecipherable text messages sent from unknown numbers?"

"No. Nothing like that."

Isabel sighed loudly on the other end of the line. "Fine, Jenessa. It doesn't truly rule it out, but I can see you're not going to let this go, and I don't need you showing up at my hotel room door, so I'm going to answer a few questions. Just a few, and keep it vague, if possible. Got that?"

"Yes, Isabel. Thank you."

"One last thing, in case the room is bugged...go in the bathroom and turn on the shower."

She did as Isabel instructed.

"Okay, now what did you want to ask?" Isabel questioned.

"I remember Ra—uh, my friend…telling me that he didn't work for a news agency after all. He was, you know, what you said. And, in that kind of job, there could be any number of people who wanted him…gone…so how will we ever find out who did it, if that's the case?"

"Slow down. You sound rattled."

"A little." Jenessa paused and took a breath. "If you don't find out who did this, will Grey Alexander rot in prison for it? It's not like the man doesn't deserve prison for any number of horrendous things he's done, but can we let him go to jail for a crime he didn't commit? Even if he's skated on all the ones he has done?"

"Whoa. What's this about Grey Alexander? How did you know—"

"I told you at the park, he's Logan's father."

"Yes, I remember now."

"What did you mean?" Jenessa questioned.

"Nothing. Something that just came up on my radar…I really can't discuss it."

"Okay, I gotcha. But then there's you know who." Jenessa was, of course, referring to their cousin Selena and hoped Isabel picked up on that.

"What about her?" Isabel asked.

"Could she have…taken care of my, um, friend?" Jenessa hoped not, but Selena did say Rafe broke her heart and stole something from her.

"She is a possibility, as much as I hate to admit it," Isabel said.

"She tried to say this person stole her heart, but I got the feeling it was something tangible, like money or jewelry, or a priceless artifact or something."

"Slow down. You're getting yourself all worked up before we know much of anything."

"Could he have stolen a file from her? A microchip? Was that what he could have been hiding behind the topaz?"

"Jenessa. Enough!" Isabel shouted.

That brought Jenessa up short. She was dizzy with questions, and the steam from the shower was starting to frizz her hair.

"Please," Isabel said firmly, "let me do my job. Your job, your only job, for this evening and tomorrow is to be a glowing bride. Enjoy your time and your handsome husband-to-be. I promise you, you will regret it if you squander this special time."

The next thing Jenessa heard was a click.

~*~

"Earth to Jenessa."

She startled and looked up to see Logan standing in the doorway of her home office. She had turned off the shower and returned to her computer a while ago. "Oh, hi, sweetheart."

"Where were you just now?"

"I'm sorry. I was just thinking about the murder case."

"I knocked, but no one answered. The front door was unlocked, so I let myself in."

"Unlocked?" She gathered up her notebooks where she had been scribbling her theories.

"You should really keep the deadbolt secured, at least until the killer is caught."

Assuming the killer is not your father. She thought it but kept it to herself.

Logan sat on the edge of the large desk. "Promise me."

She recalled her phone call with Isabel and all the potential suspects. "Yes, I will." She nodded. "What time is it?"

He peered at his watch, then stood. "It's time to put all this craziness aside for now. Let's go pick up our children."

"Our children," she echoed, raising a smile to him. "I love the sound of that."

He leaned down and planted a brief kiss on her lips. "Grab your purse and let's get there before the buses arrive."

The thought of their kids made Jenessa smile, of she and Logan always being there, for both Grayson and Lily. It filled Jenessa soul with joy.

In less than twenty-four hours from now, God willing, she was going to be their mother. Officially. What could be better than that? She was going to be a wife and a mother in one fell swoop.

"Shall we take your car, Logan?"

"Since all four of us won't fit into your little sportscar, I think that's a wise idea." Logan extended his hand to her. Jenessa took it and stood.

"Maybe I should trade it in for an SUV," she said.

She slung her purse over her shoulder and waltzed out of her office, holding tightly to Logan's hand. Soon, everything was going to be perfect. Then, after the wedding, if Isabel still hadn't solved this case, she would put her reporter's hat back on and help bring a killer to justice. But, for now, she had children to go pick up from camp—her children.

~*~

"How much longer?" Jenessa asked Logan, as they sat in the parking lot of the community center with all the other anxious parents.

Ramey and Charles were two rows back. She could see them in the side rearview mirror. What was Ramey feeling right then? Was she as anxious as Jenessa? Probably, but in a slightly different way. Charlie was a good kid, but he wasn't her biological son, like Grayson was to Jenessa.

She and Logan, Grayson and Lily, they were on the cusp of a fantastic new life together. Hopefully, Ramey, Charles, and Charlie would be soon too.

"Not much longer, I think," Logan said. "Assuming the buses arrive on time."

"That's good," Jenessa said absently. Her gaze was now fixated on a car parked three over from Ramey and Charles. It was Michael's car. Little Jake must have gone to the same camp as Lily.

It was time she got used to this. Their paths would be crossing a lot, living in a small town like Hidden Valley. She was glad that they'd had a chance to talk about things. And she was even happy that he had asked her sister out on a date.

Jenessa wasn't going to pretend it wouldn't be uncomfortable or awkward, seeing them together as a couple, but she could get over it. She had Logan and the kids. Life was good. Or at least it would be once this murder investigation was behind them.

"Over there," Logan said, pointing down the street. "The first bus is coming."

CHAPTER 42

JENESSA SAT UP AND WATCHED as the yellow school bus full of kids rambled into the parking lot of the community center. The sounds and smells of a diesel bus were never so sweet.

The bus slowed to a stop, and a swarm of parents ascended from their vehicles and moved to the line outside the bus door. Jenessa and Logan joined them, making small talk with the other parents, everyone saying how the week had been so quiet without the children home.

Jenessa's stomach bubbled with expectation. Though her week had been anything but quiet, she was every bit as excited to see the kids as every parent there. Soon, she could see Grayson nearing the door from inside the bus. She began to bounce up and down, reaching out to take hold of Logan's hand for comfort.

She looked up at him and they shared a smile. Logan squeezed her hand. He leaned toward her ear and whispered, "That's our boy," and she became almost giddy.

Then, Grayson stepped out. His face went from neutral to smiling as he noticed Logan and Jenessa standing there, waiting for him. He slung his backpack over one shoulder and hurried to them.

Logan let go of Jenessa's hand and pulled Grayson into a big bear hug. Then, he released him and ruffled the boy's cap of blond hair. "How was it, big guy?"

"It was great, Uncle Logan. I had so much fun."

Uncle Logan. The boy had grown up knowing him as uncle, though they were actually second cousins. Grayson always called him Uncle because of their age difference. But she was still just Jenessa, his uncle's girlfriend. And that was okay, for now. Soon they would be able to tell him the truth.

"We're so glad you're back." Jenessa gave Grayson a brief one-armed hug, not wanting to overwhelm him. The two were still getting to know each other. As much as it wrenched at her heart to know the truth but have to keep her distance, she did it. It was all for the greater good.

"The condo was too quiet without you guys," Logan said.

Jenessa looked toward the bus, then the road. "Where's your sister?"

Grayson pointed to another bus pulling in. "I think that one has the younger kids."

"Let's go find her," she said.

~*~

Logan had dropped Jenessa at her place after picking up the kids, so she could get ready for the rehearsal and dinner. Sara, her matron of honor, was at Aunt Renee's with her bridesmaids, Ramey and Selena. Evangeline had arrived at Jenessa's house about twenty minutes earlier.

Jenessa had wanted to spend some time visiting with Evangeline—and maybe asking a few subtle questions about Rafe and also her husband, Rudy—but time was precious, and they hadn't much of it to get ready for the night.

So, the two now stood, side by side, at the bathroom mirror, both doing their makeup and hair.

"I'm so excited for you, Jen."

Jenessa couldn't help but smile. She was excited for herself too. There was a time when she never thought this day would come. Even as recent as this very week, what with all of Grey's threats, and then Rafe's murder. But, she had to admit, it looked like this was happening.

"Thanks, Ev. And thank you for making it here tonight. I know you were busy with work."

Evangeline gave her a side hug. "Never too busy for a friend. Sorry Rudy isn't here. He was not able to get away."

Did the words *not able to get away* translate to *he's in prison*?

"It's okay. I understand," Jenessa said as she pulled the flat iron through her hair. "Sometimes things come up that are beyond our control."

Jenessa fished around in the drawer for her blush brush but couldn't find it. "Where the heck is it?"

"Where's what?" Evangeline asked.

"My big fluffy brush. I can't put my blush on without a brush."

"You can borrow mine," Evangeline said, then began digging around in her makeup bag. Unfortunately, there was not much room left on the bathroom counter, and Evangeline's bag slipped off and crashed to the floor, spilling the contents onto the woven bathmat.

Jenessa glanced down, catching a glimpse of a large topaz on a leather necklace. Was it Rafe's topaz necklace? She bent down to pick it up before Evangeline could scoop everything back up. "What an unusual piece of jewelry, Ev. Is that a topaz?"

Evangeline smiled, but it seemed a little forced, the sparkle not quite reaching her eyes. "Yes, it is." She finished putting everything back in her makeup bag and held out her hand.

"I've never seen one so big," Jenessa said, turning it over in her palm.

Evangeline took the necklace from Jenessa's hand, shoving it in her pocket, rather than placing it back in the cosmetic bag.

Jenessa studied her friend closely. Was Evangeline trying to hide something? Was she involved in Rafe's murder somehow? But she and Rafe were friends. Weren't they? They certainly seemed to be close at Evangeline and Rudy's wedding.

But then there was the whole issue about Grey saying his cell mate's name was Rudy Peters. And now Rudy was "not able to get away" to come to Jenessa's wedding. Things were going in an odd direction, getting stranger by the day, and Jenessa didn't like where they were heading. Not one bit.

"I'd love to have one like that," Jenessa said. "Where did you get it?"

Evangeline walked out of the bathroom, her back to Jenessa, so Jenessa could not read her expression. "Rafe brought them back, one for each of us, Rudy and me."

That was interesting.

"He brought it from Spain? Afghanistan?"

"No, Russia, I think," Ev replied nonchalantly, shrugging her shoulders and moving to her suitcase to get her dress for the rehearsal dinner.

"Well, it's very pretty," Jenessa called through the bathroom doorway, trying to sound casual about it too, but her heart was thumping a mile a minute.

~*~

Evangeline drove Jenessa to the country club for the dinner after the rehearsal at the church. Logan was taking the children with him, while everyone else would meet up there. Jenessa wished that Isabel would have made it to the church for the rehearsal of the ceremony. She urgently needed to talk to her about the topaz necklace she had seen in Evangeline's cosmetic bag, but she wasn't going to risk calling again.

The drive to the church had been tense, to say the least, with Evangeline seeming to be ruminating about something. Jenessa thought she knew what, too, but was careful not to mention it. It would be hard enough for her, standing up to be married, wondering if two of her bridesmaids had had anything to do with murdering Rafe Santiago. Both of them knew him. Both of them may have had motives, though she didn't know what

Evangeline's could be. She did know that Selena had been in love with Rafe—or so she said.

"Take the next left," Jenessa directed.

As far as she knew, Evangeline and Rudy had been good friends with Rafe. But...if it was Evangeline's Rudy that Grey had met in prison—and that was a big *if*—and if what Grey said he overheard was true, it meant that Rudy was a very bad man.

And, surely, his wife would have had to know what he was into—wouldn't she?—which, technically, would make her bad too.

Tension tightened around Jenessa's shoulders and began working its way up her neck. Her breathing grew shallow. This wasn't the way she should be feeling on a night when she was supposed to be preparing for, and joyously celebrating, her upcoming marriage.

"The driveway should be coming up pretty soon," Jenessa said.

If only she could sneak out and visit Isabel at her hotel, but she hadn't had the opportunity, nor the chance to call—though she doubted Isabel would pick up anyway. Ever since they were in Jenessa's bathroom getting ready, Evangeline had seemed to be keeping rather close company with her, limiting her options either way.

It was almost as though Evangeline didn't want to let Jenessa out of her sight. Sure, she played it off as though she was simply being an attentive bridesmaid, but it felt like more than that. Maybe she was just being paranoid. Or it was just Jenessa's imagination working overtime.

She had to admit, she did have a tendency to think up some pretty elaborate stories when she had a crime to solve. Not to mention that she was out of her element when trying to maneuver in the world of spooks, as Isabel put it.

Yes, it was probably nothing—merely her overactive imagination that she needed to rein in. How could she think such awful things about her own cousin and her good friend?

A man in a red vest hustled over from the portico and stopped Evangeline's car at the country club entrance, but Evangeline was scanning around for a parking spot.

"They have valet here, Ev," Jenessa said.

"Yeah, I know. But I prefer to park my own car."

Nothing wrong with that. Evangeline did have suitcases in the back, and she wasn't used to small-town life. Things were riskier in big cities. Plus, Jenessa didn't want to believe her friend could have killed someone, a man she had been friends with.

Finally, they found a parking spot and went to join the others inside.

Jenessa looked around for Logan, finding him standing next to Grayson and his buddies from college, the groomsmen. Grayson was going to be Logan's best man, which made Jenessa's heart happy.

She made her rounds, greeting friends and family that were either in the wedding or had come in from out of town, with Evangeline sticking close. Maybe it was because Jenessa was the only one she knew.

The event was much more elaborate than Jenessa would have planned. With all she had on her plate, though, she had been happy to completely turn the planning of it over to Logan's mother, even if Elizabeth would go overboard in staging the event.

Dinner was announced, and everyone made their way to their tables. Jenessa finally had a respite from Evangeline's close proximity.

As they sat down to eat, Elizabeth was seated beside her. Jenessa stood beside her chair and looked around before sitting, while Logan took his seat. "Aren't the children eating with us?"

"I've arranged for a special table for the children," Elizabeth responded. "I thought that would be more fun. While we have filet mignon and quail, they are having chicken tenders and macaroni and cheese."

"They'll like that," Logan said as he unfolded his napkin on his lap.

Elizabeth turned to Jenessa. "I heard you have Grey's mother's engagement ring. May I see it?"

Jenessa proudly held out her hand.

Elizabeth's face brightened, and a sincere smile spread on her lips. "Just as beautiful as I remember it."

"I absolutely love it," Jenessa beamed.

A wistful look blossomed on Elizabeth's face as she turned to her son. "Oh, Logan. I am so glad that ring found its way back to you. I was sure it was lost forever."

Logan smiled. "I thought so too. It was Mrs. Dobson who found it and gave it back to me."

"Ah, Mrs. Dobson. She always was very good to you, Logan. In fact, I remember when she first came here. Fresh from Russia, and—"

"She's from Russia?" Jenessa perked up at that news. She'd had no idea. The woman had a slight accent, but Jenessa had never been able to place it.

"Yes. Anna Dobstoyevsky. I helped her change it to Dobson after she arrived." Elizabeth explained. "The other one was just too hard to pronounce."

That was interesting. So now Logan's father's housekeeper was from Russia. Could she have been the one that killed Rafe?

Jenessa shook her head. She was being silly, seeing murder suspects around every corner. What were the chances that a Russian woman who came to this country more than twenty years ago to become a housekeeper for a small-town family was actually a covert agent working for the KGB?

Ridiculous.

CHAPTER 43

WITH THE DINNER OVER, Jenessa and Evangeline went out to the parking lot to join the others. Logan was saying goodnight to his mother, then he proceeded to load the kids in the car to take them home to his condo.

Mrs. Dobson was going with them, spending the night in Logan's guest room, as he had asked her to help him get the kids to bed that night and then help with them in the morning, since his bride would be preparing for the wedding.

Logan carried little Lily against his chest, her blond curls dangling over his shoulder. She had fallen asleep at the end of the dinner, and he carefully put her in his car. The kids were clearly exhausted from their fun week at camp, and they had a big day coming tomorrow.

Jenessa was grateful for Mrs. Dobson's help. There was no way she could dress Lily and fix her hair while she was getting herself ready for her wedding. The thought of Lily as the flower girl and Grayson as the best man made her heart dance.

Mrs. Dobson was sitting patiently in the front seat of Logan's vehicle. She was a sweet older woman, who happened to be Russian—that was all.

Jenessa and Evangeline said their goodnights too, and Evangeline headed to her car to go check in at her hotel. Jenessa thought she sensed Evangeline was reluctant to leave her, but probably not. It was more likely that overactive imagination again. It was just as unlikely that her friend was a covert agent as it was that Grey Alexander's housekeeper was. Now a Russian mobster's wife, maybe?

No, no, no! Stop that. Jenessa gave her head a mental shake. Too many suspicious thoughts verging on crazy.

Jenessa opened the rear passenger door and leaned in to say her good-byes to the kids, telling them she would see them in the morning. She kissed sleepy Lily on the head.

Logan came up behind her and slid his hands around her waist, resting his cheek against hers. "Um, excuse me, but no, you can't see the kids in the morning."

Puzzled, she straightened and asked, "Why not?"

"Because, dear wife-to-be, they will be with me. And the groom, as you know, cannot see the bride on their wedding day."

He had a point there.

"But don't worry, Jenessa," he spun her around to face him, his arms still encircling her. "Mrs. Dobson will be there to feed them and get them dressed."

"And do Lily's hair. Don't forget Lily's hair."

"What?" He laughed. "You don't think I'm up to that job?"

She ran her fingers gently through his thick blond waves. "Uh, no." She smiled. "Let Mrs. Dobson do it."

"Just relax. Everything is taken care of."

Jenessa peered into his adoring eyes and gave a nod. "I love you, Logan."

He kissed her lightly. "Till tomorrow, my love." He released her and circled the car to leave.

Jenessa waved at her family as they drove away, then turned to go and say her good-byes to Ramey, Sara, and Selena. Waiting for tomorrow was going to be hard. How was she going to sleep tonight, thinking of Logan and their kids?

"Are you ready to go?" Aunt Renee asked, snapping Jenessa out of her thoughts. She had agreed to give Jenessa a ride home.

"Sure." This would be her last night as a single woman. A sprinkling of joy mixed with hope drizzled over her. Tomorrow she would be a mother.

~*~

It was after midnight when Aunt Renee dropped Jenessa at home. "Can you believe it, dear? It's tomorrow already."

"That means my big day is finally here. Now, if only I can get some sleep tonight, I might manage to be a glowing bride."

"What do you have left to do?" Aunt Renee asked.

Jenessa grimaced. "I still have to pack for the honeymoon. With all that's happened this week, I didn't get around to it."

"Do you want me to stay and help?"

"No, I can handle it—but thanks. You've already done enough." She gave Aunt Renee a light embrace. "What would I ever do without you?"

"You'll never have to find out. I plan to live forever. Now get in that house and start packing. You need to get to bed soon."

Jenessa went inside and hauled her suitcase up from the basement, but her mind just couldn't focus on packing. At least, not yet. She had to call Isabel and tell her about Evangeline and the topaz. And then there was what Grey had said about his prison cell mate. She wasn't going to mention it before, because it had seemed to not have any bearing on Isabel's investigation—but now, it very well might. Jenessa couldn't take any chances, it was all fair game at this point.

She dialed the hotel and was patched through to Isabel's room, hoping Isabel would not ignore her call. Isabel answered, but admonished Jenessa to be careful what she said over the phone. Jenessa did her best to covertly fill Isabel in on all her suspicions and the necklace she had accidentally seen.

Isabel couldn't tell her much in return, wanting to keep the conversation brief, and still concerned about prying ears. But, with that off her chest, Jenessa was finally able to work on her packing, though she was still thinking intermittently of Rafe and the topaz necklace.

Was that Rafe's necklace she saw in Evangeline's bag? Her friend had seemed rattled when Jenessa saw it.

Was it possible Rafe had simply brought them each trinkets from his travels, like she'd said, as they were good friends? What did Rafe mean when he said what was hidden in the necklace was worth killing for? And was it just Rafe's necklace, or the ones he had possibly brought back for everyone else?

But then again, Evangeline had seemed surprised when Jenessa had first brought Rafe up. She had said she hadn't heard from him in years and didn't seem to know he had been in prison in Afghanistan.

Jenessa finished packing what she could, then phoned Logan to say goodnight and to tell him how much she was looking forward to marrying him and having him and the kids move into her house.

She went completely silent, an icy tingle skating down her spine.

"Jenessa? Are you still there?" Logan asked.

She lowered her voice to a hush. "I heard a noise. Logan, I think someone is in the house," she whispered. "Call the police."

CHAPTER 44

JENESSA HUNG UP ON LOGAN and switched the bedroom lamp off, grabbing a stiletto wedding shoe from the box beside her closet door. It wasn't much, but it would have to do. Then she slowly pulled her door open. The hallway was dark. She slipped out and crept toward the staircase. She peeked into the spare bedroom on the way, dimly light by moonlight, her sparkly white wedding dress laid out on the bed.

The room appeared to be empty. She carefully descended the wooden staircase in her bare feet, praying it wouldn't creak. The main living area of the house was also dark, except for a soft glow from the porch light streaming through the front window. Jenessa crept to the front door, feeling quietly to make sure the deadbolt was set. It was.

She glanced out the front window, hoping to see Logan's car or police cruisers, but no. Not yet. Maybe she had imagined the noise. Or it was simply the old house settling. Her nerves were on high alert with all the suspicions she'd been having. She wasn't taking any chances.

Jenessa headed for the kitchen, tiptoeing past the dining room, where early wedding gifts were piled high on the dining table. She peeked around the room as she passed, but nothing.

The kitchen was dimly lit by moonlight filtering through the curtained window facing the back yard and the glass in the back door to the deck. She'd better check that door, then she would check the pantry. Jenessa stepped to the door, feeling sharp pains in her foot, hearing what sounded like crushed glass as she danced back. She tried not to scream, but a gasp escaped her lips.

Someone snagged a handful of her long hair and yanked her head back. The barrel of a gun pressed against the hollow of her cheek. And she froze.

"You just couldn't leave things alone. You always were a curious little tart." Evangeline's voice was cold as she cocked her gun.

Jenessa's fingers tightened around the toe of the stiletto that hung at her side. "I thought we were friends. I was in your wedding, Ev."

Evangeline pulled Jenessa's hair harder, pushed the gun barrel closer, so that it was grating on her cheekbone. "You were so nosy, poking around where you didn't belong."

Jenessa tried to think. What was Evangeline talking about? When they worked together on the paper in Sacramento?

"We couldn't afford to have you find out the truth, so we kept you close. You and Rafe were only supposed to distract each other. Not get married. Still, that was of no consequence to me, until…"

"Until what?" Jenessa dared to ask.

"Until that narcissistic father-in-law of yours put Rafe back on the map for us. What a small world it truly is. My old friend, marrying the son of the man who shared a cell with my Rudy. What are the odds?"

Clearly the odds were better than even Jenessa had imagined, for here she was, standing in her family home, with a gun pressed to her head.

"So, actually, I owe you a thanks for that. We got a two for one, thanks to you." Evangeline laughed, a snicker really, laced with sarcasm. "We managed to get Rafe out of the picture, and also got our revenge on the conniving Grey Alexander for ratting on my husband and his business deals."

Jenessa clung tightly to the shoe. It was all she had to defend herself. She thought of a joke she had once heard. The punchline was "Never bring a knife to a gunfight." Jenessa was certain it was an even worse idea to bring a shoe to a gunfight. But it was all she had, so she tucked it close at her side, keeping it ready if the opportunity presented itself.

Where were the police?

Jenessa listened for sirens, though she wondered if they would even use them in a situation like this. It might be smarter for them to arrive on scene quietly, so as to catch the prospective burglar by surprise. There was no traffic noise either, though, and that frightened her.

Sensing a quiet pause with Evangeline, Jenessa spun around and swung the high-heeled end of the shoe at Evangeline's head with all her strength. Her friend stumbled back. Jenessa bolted out of the kitchen, toward the front door, pulling down the small bookcase housing all her mother's cookbooks to block Evangeline's way.

The gun flared, and a shot whizzed past Jenessa as she ran, narrowly missing her, judging by the splinters that flew off the doorjamb as Jenessa reached the front door. She scrambled to unbolt it and swung the door wide open.

Logan raced through the doorway, just as Evangeline raised her gun again to fire, but Logan pushed Jenessa out of the way as she shot, willing to take the bullet for her.

Jenessa was on the floor as two shots rang out. Gripped in the throes of fear, she hesitated to look beside her, squinting her eyes shut. If she looked, she was certain she would see Logan, dead, lying in a pool of blood.

But, as Jenessa finally allowed herself to look up, Evangeline dropped to the floor, revealing Isabel standing behind, her gun raised. Isabel quickly holstered her firearm, as George Provenza and a couple of uniformed officers charged in through the open front door.

Isabel rushed to Jenessa's side. "Are you okay?"

Jenessa nodded and her gaze flew around, seeing Logan down. She screamed, "Logan!"

"He's fine, don't worry." Isabel glanced to the side, where Logan sat, his back against the wall, clutching at his arm. "Looks like the bullet just grazed him."

Logan nodded, a grimace on his face.

"Paramedics are on their way," George said.

Jenessa shifted her attention to Detective Provenza, standing beside Logan. "What are you doing here?"

George came close and helped her to her feet. "I heard the call on the police scanner...I listen to it sometimes after work...this is my town, after all. Sometimes it's hard to let go."

How was George ever going to retire?

"Yes, it is hard." Jenessa sat down beside Logan. "How are you doing?" she asked him, blood seeping through his shirt sleeve.

"I've been better." He winced.

"I called Isabel as soon as I heard it was your address," George explained.

"Thankfully."

"The truth is," Isabel began to say, "I didn't go to the rehearsal dinner because I didn't want to alert a potential killer that I was in town. You know, just in case it was someone close to you."

"Like my cousin or my good friend?" Jenessa asked.

"Yes, there's that. Plus, I was afraid someone at the dinner might mention I worked for the FBI."

"Like Ramey?" Jenessa asked.

"Maybe." Isabel grinned. "Actually, after you phoned me, I did some digging on Evangeline and thought I'd better tail her. I was outside in my car when Provenza reached me."

"You're a lifesaver, Isabel," Jenessa said. "Literally."

"I appreciate your saying that, but if it hadn't been for your initial information on Evangeline, and your tip about the topaz necklace, it might have taken me another day or two to figure out what was going on. You're the real hero, Jenessa."

CHAPTER 45

JENESSA WAS TIRED, BUT ELATED, as she stood in front of the full-length mirror in the bride's dressing room at the church. Ramey was buttoning up the back of Jenessa's wedding gown and smiling. Jenessa's dark hair was swept up with a few curled tendrils at the sides.

"I can't believe that while I was home in bed, you were living through that nightmare."

"Me either," Jenessa said. "It still seems so surreal."

Ramey attached the long veil to the back of Jenessa's up-do with the rhinestone-encrusted comb.

"Thank God you were paying enough attention to hear that noise and take it seriously," she said.

"You can thank George Provenza and my cousin Isabel, too. And, of course, Logan."

"Scary thing, but how romantic that he threw himself in front of a bullet for you, Jenessa. That is true love. Movie love."

Yes, yes it was. On both sides. There was nothing that Jenessa wouldn't do for Logan either. Or those two children. Jenessa twisted around to see the lacy veil in the mirror.

She smiled to herself. It was like Ramey said, right out of the movies.

"So, tell me, why did your friend Evangeline murder Rafe?" Ramey asked.

"That's a long story."

"We've got time," Ramey said with a look of anticipation. "So spill."

Jenessa told her it all started when Grey had overheard a conversation Rudy had with someone, about the hit on a government official, and he then used that info to get himself out of prison early, which would get Rudy a longer sentence.

Isabel had discovered, because of Rafe's intel, that Evangeline and Rudy were Russian assassins, and she was sure Rafe had information on the microchip in the topaz necklace that would have proved it. But that microchip was probably long gone.

And, just like Mrs. Dobson had changed her name, so had Rudy Peters. His name had been Rudy Petrikov, and Evangeline's maiden name was Smith, changed from Smirnov.

Apparently, the pair had come to the US when they were each nineteen, had help blending in, and had falsified backgrounds that they were American born.

They went to Sacramento State University while acclimating to the American way of life and learning American slang and language, both getting jobs at a Sacramento newspaper as a cover.

"That's where they met Rafe," Jenessa told Ramey, "and used him to get information and help with research. He began suspecting what they were doing, but then was assigned to the Middle East and was captured for a few years."

"That is freakin' crazy," Ramey said. "I'm so sorry you had to go through that, Jenessa." Ramey gave Jenessa a warm, comforting hug. "Your cousin Isabel sure found out a lot about them."

Jenessa nodded. "Once I told her about seeing a topaz necklace in Evangeline's makeup case, she filled in the blanks with everything else she already had in Rafe's file. She just never had the names and faces to go with the facts, until I gave them to her."

Something sparkled on Ramey's hand that drew Jenessa's attention.

"Is that what I think it is?" Jenessa asked with elation.

Ramey stuck out her hand and displayed a diamond engagement ring, a single solitaire set on a simple platinum band. "Isn't it perfect?"

"When did this happen?"

"Last night," Ramey said, "when Charles drove me home after the rehearsal dinner."

"And is Charlie on board with this?"

"Yes, finally." Ramey was grinning. "He was in the backseat when his dad proposed. He said it was time he had a mom again."

~*~

"Are you ready?" Ramey tucked a loose strand of Jenessa's dark hair behind her ear.

"Ready as I'm going to be," she replied, hoping happiness could conquer her nerves.

"Let's go then, shall we?"

Jenessa took her friend's arm and they moved through the doors that led down the wide hall to the church's auditorium. The organist was playing the theme from *Love Story,* and the wedding party was already lined up at the double doors, waiting to go in.

Lily was all smiles when she saw the bride in her flowing wedding gown. The six-year-old looked like a little angel with her halo of blond curls and her own white dress of lace and tulle. "Pretty," was all Lily said before Ramey took her hand to lead her away.

"Sweet little girl," Aunt Renee remarked as she took Jenessa's arm. She had been asked by the bride to walk her down the aisle. "You're going to be a wonderful mother."

"I hope so." Jenessa's heart was beating so wildly she was afraid she might faint. She drew a couple of deep breaths, hoping to calm it down. "Right now, I just need to get through this wedding."

"Your mother and father would be so proud of you."

"I miss them." Jenessa's eyes began to mist and she blinked back the tears. "Thanks for stepping in."

"My pleasure."

The wide doors opened, and the wedding party slowly filed in, little Lily being last as she scattered white rose petals along the aisle, from her pink woven basket.

The organ music changed to Mendelssohn's "Wedding March," the cue for the bride to enter the auditorium. As Jenessa and Aunt Renee walked in, everyone rose to their feet. Jenessa clung to her aunt's arm, when awe and gratitude filled her heart at seeing the church packed with people that had come to celebrate with them.

In her excitement, she was only able to pick out a few faces as she floated down the rose-covered path. Isabel was on the aisle. Charles and Charlie were nearby. There was the mayor and his wife, Alice from the newspaper, Maddie from the market, and of course George on one side of the aisle and Elizabeth on the other.

Jenessa's breath caught in her throat when she first saw Logan standing at the front, looking especially handsome in his deep gray tuxedo, his left arm in a dark sling, held tightly next to his body. He had taken a bullet for her. Her chest vibrated with emotion at the thought.

Logan stood tall, every bit the man she needed. Gone was the image of a selfish teenage boy, one who let his father ship Jenessa off to give birth to their son. That boy was replaced by a strong and loyal man. One who would literally do anything for her...including lay down his life.

And beside him was their son, Grayson, the baby boy she had feared she would never see again. Yet, here he was—the spitting image of Logan.

Jenessa continued down the aisle on Aunt Renee's arm, fighting back happy tears that welled up at the sight of her groom. She came to stand beside Logan and took his warm, gentle hand.

His lips spread into an enticing smile, then he mouthed, "I love you," to her. Warmth engulfed her, from her head to her toes, knowing how true that was.

Just then she felt a little tug at the bottom of her dress. She looked down and Lily was beaming up at her. "Does this mean you're going to be my new mommy now?" the little girl asked.

Jenessa looked at Logan through tears threatening to spill over, staring deeply into his watery blue eyes. His were tears of joy, as were hers. In that moment they both knew that, for them, a beautiful life was just beginning.

~ THE END ~

Thank you so much for reading my book,
The Gate House Secret.
I hope you enjoyed it very much.

Debra Burroughs

The highest compliment an author can get is to
receive a great review, especially
if the review is posted on Amazon.com.

Debra@DebraBurroughs.com
www.DebraBurroughsBooks.com

Other Books

By Debra Burroughs

The Lake House Secret, *a Jenessa Jones Mystery,*
Book 1
The Stone House Secret, *a Jenessa Jones Mystery,*
Book 2
The Boat House Secret, *a Jenessa Jones Mystery,*
Book 3

Three Days in Seattle, *a Romantic Suspense Novel*

The Scent of Lies, *Paradise Valley Mystery Book 1*

The Heart of Lies, *Paradise Valley Mystery Book 2*

The Edge of Lies, *Paradise Valley Mystery Short Story*

The Chain of Lies, *Paradise Valley Mystery Book 3*

The Pursuit of Lies, *Paradise Valley Mystery Book 4*

The Betrayal of Lies, *Paradise Valley Mystery Book 5*

The Color of Lies, *Paradise Valley Mystery Short Story*

The Harbor of Lies, *Paradise Valley Mystery Book 6*

The House of Lies, *Paradise Valley Mystery, Book 7*

ABOUT THE AUTHOR

Debra Burroughs writes with intensity and power. Her characters are rich and her stories of romance, suspense and mystery are highly entertaining. She can often be found sitting in front of her computer in her home in the Pacific Northwest, dreaming up new stories and developing interesting characters for her next book.

If you are looking for stories that will touch your heart and leave you wanting more, dive into one of her captivating books.

Sign up for Debra's New Release &
Giveaway eNewsletter at:

www.DebraBurroughsBooks.com

*You will never be spammed or your email address sold,
and you can unsubscribe at any time..*

Made in the USA
Las Vegas, NV
15 April 2023

70637748R00229